71,400 words.

Bloodrise

by Grant Atherton

with grateful thanks to

JAKOB PAULUSSEN

for all his valuable help and advice

Cover art by
SelfPubBookCovers.com/BeeJavier

Grant Atherton's Website
GrantAtherton.co.uk

WARNING

This book contains adult language and may be considered offensive to some readers.

Bloodrise, Copyright (c) March, 2023 by Grant Atherton

All rights reserved. This copy is intended for the purchaser of this e-book ONLY. No part of this e-book may be reproduced, scanned or distributed in any printed or electronic form without prior written permission from the author. Please do not participate in or encourage piracy of copyrighted materials in violation of the author's rights. Purchase only authorised editions.

This e-book is a work of fiction. While reference might be made to actual historical event of existing locations, the names, characters, places and incidents are either the product of the author's imagination or are used fictitiously, and any resemblance to actual persons, living or dead, business establishments, events or locales is entirely coincidental.

CHAPTER ONE

The best of memories are made on days like this, precious moments woven from a mix of simple pleasures.

It was a day to match my mood. Bright and cheerful. A large, red autumn sun shone in a clear blue sky, lending its sparkle to everything it touched with its warming rays and, beside me, Nathan hummed a merry tune as he drove us through the town.

I reached up above the windscreen and lowered the passenger-side sun visor against the glare.

"Are we going to tell them?" I asked.

"Of course we are." Nathan shifted down a gear, took the turn off the High Street, and drove the Astra along the Esplanade towards the Fairview Guest House.

As we approached our destination, I unbuckled my seat belt. "Karen will try to take over," I said. "You know that?"

Nathan pulled over the road and, as he parked at the bottom of the steps leading up to the Fairview's terrace, he said, "You want to take a wild guess at how she'll react if we don't tell her?"

It took me all of one second to imagine her reaction, and I shuddered at the thought. "You're right, of course. Might as well get it over with."

First out of the car, I grabbed the bottle of Champagne from the footwell, slammed the door, and headed for the stairs.

Nathan caught up with me at the top of the steps and we crossed the terrace towards the sliding glass doors leading into the reception.

We were about to dine with Richard and Karen, our closest friends. We often socialised together, and our Saturday night dinners were a regular occurrence.

But tonight was different. Tonight was going to be a celebration.

Karen spotted us from inside and opened the door to greet us. She saw the bottle in my hand and raised a quizzical eyebrow. "Champagne? Special occasion?"

"Isn't dinner with friends always a special occasion?" I handed her the bottle. "Best stick it in the fridge for a while."

I'm not sure my explanation convinced her, but she took the bottle anyway and led us through to their private quarters on the other side of the reception area where Richard was waiting for us. "Nice tans," he said, rising from his chair as we stepped into the living room. "Good holiday?"

"You know me," I said. "Always happy to lie around on a Mediterranean beach. But Nathan gets restless if he's not on the move all the time."

"I like to take in the sights," said Nathan. "If I'd wanted to lie on a beach all day, I would have stayed at home."

"Oh, yes? Bit of dissension was there?" said Karen.

I glanced at Nathan and gave him a conspiratorial wink. "It was a great holiday. One of the best."

"You can tell us all about it over dinner," said Karen and headed to the kitchen with the bottle of Champagne.

She returned with a tureen and ushered us through to the dining room. Richard acted as host and ladled French onion soup into our bowls as we seated ourselves.

Karen opened a bottle of Merlot and filled our glasses. She said, "Nathan tells me you came home to bad news, Mikey. Not the best way to end a holiday."

"I'm trying not to dwell on it until I've talked with Cara's solicitors," I said. "I've made an appointment for Monday."

"What did they tell you?" Karen asked.

"Not a lot. They didn't want to say too much on the phone."

"How did she die?" Richard asked.

I grimaced. "No idea. It seems she'd been ill for some time. But that's all I learned."

Karen said, "I didn't know you'd stayed in touch."

"We didn't. Which is why the call was such a shock. We'd not seen each other since the divorce. And that's getting on for twenty years."

"She must have left you something in her will," said Richard.

"Nathan thinks that too," I said. "But I can't imagine why."

Nathan said, "Not sure what else it could be."

"After all this time," I said, "why would she give me even a second's thought?"

"I guess you'll find out soon enough," said Nathan.

"And in the meantime," said Richard, "you can tell us what a great time you had on holiday while the rest of us were slogging our way to work through endless days of rain. Don't let today's weather fool you. It's been dire."

I laughed. "Must admit, it was good timing. But we're always glad to get back home, whatever the weather."

The next hour was taken up with talk of our holiday and catching up with news from back home. We were finishing the main course of Coq au Vin when Nathan decided to break the news. He shot me a guarded look, gave the briefest of nods, and said, "I think it's time for that Champagne."

"Champagne?" said Richard. "We have Champagne?"

"Apparently, we're worth it because we're special," said Karen and went to the kitchen.

She returned with the Champagne and a set of flutes. Nathan took the bottle from her and opened it. As he filled our glasses, he said, "That's not the only reason." He held up his glass in readiness for a toast. "While we were away, Mikey and I had time to talk things over, and we've decided to take the final step. We're getting married."

A brief shocked silence was followed by cries of cheers and congratulations as we clinked glasses, and Karen said, "Not before time."

"These things can't be rushed," I said.

"You've been living together nearly four years," said Karen. "Though I suppose it took that long to get you under control."

"I shall pretend I didn't hear that," I said.

Nathan grinned and chimed in. "That was never going to happen. I gave up on that long ago."

"Okay, you jokers. Enough."

"So who asked who and when and where?" Richard asked.

"I'm telling everyone Nathan proposed on the apartment terrace over a glass of wine and overlooking a Moroccan sunset. That's the official version. But it was actually over morning coffee in a back street cafe." I rolled my eyes. "Ever the romantic."

"It was a very nice cafe," said Nathan, "and the coffee was excellent."

"Ahh," I said as if coming to a sudden realisation. "So it was the coffee that swung it?"

Nathan, still grinning, leaned over and planted a kiss on the side of my head. "That and your weird sense of humour."

"Have you decided on a date yet?" asked Karen.

"We haven't had much of a chance," said Nathan.

"Let me know as soon as you do," she replied. "We need to get things rolling. The reception will be here, of course, but you'll need to let me have a list of guests so I know the numbers."

"We don't want to make a big thing of it," said Nathan. "Just a simple ceremony with you and Richard as witnesses."

"Nonsense," said Karen. "All your friends will want to share your day."

"You see," I said to Nathan, "I did warn you."

"Warn him of what?" Karen asked.

"That you were going to take over," I said.

"Of course I am," she responded.

The conversation and banter continued for a while after that. We chatted until well into the night. Just four good friends enjoying each other's company and sharing in our good fortune.

All was well with the world.

CHAPTER TWO

The offices of Carrington Reed Solicitors stood behind the facade of an imposing Victorian terrace in Almchester's professional district. A solid, formidable structure of painted brick and ornate gables.

I left the Elan in a nearby parking bay within sight of the building and hurried towards it. It was the following Monday, and I was eager for answers to the many perplexing questions that had troubled my thoughts over the weekend.

Carrington himself wouldn't have looked out of place in the Victorian era. He was the old-fashioned type, all starched collar and waistcoat with centre-parted Brylcreemed hair, a style that made him look like a centuries-old leftover from Britain's colonial past.

My own casual style, jeans and sweatshirt, earned me a disdainful look as Carrington peered at me over the top of his spectacles before introducing himself and offering his hand.

As I shook it, he said, "I'm sorry to have brought you all this way at such short notice, Mr MacGregor, but as I explained on the telephone, it is a matter of some importance and I thought it best to meet face to face."

Formal introductions over, Carrington led me into his office, a dark, wood-panelled room at the back of the building. It smelled of furniture polish and dust, an ironic mix. Floor-to-ceiling bookcases sagging under the weight of heavy, legal tomes lined the walls.

A large mahogany desk inlaid with red embossed leather stood in the centre of the room and he offered me a seat facing it before settling into a matching leather-cushioned swivel chair on the other side.

He seemed ill at ease, tugging at his shirt cuffs and swallowing several times before reminding me he needed to discuss what he referred to as 'a somewhat sensitive matter'. He struck me as someone trying to delay the breaking of bad news.

I took the lead, eager to learn why I was here. "Naturally, learning of my ex-wife's death was a shock. But I was surprised to hear from you even so. Cara and I lost touch with each other many years ago."

"I have to admit," he said, "your lack of recent contact made it rather difficult to establish communication with you. We had to seek the aid of the radio station that airs your programmes."

"Yes, they contacted my agent. But I'm at a loss to understand my position in this matter."

He nodded briskly. "I should give you some background information. It will help to explain the present situation." He drew in a deep breath. "This firm acted for Ms Welles for some years. During that time, we handled both her personal and professional matters."

"Professional?"

"Ms Welles and her partner run… sorry, ran… a very successful advertising agency, Springboard Creative. They were a local firm but had a large, extensive client base."

"She had a good head on her shoulders. I always knew she'd do well."

"Indeed. She was an accomplished businesswoman. Unfortunately, a few years ago, she developed a progressive neurological illness which had implications for her future wellbeing."

My heart sank and, in my mind's eye, I conjured up the smiling face of the woman who had once meant so much to me.

Our journeys through life often lead us away from those we once held dear, our paths diverging ever more as we each move towards our separate futures. Sometimes, in quieter moments, we may think back to those times and those people and wonder where their journeys led them, and if they survived the trials along the way. In such quiet moments, I sometimes thought of Cara, of the good times we had shared before it all went wrong, and I had hoped that, like me, she had finally found what she was looking for. It pained me to think she had suffered, and had died at such an early age.

"Was it the illness that led to her death?" I asked.

"Not directly. Despite her illness, she still had many years ahead of her. But as a result of her condition, she was subject to fainting spells. It seems during one such episode, she sustained a head injury from a fall, which led to her demise. At the time of her accident, she was at home and her body lay undiscovered for several hours.

"She was home alone?"

"Ms Welles lived alone. She was in a relationship, but she and her partner lived separately. She also had a son, Jordan, with whom she was close. But the young man no longer lived with his mother, having recently moved into accommodation of his own nearby. I understand he was looking for a more independent lifestyle and thought it time to fly the nest."

The more Carrington told me of Cara's circumstances, the more confused I was. Cara had moved on with her life, achieved some success, and formed new relationships before her unfortunate and untimely end. But it was a life in which I played no part, and I was no nearer to understanding what any of it had to do with me.

I said, "Where do I fit into all this?"

Carrington shuffled in his chair before continuing. The leather squeaked beneath him. "I'm just coming to that," he said.

He tugged at his cuffs again, a clear sign of his increasing discomfort, and I had an uneasy feeling I was about to learn something not to my liking.

Carrington continued. "Given the circumstances of Ms Welles' demise, the signing of the death certificate requires authority from the coroner. I anticipate no problem there. It's no more than a formality. But until the signing of such certificate, this firm is not able to deal with probate. These formalities should be settled within the next few days, but in the meantime, I thought it expedient to apprise you of certain provisions in my client's will that you should be aware of."

His fidgeting increased, and I tensed. I figured I was about to be delivered a blow.

"Obviously, Ms Welles made provision for her son," said Carrington, "but as he had not yet reached the age of majority on her death - the young man is aged just seventeen - she also made provision in such circumstances for a trustee to be appointed with discretionary powers to handle Jordan's legal and financial affairs until he comes of age." Carrington swallowed and cleared his throat. "She specifically requested that you take on that role."

I shook my head, trying to clear my thoughts. "I don't understand. Why me? Surely, Jordan has family to take care of his needs."

"Ms Welles had been estranged from her parents for some time."

"I can't say I'm surprised. But there must be other family?"

Even as I said the words, the answer came to me.

And that's when the blow landed, when it finally dawned on me why I was here.

What an idiot I must have been not to see it coming.

As Carrington opened his mouth to respond, I held up a restraining hand, allowing myself a moment to let the truth sink in.

"Seventeen, you said?"

Carrington answered with a slight nod and a weak, understanding smile.

I made a quick mental calculation. The numbers fell into place, confirming what I now knew. "I am his family, aren't I?"

"Yes, you're his father."

I tensed and dug my hands into the arms of the chair as the world slowed and closed in around me, my mind fixed on that one thought.

My heart pounded.

Father.

The word bounced around in my head.

I said it out loud as if, by doing so, it would make more sense. "His father?"

Carrington nodded again. And when he spoke, he sounded relieved, as if, in making his disclosure, he had shaken off a heavy burden. "I know it must come as a shock," he said, "and I should tell you I tried to persuade Ms Welles against such a revelation. At least, the manner in which she chose to make it. She did not take my advice."

The blood drained from my face. "There's no mistake?" But of course, there wasn't. I was still struggling to come to terms with the truth of it.

"There's no mistake." Carrington's tone was sympathetic. He leaned forward, hands clasped on the desk before him. "Ms Welles and I discussed the circumstances of your relationship at some length. I understand your marriage was short-lived."

I nodded. "It was less than a year."

"Ms Welles learned of her pregnancy following your separation. Fearing you may wish to re-establish your relationship as a consequence - something she deemed not to be in the interests of either of you - she chose not to inform you of the pregnancy. I understand there was some pressure from her family, too. In essence, she chose not to burden you with the responsibility or call on you for financial support."

As the initial shock subsided, another feeling took its place, a slow-growing resentment that swelled inside me. "To hell with the financial support," I spluttered. "For seventeen years, I've been a father, and no one thought to tell me? No one thought maybe I had a right to know?"

Another notion struck me. "If it hadn't been for Cara's premature death, I may never have known I had a son."

"My understanding is that she fully intended to tell the young man of your existence once he reached the age of majority, leaving him to decide whether or not to establish contact."

"You have to wonder why she bothered to involve me now." I tightened my grip on the arms of the chair and struggled to suppress the mix of emotions threatening to overwhelm me.

Carrington leaned back in his chair, fingers steepled, and nodded. "I understand your reaction and I sympathise. In your place, I'm sure I would feel the same. In my client's defence, she believed she was making the right decision at the time. A decision she later regretted. But by then the deed was done, and she thought it best to let it be."

"Until now. Now she can no longer be held accountable." I flinched. "I'm sorry. In the circumstances, that may seem unkind. But I can't help feeling... I don't know what it is... betrayed?"

"Understandable. And if you chose not to take on the responsibility of trustee, I would understand that too."

Until then, I hadn't considered the matter. It was the least of my concerns. But for now, I needed to keep my emotions in check and think this through objectively. This wasn't just about me. "What about my... what about the boy? Does he know... does he realise...?"

"I spoke with him at some length yesterday. Until then, he was no more aware of your existence than you were of his. I'm sure you will appreciate he was as shocked as you."

I turned and stared out of the window into the growing gloom, trying to gather my thoughts. Carrington switched on a desk lamp, but it did little to brighten the dark and sombre room.

The sound of raised voices filtered through from somewhere nearby.

"Before I make a decision," I said, "perhaps I should meet the boy."

Carrington agreed. "I had already anticipated such a meeting," he said. "I suggested to Jordan that you meet here under my guidance. However, he expressed a preference to see you privately at his mother's home. And he asked if that could be as soon as possible. Tomorrow if you're agreeable. Personally, I thought it better to meet here, but he was adamant."

I agreed to the arrangement.

Carrington reached across his desk, picked up a manila envelope, and offered it to me. "I took the liberty of putting together some information you will find useful; Ms Welles' home and business addresses, contact details of her business partner, and the young man's contact details."

My hands were shaking as I took the envelope from him. "Given the circumstances," I said, "it may be best if I stayed over for a few days."

"I can help with that too," he said and reached into a desk drawer. He produced a set of keys. "These are the keys and the remote for the security system to Ms Welles's property. It may be a little premature, but accepting Ms Welles's last wishes would mean taking control of her assets, anyway." He handed me the keys and added, "If I may have your assurance that you will return them to me if you decide not to take on the role."

I agreed and took the keys from him.

Carrington brought our discussion to a close after confirming he would arrange a meeting with Jordan, and I left his offices in a daze.

For a while, I sat in the car as the late autumn shadows lengthened around me, trying to come to terms with what I'd learned. My world had changed, and I was having a hard time taking it in.

With a shaking hand, I reached into a pocket for my mobile and called Nathan.

"Was I right?" he said. "Was it the will reading? Did she leave you something?"

I drew in a deep breath before answering. Might as well tell it like it was and get it over with.

"She left me a son."

CHAPTER THREE

"She certainly liked to live in style," said Nathan. "This floor is marble. And I'm betting that painting over the fireplace didn't come cheap."

We were standing by the sitting room window of Medway Hall, Cara's home, waiting for Jordan's arrival, and Nathan was trying to distract me, a futile attempt to put me at ease. But it wasn't working. My mind was focused on the impending meeting, and I was getting more and more wound up by the minute.

Once the initial shock had worn off, Nathan had taken my news surprisingly well. Something I was grateful for.

I shot him a sideways glance. "Thanks for coming," I said. "Not sure I could have done it alone."

"Of course I was going to come."

"I wasn't sure you'd want to. I thought you'd be angry."

He frowned. "Why would you think that? It was a lot to take in, of course it was. But why would I be angry?"

"Yet another screw-up from my disreputable past. Something I seem to make a habit of."

"Being a father? A screw-up?"

I shrugged. "What would I know about being a father? Cara knew I'd be hopeless. Why else keep me in the dark? I was such a selfish prick back then. Too wrapped up in my own pathetic problems."

"Hey, come on." He squeezed my arm. "Don't be so hard on yourself. It all worked out in the end, didn't it? Isn't this where you want to be?"

"Of course it is. You need to ask?"

It's not as if our relationship had been without its troubles. Mostly down to me and my amazing ability to fuck up. But we had worked our way through the bad times, and now here we were, living our version of domestic bliss. We'd lived and loved together these past four years since finding each other again, and the last thing I needed was to land myself in another mess.

"So lighten up," Nathan said. "Why worry over something you can't change? What matters is where we go from here."

I looked into those warm green eyes and wrapped an arm around his waist. "You're here right now," I said. "That's all that matters."

"It's not like I had much choice," he said. "It was that or leave you without a change of clothes for the next few days. And much as I love your smell, there are limits."

I laughed and said, "You always were a bit weird."

After I'd brought Nathan up to speed on my discussion with Carrington, and told him of my agreement to meet Jordan, he had insisted on travelling up to Almchester to support me, and we had met up here at Medway Hall.

Cara's home was a large Georgian house, one characterised by its restrained symmetry, and typical of those houses built for country living before nearby cities encroached upon and surrounded them. It was set well back from the road in extensive grounds and accessed through a gated entrance framed by high, manicured hedges. A wide sweeping drive led up through a cultivated lawn to the front of the building where robust ivy trailed the brick facade.

The house had been extensively remodelled, and the room we stood in looked more like the reception of one of London's more expensive hotels, spacious and airy.

I could understand why Cara would want to live in such a large home. She would need all that space to contain her expansive personality.

"I thought about her sometimes," I said, "and wondered how she was. I wish we'd found a way to stay in touch."

"Why didn't you?"

I snorted. "Not after the mess we made of things."

"So what happened?"

"We got married is what happened. We were a couple of idiots who did it for all the wrong reasons." I glanced out of the window, keeping an eye on the entrance gate, then turned away and leaned back against the sill. "I was struggling with a lifestyle that didn't suit me, and she was trying to escape from an overprotective family."

"Not the best of foundations for a stable relationship."

"It was a mistake," I said. "We both knew that. And it was over in less than a year. She went back to her family, and I moved on to make an even bigger mess of my life. But I wish it could have been different."

I let my mind travel back to those days, to a time of turmoil, a time when Cara's friendship was a brief welcome interlude that helped me through those troubled times. I remembered too the pleasure we had taken in each other's company, the silly things that had made us laugh, the shared moments that became happy memories. And how we had finally lost that special connection.

With a shake of the head, I pulled myself back to the present. "I was so stupid then," I said.

A rueful smile from Nathan. "No argument from me there."

I pulled a face. "I'm not so stupid I don't know when I'm well off now. The saddest part of that whole sorry episode is that if we hadn't taken that final fatal step, we might still have been friends."

"Couldn't you have stayed friends afterwards?"

I snorted. "No way. Her father was a total control freak. He micromanaged her every move. I think she only married me to spite him. The guy hated me and, once the divorce was settled, he wouldn't let me anywhere near her."

"Not sure you can blame him for that. She didn't make the best of choices."

"Perhaps. But he's the one who drove her to it in the first place."

"But you parted on good terms?"

"Sure, but it didn't stop the media raking over my past once I'd made a name for myself. They set me up as some sort of callous jerk who dumped her."

"Nothing new there then."

"I'm surprised they didn't find out about Jordan. They missed a chance to make me out to be an absent father too."

"They were no more likely to learn he was your son than you were. She obviously went to great pains to keep it a secret."

Struck by a sudden pang of regret, my throat constricted. I swallowed and said, "She was a joy to be with. One of the most intelligent people I knew. So much energy. And full of big ideas. I'd like to think she made the most of her brief life."

"She sounds the type to make sure of that," said Nathan.

I grunted, glanced at my watch, and checked the gate again. Jordan was due to arrive any time soon, and I was growing ever more tense as the minutes passed.

Nathan gave my shoulder a reassuring squeeze. "Still nervous?"

"Nervous? Nervous doesn't come close. Try terrified."

"Just remember that he's going to be feeling the same."

"He must be quaking in his boots then."

I pushed myself to my feet and turned to face the window again.

He slipped an arm around my waist. "You know I'm here for you," he said. "But I have to go back this evening. I have a meeting set up for tomorrow."

"You're here for the main event. That's the important thing."

"You know me. Always happy to take a break from the office. If only for a day."

There was a wistful edge to his tone. His duties kept him tied to his desk more often than not these days, and he missed working out in the field with his men.

"I don't get out half as much as I used to," he said. "If I'm not careful, I'll end up going to seed behind that desk."

I smiled. There was no danger of that. He was still in great shape. All firm flesh and hard muscle.

Over the years, he had changed little. A few extra crinkles around the eyes maybe, and a bit greyer at the temples, but the energy and verve hadn't diminished one jot and those molten green eyes were still full of fire.

I turned towards him and wrapped my arms around his neck.

He drew me toward him and held me close. "Need a hug?"

"Believe it or not," I said, "I do sometimes remember how lucky I am to have you."

"Only sometimes?" he said and chortled.

"Don't push your luck." I pulled away and gave him a playful punch on the arm.

Before he could respond, a sound from outside interrupted us. I spun around to face the window once more in time to see the automatic metal gates at the entrance to the grounds swing open on creaking hinges. A grey Ford Focus pulled through.

I flew back into panic mode and my muscles tensed. I gripped Nathan's arm and held it tight.

The car swung around and headed up the gravel drive towards the house as the gates closed behind it.

Given his mother's apparent wealth, I had half-expected Jordan to turn up in a sports car. I was glad to see he hadn't been overindulged.

It struck me then how very different our backgrounds must be. I was raised in a small, sleepy, backwater, the son of the local priest; Jordan had been raised in a large city with all the advantages that allowed. And whilst my family were financially secure, and had never denied me any material benefits, I suspected Jordan was used to a level of material comfort far above anything I had enjoyed as a young man. All that I now was and everything I had was achieved through my own endeavours. I wondered what Jordan's life experience had been like till now and how much he would need to strive to satisfy his future material needs.

Nathan pulled away from the window, releasing my hand from his arm. "Time to make myself scarce before he sees me," he said. "I'll go wait in the dining room. I'll be able to hear you from there. Call me back when you're ready."

And he was gone.

And even though he was nearby, I felt so alone.

The door of the Focus opened and a young man stepped out.

Here at last.

My son.

I took a deep breath and braced myself.

CHAPTER FOUR

I don't know what I'd expected, but the young man on the other side of the window didn't quite fit the image I'd conjured up in my imagination. Far from it.

In my mind, I'd pictured a younger version of myself. Dark-blond hair, bronzed skin tone, muscular build. What I got was a thin, pale-faced youth of average height with long tangled brown hair. Obviously, he favoured his mother's looks.

We didn't share the same dress style either. Casual was fine. But casual scruffy was way beyond my idea of fashionable shabby chic. Maybe the dishevelled look was in vogue at the moment. Or maybe I was getting too old to appreciate current trends.

The well-worn, paint-speckled, tan jacket was matched with torn, patched jeans and black, scuffed, leather boots that hadn't seen a lick of polish for some time.

As he turned and headed towards the door, what I noticed most after the dress style was the grim, tight line of his mouth.

My stomach churned, and a knot formed in my throat.

I wasn't prepared for what lay ahead.

It's not as if I hadn't been in difficult situations before, but this was up close and personal. I was way out of my depth and hadn't a clue how to play it.

How was I supposed to introduce myself to a son I had never met? Hug him? Shake his hand? Perhaps it was best just to wait and see how he reacted.

I didn't go to meet him. Instead, I took some more deep breaths, stood my ground, and followed the sound of his progress into the house and across the hall to where I waited in the centre of the sitting room. The door opened and, a moment later, he was standing in front of me, the same grim expression on his face.

For several seconds, we faced each other in deafening, stilted silence. I was the first to break it. Pointing towards the nearby couch, I said, "Why don't we sit? Make ourselves comfortable?"

"No."

Short and to the point. And not very encouraging.

I tried again.

"We should introduce ourselves," I said. "I'm not sure what you've been told about me."

"Nothing I didn't already know." His tone was hard. "There was some stuff about you in the news."

Given the hammering I received from the media following my second divorce and the reasons for it, I can't imagine it would leave him with the best of impressions.

"Remind me," I said.

"They said you were a faggot."

I stiffened. "Did they indeed?" So this is how it was going to play out. "I'm not sure that's how they would have phrased it," I said, "but they got it more or less right."

Jordan shrugged and pulled a face. "They reported some other stuff, too. You were screwing around with other men. Is that why mum dumped you?"

Here we go again. I groaned inwardly and tried not to let the irritation show. There were times in my life when I hadn't exactly covered myself in glory. Those days were long gone. But plainly not forgotten.

I took a breath, and said, "That's not why we parted, no. Do you want to know the real reason, or would you prefer to stand there and throw a few more insults my way?"

"I don't want anything from you. Just what's mine."

"And what might that be?"

He swept a hand across the room. "This place. And everything else mum left me. I'm not buying all that bullshit about a trust fund or whatever. You have no right to keep what's mine."

"Is that why you're here? To stake your claim?"

"Why else? What did you think this was going to be? A happy-sappy family reunion? Tears and hugs all round?" He curled his lip and sneered. "Do yourself a favour."

I drew in another breath and exhaled slowly. Trying to control my voice, I said, "I'd hoped this would be a chance to get to know each other."

"You've had seventeen years to do that."

"Until the other day, I wasn't even aware you existed."

"Bullshit. How could you not know?"

"Your mother and I divorced some months before you were born."

"So? Why would she not tell you about me?"

"I don't have the answer to that. I wish it were otherwise."

"She said my father was dead. She wouldn't do that unless she wanted to protect me from what really happened. You deserted us and you didn't give a damn about me."

"That is so not true."

Again, his mouth twisted into a sneer. "It might be better if you had been dead. I've managed without a dad all these years. And it's not like I need one now."

This was going nowhere. He'd already cast me in the role of villain and nothing I said was going to convince him otherwise. Time for a change of tack.

I nodded briskly. "In that case, let's stick to the essentials, shall we? The trust fund."

I turned away and seated myself on the couch. "So here goes. I have no idea why your mother appointed me as your trustee, and I have to admit, I was reluctant to take on the task. But I'm sure she had her reasons. And I'm prepared to trust her judgement. So like it or not, from now on, I'll be overseeing your financial needs."

He scowled and clenched his fists. "That's just so fucking dumb. I'll be eighteen next year, and it will all come to me, anyway. So what's the fucking point?"

"The point is, you'd better change your manners and your attitude or I'm going to make sure it's one hell of a long year."

That probably wasn't the best way to respond, but I'd heard enough of this and my patience was wearing thin.

He stared down at me, tight-lipped, eyes blazing, clenching and unclenching his fists. And then, without another word, he turned on his heel and stormed out of the room, slamming the door behind him.

I pushed myself up from the couch and crossed over to the window in time to see him climb into his car.

A moment later, Nathan was back by my side, his arm around me. We stood in silence and watched Jordan speed down the drive and out of sight through the open gates. The sound of his engine died away into the distance.

For a while, neither of us spoke. Eventually, Nathan said, "I'm sorry you had to go through that. It can't have been easy."

"I don't suppose it was easy for him, either."

He turned and stroked the side of my face with his free hand. "You okay?"

I gave his arm a reassuring squeeze. "I've had more productive meetings. But I'll get over it."

He arched an eyebrow.

"It could have gone better," I said, "but this whole thing was as much a shock to him as it was to me."

"Not sure that excuses some of the things he said."

"Everything he thinks he knows about me, he learned from the media. And let's face it, they've not portrayed me in the best of lights over the years, have they? And with just cause. He was bound to think the worst."

He grunted. "So what now?" He took me by the hand and led us over to one of the couches.

We settled ourselves side by side, and I said, "I'll get in touch with the solicitors later. Carrington will need to know how the meeting went. And I'll tell him I intend to honour Cara's wishes and take on the responsibility of trustee."

Nathan tilted his head to one side and regarded me with wide eyes. "You surprise me. After what he just put you through."

I reached out and squeezed his thigh. "It's possible Cara regretted keeping Jordan and me in ignorance of each other. Why else would she choose to enlighten us now? This could be her way of making amends for that decision. Better late than never?"

"But why like this? Wouldn't it make more sense to let the solicitors take care of Jordan's needs? Why you? After all this time."

"I wondered about that too. But now I think I understand."

Nathan didn't look convinced.

"Cara was close to her son," I said. "And perhaps she knew this would happen, that he might reject me. And if so, what better way to thwart that intention than by binding him to his father in a relationship of financial dependency?"

"A relationship he couldn't walk away from."

"Exactly. A chance to learn more about each other, come to terms with the past, and, hopefully, find a way to build a more harmonious relationship."

"It won't be easy."

"I know that. And, in the end, it may come to nothing. But it has to be worth a try. I guess this is where the hard work begins, where I learn how to be a father."

CHAPTER FIVE

Uneasy dreams disturbed my sleep that night and, the following morning, I woke exhausted, my mind buzzing and full of troubled thoughts and unresolved tensions.

It was still first light, but I rolled out of bed anyway, unable to sleep any longer.

For most of those early hours, I wandered aimlessly around Medway Hall's large silent rooms. Later, I would call George Carrington and let him know about my disastrous meeting with Jordan. But, right then, I was finding it difficult to concentrate and couldn't settle to anything.

Concerned and caring as ever, Nathan had wanted to stay over, worried about leaving me to brood alone. He'd suggested we find somewhere to eat in town, forget about the confrontation with Jordan for the moment, and try to unwind. But I was having none of it. Knowing how much pressure he was under at work, I insisted he return home, promising to keep in touch over the next few days. He took some coaxing, but finally acquiesced and left for home that afternoon, albeit reluctantly.

Now, I wished I'd asked him to stay. For all its grandeur and its expensive furnishings, there was something cold and uninviting about this house, and I would have welcomed the warm companionship of my man.

A glance at my watch told me there was still time to spare before Carrington's office opened for business. Enough time for breakfast. And at least it would keep me occupied while I waited.

From the conservatory, I made my way to the kitchen at the back of the house. I'd just poured myself a fresh mug of coffee and was settling down at the table to a bowl of Weetabix when I heard the voices.

I tensed and almost dropped my spoon.

It wasn't so much the sound itself that startled me, more the sudden shattering of the silence.

I pushed my bowl to one side and strained to hear. The voices seemed to come from the front of the house, two people talking together. Male voices. I hadn't heard the gates open, but I was so wrapped up in my thoughts, I wouldn't have heard anything from outside, anyway.

Only on hearing echoing footsteps on marble did I realise my mistake. They weren't outside. They were in the house.

I pushed myself to my feet and hurried towards the source, heart racing, and came to a sudden halt in the hall.

Two uniformed police officers stood by the front door, a young fresh-faced constable and a sergeant, an older, moustachioed man with greying hair.

They were in conversation, but broke off and turned to face me as I appeared before them. They seemed as surprised to see me as I was to see them.

"I'm sorry, sir," said the constable, "we weren't expecting anyone to be here."

"Obviously not," I said. "How did you get in?"

"We got the keypad entry code from the owner."

"The owner?"

The sergeant interrupted us. "And who might you be, sir? Are you here with the owner's authority?"

"The name's MacGregor, Michael MacGregor, and I'm here as the deceased owner's legal representative."

Jordan must have allowed them access. Clearly, he was having a hard time understanding the legal implications of my pending trusteeship.

"As far as I can see," I said, "you're the ones here without authority. Perhaps you'd like to tell me what this is about?"

The two officers glanced at each other, a look of bewilderment passing between them. The sergeant took charge of the conversation. "Our information is that the property is now in the ownership of the deceased's son, Jordan Welles."

"Then your information is wrong."

"And what was your relationship to the deceased, sir?"

"She was my ex-wife. Though I'm not sure that's relevant in the circumstances."

The sergeant seemed more interested. "When did you last have any contact with your wife, sir? Were you on good terms?"

"I haven't seen my ex or had any contact with her for the past seventeen years. Now, are you going to tell me what this is about?"

The two officers exchanged glances again.

"We're here to secure the property, sir," said the constable.

I threw up my hands in a show of exasperation. "You're not making sense. The property is secure. And presumably, your presence here requires a warrant." I held out a hand. "I'd like to see it, please?"

The sergeant puffed out his chest. "We don't need a warrant, Mr MacGregor. We have express authority under the Police and Criminal Evidence Act to secure the property as a crime scene."

"Crime scene?" My heart skipped a beat. There was only one reason I could think of for such an action. "You're not saying..." The words died in my mouth.

The two officers stared at me, stony-faced.

"Is this a murder investigation?" I asked.

"Sir, our instructions are to secure the property pending a forensic examination," said the sergeant. "That's all I can tell you for the moment."

A tightness gripped my chest, and I stared at them, momentarily lost for words.

"And in the meantime," the sergeant continued, "we're going to need details of everyone who's been staying at the property. Do you have any means of identification, Mr MacGregor?"

In response to the sergeant's words, the young constable took a notebook and pen from his breast pocket and stood poised and ready to take notes.

In a half-daze, not quite believing what was happening, I gave the constable details of my full name and address and produced a calling card. I handed it to the sergeant and said, "My driving licence is upstairs if you need formal identification."

He glanced at the card and raised a quizzical eyebrow. "A Forensic

Psychologist?" He narrowed his eyes and studied me more closely. "You're the guy who does that crime series on radio?"

"Amongst other things," I said.

"And you work with the police?"

"I help with profiling and crime scene analysis."

He nodded and, with a knowing smile, said, "So you'll know how this goes, the procedures involved?"

"Some."

"Then I'm sure you'll be aware we'll need you to vacate the property," he said.

I nodded my understanding.

"And were you here alone, sir?"

"No, my partner was here too?"

"And is she here now?"

"He..." I stressed the word to show my disapproval at his presumption "... is at work at the moment."

A pause while he stared at me. "And where might that be, sir?" The 'sir' had taken on a more contemptuous tone.

"Police Divisional Headquarters in Charwell."

The constable stopped writing and raised his eyes to look at me, a guarded expression on his face.

I said, "Detective Chief Inspector Nathan Quarryman."

"He"s your partner?" The scepticism in the sergeant's voice wasn't lost on me.

"I have his number, if you wish to call him."

"No need for that at the moment, sir." This time, the 'sir' had taken on a more neutral tone. It was amazing what a difference having the right connections could make.

"Anyone else, sir?"

That's when I remembered Jordan. The shock of realisation at what was happening here had put him out of my mind.

"My son was here yesterday, too. I presume he knows why you're here?"

Both officers frowned, and the sergeant said, "Your son?"

"Jordan Welles."

"Jordan Welles is your son?"

They seemed surprised.

The sergeant said, "The young man told us he had no other family."

I sighed in exasperation. "The young man may well like to think he hasn't. But I'm sorry to say he misled you." I added, "And why would that be an issue, anyway?"

The sergeant responded, "Because he's in custody awaiting the appointment of an Appropriate Adult to represent his interests."

"In custody?"

"Jordan Welles is being held for questioning pending possible arrest for the murder of his mother."

CHAPTER SIX

"Your son doesn't wish to see you, sir." Inspector Gibson's tone suggested his declaration was the last word on the matter.

He was about to learn otherwise.

"What my son wants is irrelevant," I said. "The appointment of an Appropriate Adult is at the discretion of the Custody Officer, not the detainee. Is there any reason you would deny that role to the boy's father? Or do I need to take this to a higher authority?"

Police stations are seldom known for their warm and friendly atmosphere, but I could have hoped for a better welcome.

I was in a sour mood and wasn't going to be fobbed off by some misguided presumption about who was in charge here.

Gibson looked me up and down from the other side of the glass partition that divided the despatch room from the reception area. He was a short, freckled guy with fiery red hair and an attitude to match.

I folded my arms, caught his gaze, and fixed him with a cold, hard stare. Somewhere in the distance, a ringing telephone went unanswered.

Gibson was the first to cave. He broke eye contact and, when he spoke again, he sounded less confident. He dithered for a moment and said, "I'm sure we can sort something out, Mr MacGregor. I'll see what I can do."

He came around to the front of the counter and shot off down a side corridor.

He was an officious little man who had already rubbed me up the wrong way. I'd overheard him in discussion with the desk sergeant refer to Jordan as 'the perp', as though guilt was a foregone conclusion. Not that I was in the best of moods to start with. Once I'd learned of Jordan's detention, I'd thrown my few belongings into the car, called Nathan to apprise him of the situation, driven as fast as I could to the local police station, and was now standing in the custody suite. I was flustered, out of sorts, and not in the mood for any opposition. Bad enough that I had to face a recalcitrant Jordan again in these circumstances.

A few minutes later, Gibson marched back. "I had your son moved to one of the interview rooms. Follow me." His tone was curt.

He led me down an airless corridor towards a row of doors at the far end.

He brought us to a stop at the nearest door where a constable stood guard, paused with his hand on the door handle, and said, "It would be in your son's best interest to tell the truth and make a full confession."

I bristled. "You need to decide which it is you want," I said, "a confession or the truth."

His voice took on a mocking tone. "I think we both know where this is going, sir." He made the "sir" sound like an insult.

"You may think you do, Inspector," I replied, "but you need reminding that your job is to examine the evidence, not to make presumptions. Perhaps if the police weren't so eager to act as judge and jury, we'd have fewer miscarriages of justice."

Okay, so maybe I was pushing my luck a bit. But this guy was seriously pressing all the wrong buttons, and I wasn't about to suffer his bullshit in silence.

Gibson didn't respond directly, but his jaw tightened and the knuckles of his hand on the door handle turned white.

He swung the door open and said, "Let the constable know when you're through, Mr MacGregor." The ice in his voice was a sure sign I had made no friends that day.

I acknowledged his directive with a brusque nod, stepped through the door, and closed it behind me.

In the centre of the small windowless room stood a desk. Jordon was seated on the other side of it. He glared up at me, eyes aflame. If looks could burn, I'd be a charred heap on the floor by now.

"I told them I didn't want to see you."

Here we go again. It was turning out to be another one of those days. It felt like wading through treacle.

I pulled back the chair facing the desk and dropped into it. "You don't get a say. And if you had any sense, you'd realise it was in your best interests to see me."

"Oh yeah?"

The sneer told me he wasn't buying it.

I clasped my hands on the table before me and leaned toward him. My exchange with Gibson had left me rattled but, when I spoke, I tried to keep a neutral tone. "Let me tell you how this goes. Like it or not, until you're eighteen, you're legally a child. Which means you can't be interviewed without an Appropriate Adult being appointed to sit with you and represent your interests."

"They already told me that. But it doesn't have to be you."

"You'd rather have a total stranger looking out for you?"

He snorted. "So what do you think you are? I don't know you."

"Perhaps not. But at least I have a personal interest in getting to know you. And I care enough to want to help."

He leaned back, crossed his arms, and stared at me in silence. I hoped his lack of response was a sign I was getting through to him.

Softening my tone, I said, "Just think about it. I work closely with the police. And my partner can help too. He's a senior police officer. Who better to help?"

He pressed his lips together in a tight line and then said, "Your partner's a guy?"

"Yes, my partner's a guy." I leaned back.

I was about to continue when he interrupted, blurting out his words. "If you're gay, why the fuck did you marry my mum?"

That came out of nowhere, and it threw me.

I studied his face. His brow was creased and his eyes full of questions.

He deserved an explanation, but what was I supposed to tell him?

"I wish there was an easy answer," I said, "but there isn't."

He shook his head and looked away, his jaw set firm.

"Sometime soon, if you'll let me," I said, "I'd be happy to talk about my relationship with your mum. It was complicated. But I don't want you thinking I didn't love her, 'cos I did."

He faced me again, and nodded, but said nothing.

"But that's a discussion for another time," I said. "Right now, we need to get you sorted out, okay?"

He gazed over my shoulder, a faraway look in his eyes, his jaw still clenched. Turning back to face me, he nodded, as if coming to a decision, and said, "So what happens now?" His tone was sharp.

It seems we'd come to some sort of tacit agreement about my offer of help. A begrudging acceptance, maybe, but better than nothing.

But now came the tricky part. A question. Not an easy one, and not one that would endear me to him. But it had to be asked.

"Before we go any further," I said, "There's something I need to ask you. It's a question I have to ask, and I'm sorry for it, but please try not to get upset. Just give me a straight answer."

I took a breath and swallowed hard. "Did you have anything to do with your mother's death?"

Reading body language was an essential part of my skill set when working with the police, and I'd honed that skill well over the years. I had a keen eye for all those tics and traits that told me when someone was lying; the darting eyes, rapid blinking, flushing, the pacifying hand movements.

Now was the time to put my training to good use.

It wasn't something I relished doing in the current circumstances, but I had to know, one way or the other, what we were facing here.

I expected an emotional outburst, a heated denial and angry words. Instead, his face crumpled and tears welled up in his eyes. "I loved my mum. I would never hurt her." He fell forward onto the desk, face buried in his hands, and wept, his shoulders heaving with each gasping sob.

A small bowed shape, he looked so helpless, all his anger gone.

He was telling the truth. I was sure of it.

I reached out a hand, hesitated, and then squeezed his shoulder. "Let's put this right then, shall we?"

He sat upright, shook my hand from his shoulder, and wiped a sleeve across his eyes. He avoided my gaze, staring past me, his mouth set in that same grim line I had seen before.

I so desperately wanted to reach out and hug him, to let him know I was here for him. But it wasn't to be. My emotional support was the last thing he wanted. Even so, I could at least try to give him some practical help.

I waited a moment to be sure he had calmed himself and was ready to move on. Someone passed the door, their footsteps echoing down the corridor, and from somewhere in the distance came the muted sound of laughter.

"I understood your mother's death to be an accident," I said. "A head injury following a fall. Why are they now treating it as murder?"

"They're saying it wasn't the fall that killed her. They're saying she was smothered or choked to death. And something about cushion fibres."

"The police seem to think they have a case against you," I said. "Why are they so sure?"

"I was there that day, the day they found her. I went to the house, but it was locked from the inside, and I couldn't get in."

"Your presence alone is hardly a good enough reason to assume guilt. Was there anything else?"

"Not sure." He lowered his gaze to the table and ran the back of a hand across his mouth.

Something about his response gave me cause for concern. It was evasive, and I felt sure he was holding something back. I watched him for a moment, but he kept his gaze on the table.

"That's a matter to talk about later," I said. "For now, we need to arrange your release as soon as possible."

He raised his head and stared at me intently, a pleading look in his eyes. "They'll let me go?"

"If they had sufficient evidence to charge you," I said, "they would have done so by now. Which means they'll have to release you. Because of your age, they can't keep you in custody overnight without very good reason. So, I'm guessing you'll be released on bail but with conditions imposed, including discharge into the care of an adult."

"That would be you?"

"That would be the easiest option all round." I rose from my chair. "They won't release you straight away. But I'll find out what's happening and make whatever arrangements are necessary. In the meantime, you need to let them know you'll only be interviewed in the presence of a solicitor. I'll take care of that too."

He nodded his assent.

Trying to put him at ease, I assured him I would arrange his release as soon as possible.

As I rapped on the door to attract the constable's attention and signal my intention to leave, I took one last look at the small hunched figure sitting alone in the centre of that cheerless room.

The previous day, I had been grateful for a reason to keep Jordan close enough to build a relationship with him. Given the current circumstances, I could have hoped for a better reason.

CHAPTER SEVEN

After several phone calls and a hasty lunch, I drove to the town centre car park, where I'd arranged to meet Nathan.

He arrived about fifteen minutes later, and I hurried over to where he had parked and slipped into place beside him.

"Thanks for coming back," I said.

Nathan apologised for being late. "Had to make a call on the way," he explained. "So how do things stand at the moment?"

"I've sorted out a solicitor. We're meeting at the station this afternoon for Jordan's interview and statement. And they've agreed to release him into my custody."

"And you're okay with that?"

"It's something we have to talk about." I hesitated. "I know we're only an hour's drive away, but they weren't happy about him leaving town, and I'm not sure it's a good idea to disrupt his routine, anyway. Perhaps it's best if I stayed with him down here for a while."

"Had a feeling you might say that."

"It's either that or a bail hostel. And no way will I let him stay in one of those God forsaken places. If I can find somewhere local, it would be easier on him."

"And it would make it easier for you to insinuate yourself into the investigation and do some snooping around."

Bristling, I said, "There's no question of snooping." I squirmed in my seat and swallowed. "Of course, if I'm down here anyway, there wouldn't be any harm in making a few discreet local enquiries."

"That's what I said. Snooping."

I hardened my tone. "Discreet enquiries."

"And how do you intend to do that?"

"It shouldn't be a problem. I'll need to talk with Cara's business partner anyway. There'll be financial matters to discuss. I can start there and find out about Cara's other relationships. Jordan should be able to help, too."

Before he could raise any objections, Nathan's mobile interrupted us. He dug it out of his pocket and checked the screen. "I need to take this," he said. "It's Karen."

He answered the call and grunted a couple of times. And then, "Hang on a sec." He reached into his glove compartment and took out a pen. "Okay, go ahead." He hunched his shoulder to hold the phone in place and wrote something on the back of his hand. "Thanks, Karen, I owe you. Speak later," he said and ended the call.

As he shoved the phone back into his pocket and replaced the pen, he said, "It pays to have someone in the trade."

"What was all that about?"

He showed me the back of his hand. He had an address written on it. "Karen found us a local furnished let. We have it for a month with an option to extend."

"How did you know I was going to stay? And what do you mean by 'we'?"

The corner of his mouth quirked, and he said, "You think I haven't learned to read your mind by now? And by 'we' I mean 'we'."

"You're staying too?"

"You seriously think I'm staying home worrying about what trouble you're getting into snooping around?"

"I won't be snooping around or getting into trouble."

"Damn right you won't. Not with me here. I'll make sure of that."

I should have been miffed at his continuing refusal to listen to my protestations. But I wasn't. I was just grateful he was here. And feeling guilty about having dragged him away from work. "I know how busy you are," I said.

"This is more important. I took some leave. And Karen and Richard are looking after the dog."

Karen and Richard were always happy to help out when needed. Which is why they were such close friends. I was glad of their support. And for Nathan's too. "I don't care why you're here. Just pleased you are."

"Just as well. 'Cos you're not getting a choice." Jerking his thumb behind him, he said, "There are a couple of cases in the boot. Extra clothing and a few essentials. Anything else we need, we can get down here." He switched on the ignition. "Right now, we'd best get over there. One of the neighbours is waiting for us to collect the key. And then we'll go to the police station."

"I'll be right behind you." I opened the door, made my way back to where I'd parked, and followed Nathan through the afternoon traffic to a quiet suburban street. The house was a large semi behind a well-tended narrow front garden and bordered by a privet hedge.

Nathan collected the key while I fetched the cases from the boot of his car and, minutes later, we were standing in the centre of a spacious living room.

I dropped the cases at the side of a worn but comfortable-looking couch set in front of a large picture window at one end of the room.

A matching couch faced it from the other side of the room and, in between them, a teak, glass-topped coffee table stood on a thick, fawn, wool carpet with a couple of matching armchairs nearby. The room was bright and cheerful.

"Nice house," I said. "Pity we're not on holiday. It would have made a comfortable chill-out place."

"Any time away from my desk is a holiday."

"I'll take these upstairs," I said and reached for the cases.

Before I could pick them up, Nathan took hold of my arm. "Later. We need to talk." He ushered me over to the nearest couch, seated himself, and pulled me down beside him.

He was wearing his serious face.

"What is this?" I said.

"I called in at the police station on the drive over. That's why I was late."

I sensed bad news was on the way.

Nathan continued, "I had an interesting chat with the desk sergeant. Seems they're pointing the finger at Jordan because his story didn't add up. When they told him his mother's death was now a murder enquiry, he claimed he hadn't seen her the day she was killed. He lied. They have a witness who placed him at the house."

My heart sank. When I'd broached the subject with Jordan, he had been evasive. I'd let it pass, but maybe I should have been more insistent.

A thought struck me and I brightened. "What he told them can't be used in evidence, anyway. They can't use anything he says unless an Appropriate Adult or solicitor is present."

"You're missing the point here, Mikey. He lied. People don't lie without good reason."

A heaviness settled on me. "I asked him outright if he had anything to do with his mother's death. He said not, and I believed him. There were none of the signs that would suggest he was lying."

But of course, that wasn't entirely true. And I had to ask myself why I'd not pushed him harder when I'd sensed he was hiding something. Was it because I wanted to believe him despite any misgivings I may have had? I hoped not. I hoped I hadn't got it wrong.

"You want to think the best of him," Nathan said. "I know that. You just learned he's your son. But you don't know him. You know nothing about him and what he's capable of. And you need to face the possibility the police have their killer."

"If you'd seen him at the station, how helpless and alone he was, you may not be so sure of that."

"Perhaps not. But you can't let your emotional responses cloud your judgement. You need to think objectively."

He was right, of course. As usual. I had a habit of letting my emotions get in the way. But maybe that wasn't always a bad thing.

"It's you I'm thinking of," said Nathan. "I don't want you getting hurt."

"I know that. But for a moment, let's presume he's innocent. Now try to imagine what he must be going through. He's lost his mother in the most dreadful of circumstances, is accused of her murder, and is reliant for his welfare on a father he never knew he had. His world has been turned upside down, and he's alone and afraid. And that being so, he needs someone in his corner looking out for him."

"Just so long as you know where this may lead," Nathan said.

"I hear you. And I promise I'll keep what you say in mind. But I'd rather support him and be wrong than let him go through this on his own." I rose to my feet. "Now let's get those cases sorted out."

Nathan rose too and glanced at his watch. "The cases can wait. Time's getting on. We'd best get over to the station."

Nodding, I sighed and buttoned up my coat. "I have a feeling this is going to be a long, long day."

CHAPTER EIGHT

I left Nathan in the car and went over to the station to seek out our solicitor.

John Grayson struck me as one of those world-weary types who'd spent too much time in police stations fighting lost causes for lost people. But he had come highly recommended, so I was happy to give him the benefit of the doubt.

In the event, securing Jordan's release was nothing like the hassle I'd thought it might be. Almost a letdown. Grayson did a sterling job. He guided Jordan through his statement, making sure it was limited to a denial of any charges that may be brought against him and took issue with the investigating team for questioning Jordan about his whereabouts at a time when he was shocked and confused at learning of his mother's death.

I'd gone into the interview room all geared up to do battle, but within the hour, Jordan and I were saying our goodbyes to Grayson before leaving for home in Nathan's car.

Jordan seemed less appreciative of the ease with which we had secured his release. He slumped down in the back seat, arms folded across his chest, face set in a scowl. "I don't see why they get to tell me what I can and can't do and where I have to live. It's not like I've done anything wrong."

I said, "You'd rather they kept you locked up?"

Nathan shot me a dark look and said, "It won't be anywhere near as bad as you think, Jordan. We just need to make some adjustments."

Jordan grunted but said nothing.

"So, how did it go in there?" Nathan asked.

"They imposed some restrictions," I said. "Jordan has to live under our supervision, and he has to report to the local station once a week. But nothing too severe. It's obvious they don't have enough to press charges. No hard evidence. They had no choice but to let him go."

Jordan butted in. "It's not like there was anything to tell them, anyway."

Nathan and I exchanged glances. There was plenty to tell, given Jordan's dubious alibi. Something we would need to talk to him about.

"Will I still be able to work?" Jordan asked.

Only then did I realise how little we knew about him. His daily routine. His work. His friends. So much had happened so quickly, there had been no time to get to know much about him.

"I don't see why not," I said, "as long as you stick to the curfew. So, what is your line of work?"

"I'm a sculptor and potter. I work with clay or metal depending on the current project."

"An artist?" said Nathan. "I'm impressed."

"Do you work nearby?" I asked.

"Me and my friend Danny from art college share a workshop in town."

"I can't see a problem then."

"I've moved some of my metalwork stuff to my mum's place, though. There are some old buildings at the back of the house where I can store my gas cylinders and equipment. I was setting it up before all this happened."

"That might be more of a problem," I said. "It depends how much of the property has been secured as part of the crime scene. I'll check with the station."

I got a begrudging thanks in return.

Nathan said, "I asked for a copy of the crime report when I stopped off at the station. I checked in at the desk just now and they tell me they passed on my request to the senior investigating officer. They're under no obligation to let us have a copy, but I can't see it being a problem."

"It would give us something to work with," I said.

The rest of the journey home passed in relative silence despite my attempts to get Jordan to open up and tell us more about himself. He wasn't in a communicative mood.

Once back home, Nathan allocated sleeping quarters, and I carried the cases up to our room and unpacked them while Nathan and Jordan explored the rest of the house.

Within a short time, they were chatting together amicably enough, and I was surprised at how well they were getting along, given Jordan's obvious animosity towards me. Maybe he was finally beginning to thaw. Or, more likely, his hostility was reserved for me alone. Maybe he still found it hard to accept me as anything other than the father who had abandoned him. Something I needed to work on.

Back downstairs, Nathan announced it was time for a serious talk. He shunted us through to the sitting room and told us to sit. "We need to get a few things sorted out," he said.

I guessed what was coming and, as we settled into place, I steeled myself, ready for a heated exchange.

Nathan nodded to Jordan and said, "We can start by discussing the police case against you."

I interrupted. "Can't this wait?" It shouldn't, of course, but I was hoping to give Jordan a break from yet another interrogation and give us chance to settle in and get to know each other first.

"The police aren't going to wait," said Nathan, "and neither can we." He turned his attention back to Jordan. "Let me tell you how this works. Investigations of this nature follow a pattern. The investigating team focus attention on those closest to the victim and gradually widen their scope to include other relationships. Which is why their initial focus is on you. You're family. Which puts you right at the top of the list."

I interjected. "Anyone who had a close relationship with your mother is a potential suspect. It's nothing personal."

"If it's nothing personal," said Jordan, "how come I'm the only one on bail?"

"Because you lied," said Nathan. "You gave them a false alibi. And you must have realised that would set off alarm bells. So let's start there. Why?"

Straight to the point, as ever.

Jordan flushed and looked away, avoiding Nathan's gaze.

"You're not doing yourself any favours by lying," Nathan said. "It should be obvious it would arouse suspicions. And whatever resources the police have are now going to be concentrated on making a case against you."

He paused for a moment, but Jordan stayed silent.

Nathan continued, "Your father tells me he accepts your claim not to have been involved in your mother's death, and I trust his judgement. So we need to put this right. We need to ensure the local force direct their resources elsewhere."

Father? I baulked at that. Not a title that settled on me easily. It was going to take some getting used to.

Jordan bit his lip and nodded. Nathan's tone didn't allow for argument or dissent. It kept Jordan in check. Something I was grateful for. He said, "We argued. Big time. I thought if I told them we'd rowed, it would look bad. And I panicked."

"What was it about?" I asked.

"She was always on my case," he said. "You can't do this. You can't do that. It's why I left home. I got so sick of it. I'm old enough to make my own decisions. I don't know why she couldn't see that?"

"I guess she was just looking out for you," I said.

"And then she tried to blackmail me into moving back. Threatened to cut off my allowance. That was so unfair."

I exchanged a knowing glance with Nathan. Jordan had just given us a viable motive for murder.

"It's probably best if we discuss the way forward with your solicitor," I said, "but, for the moment, don't talk to anyone else about this."

Nathan said, "And that was the day they found your mother's body?"

Jordan shook his head. "It was a couple of days before. I went back that morning to make the peace. But I never got a chance. The door was locked and she wouldn't answer it. I guess she didn't want to see me." He folded his arms and looked down at the floor.

"I can understand why you lied," said Nathan, "but it wasn't the best of moves. It was bound to throw suspicion on you."

"Your mum's solicitor told me she was in a relationship with someone," I said. "He'll be of interest to the police, too. What can you tell us about him?"

"Austin Brady. She met him through some client at work. I don't know much about him. She hadn't known him long."

"Have the police interviewed him?" I asked.

"No idea. They wouldn't tell me anything."

To Nathan, I said, "Is there any way you can use your influence down at the station? Get them to hurry up with that report."

"I'll do what I can, but I'm sure we'll get it soon enough."

"It should help us do some digging around."

Nathan pointed a warning finger at me. "I won't try to talk you out of getting involved. That would be a waste of time. But you need to make sure you don't tread on any toes."

"I promise I'll be discreet."

"I have no authority here," he continued. "This region is outside my jurisdiction. So any help we get from the local force would be a courtesy only. And they would have every right to refuse that help if they thought we were getting in the way. Okay?"

"Okay, I get it." He meant well, but I wished he would credit me with a bit more common sense at times.

"I'll get in touch with Cara's business partner and take it from there," I said. "She's sure to know about Cara's other relationships and it'll give me an excuse to ask about them. So no need to worry. I'll be on safe ground."

Nathan grunted. A reluctant acknowledgement.

"In fact, I'll call her now," I said. "See if I can't set up a meeting for tomorrow. She must be eager for news after recent developments."

I dug my mobile out of my pocket.

"In that case, we'll leave you to it." Nathan rose to his feet. "Come on, Jordan. Let's go get your stuff. Might as well get you properly settled in."

I paused in the act of calling Cara's business number. "Are you sure you're okay with that? I'd be happy to run Jordan over to his place." I'd been hoping for a chance to talk with him one on one, try to build up some rapport between us.

"No problem," said Nathan. "we've got it covered."

"I can show you some of my work," said Jordan as they headed for the door.

So that was it. Any hopes of getting some prime time with my son were put on hold.

But at least we could now get down to some serious work and help

him out of this mess.
　　I made the call.

CHAPTER NINE

As I predicted, Cara's business partner jumped at the chance to see me and agreed to a meeting early the following morning. Any pretext of discussing financial matters was unnecessary. Reagan Francis was concerned only with the fallout from Cara's death and anxious to learn as much as possible about any developments.

But that could wait.

With little more to do that afternoon, I had hoped to spend time with Jordan. Not only an opportunity to get to know him but also to question him about his mother's relationships. The more I learned about her social and business contacts, the more I could increase the number of likely leads to follow up on.

But I was out of luck.

Once Nathan had dropped him off at his flat and he'd taken back charge of his own car, Jordan had driven off to his workshop after promising to pick up his belongings and bring them over to the house that evening.

It was nearer to ten when he returned, and he went straight up to his room, declining an invitation to join us for a chat before turning in for the night.

"Not exactly sociable," I said to Nathan.

We were in the living room sharing a bottle of Pinot Grigio and catching up with the news on Radio 4.

"Be patient," he said. "It's going to take time. And he is beginning to thaw."

"With you. But he's avoiding me."

"Could be he's just embarrassed. He didn't make the best of starts."

"I hope that's all it is."

"You'll get there in the end."

I resolved to engage him in the morning but, once more, I was thwarted. He was up and out of the house while Nathan and I were still in bed. And so I set off for my meeting with Reagan Francis, having failed to spend any quality time with my newly acquired son.

My first impression of Springboard Creative wasn't good. It was one of those soulless ultra-modern offices, all glass and chrome and fake potted plants.

On the plus side, the waiting area had some of those comfortable leather chairs that let you sink into them when you seat yourself. It also had magnificent views over the old town. Not that I had time to sit and admire them; Cara's business partner, Reagan Francis, came to greet me within minutes of my arrival.

She was an attractive woman, mid-thirties I guessed. Slender with shoulder-length auburn hair.

As I rose to my feet, she reached out and greeted me with a handshake. "Let's go through to my office," she said and guided me across the large reception area and into a glass-walled room nearby.

Reagan Francis was the first person I'd seen here in traditional office wear - a fitted grey business suit and plain white blouse - totally out of sync with the casual jeans-and-sweatshirts style of most of her colleagues. Her choice of attire was matched by a self-assured and businesslike manner.

"I'm so pleased we could finally meet." She waved me over to a leather couch and seated herself in an adjacent matching chair.

She crossed her legs and leaned forward, hands clasped together on her raised knee.

"The entire company is in total shock," she said. "Bad enough we should lose Cara in such a way. But to hear that Jordan..." She broke off and shook her head. "I can't quite believe it."

"I should tell you, he vehemently denies any involvement in his mother's death. And he has my full support."

She nodded. "I didn't doubt it for a moment. His relationship with Cara could be stormy, but he would never hurt her. I just hope he's bearing up."

I explained his present circumstances and brought her up to date on where the police were with the investigation - which was precisely nowhere - and assured her we were taking care of Jordan.

"It's good to hear he's in safe hands. I've been so worried. You must tell me if there's anything I can do to help. I've always been very fond of Jordan."

I told her I would and added, "Do you know what they were arguing about? He's being cagey about it."

"They rowed all the time. They were both volatile by nature. But you may learn more from his girlfriend."

"His girlfriend?"

"Yes. Sophie."

I stared at her blankly.

"Sophie Barber. They share a rental in town. You didn't know?"

My face flushed. "I'm embarrassed to say I know very little about Jordan. So much has happened these last few days. I haven't had a chance to get to know him."

"You both have a lot of catching up to do," she said. "It must have been a shock to learn you even had a son."

"I take it your solicitor filled you in on the details."

She nodded. "It was a shock for me, too. I'd always presumed you were part of Cara's dim and distant past."

"Me too."

"If there's any way in which I can help, please ask. Whatever you need. Cara wasn't just my business partner. She was a dear friend. And I'm happy to help in any way I can."

"Were you aware of any concerns she had in the days before her death? Anyone she was having problems with?"

She shook her head. "If there had been, she would have told me."

"So nothing out of the ordinary?"

"Nothing to worry about. We'd recently taken on a new client with several businesses. Eliott Garcia. It was a very lucrative contract. We had a party to celebrate at our offices the night before Cara's death. Elliot Garcia and his fiancée, Leila Rivera, were guests of honour. Everyone was having a good time. Cara overdid it on the wine. Not like her. But it was a special occasion after all and, like the rest of us, she was in good spirits.

"It must have been a particularly cruel blow to lose Cara just when everything was going so well."

She sighed deeply. "Not only did we lose a dear friend and colleague, but her loss will have a negative impact on the business."

"I'm sorry to hear that."

She must have noticed my puzzled look. "I work on the financial side," she said. "Cara was the creative one, and losing her will make a difference. We have other creatives, of course, but none as talented as Cara. We were very much dependent on her skills."

I expressed my concerns and wished her well in her future endeavours before moving on to another area of interest. "Jordan tells me his mother was in a relationship. Someone she met through work. Austin Brady. Do you know him?"

Her face hardened, and she frowned.

The moment passed, and her face lightened again. "Why don't I get us something to drink?" She rose to her feet and crossed over to the phone on her desk. "Tea? Coffee?"

I asked for tea. She phoned through the request and returned to her seat.

Something about her reaction to hearing Brady's name made me suspicious. I got the impression she was stalling, playing for time while she considered her reply.

She paused for a moment and then said, "During initial negotiations, we worked on a marketing strategy for our new client. He has several businesses across the country. This was a local one. A gymnasium. Beefed Up. It's just down the road from here."

I pulled a face, and she raised a hand in response. "I know. Terrible name. Something we need to work on." She continued, "Austin Brady works there as a personal trainer. He and Cara met during our first visit a couple of months ago. Elliot Garcia's fiancée is the manager there, and she let us check out the place to formulate an appropriate marketing plan. It seems Cara had her mind elsewhere."

The sarcasm in her voice wasn't lost on me. "You disapproved?"

Before she could respond, we were interrupted by the sound of the door opening. A smiling young woman brought in a tray bearing a pot of tea and crockery. She placed it on the coffee table before us and departed without a word.

Reagan watched after her until she left the room before speaking. "I'm not sure I considered Austin Brady suitable relationship material." She reached for the teapot. "Milk and sugar?"

"Just milk."

She finished pouring the teas and settled back in her chair, cup in hand. "Maybe it's just me," she said. "I'm old-fashioned enough to believe that business and pleasure don't mix."

"It wasn't him, in particular, you objected to then?" I picked up my cup and drank from it.

Her face clouded again, and she considered this for a moment. "I'm not sure it matters what I think," she said. "Cara was happy with her choice and that's what counts, isn't it?"

Or maybe not. I felt sure Reagan was holding back, keeping her true thoughts to herself. Which did little to help me form a positive impression of this guy. I made a mental note to check him out.

"The police must have interviewed him anyway," I said.

"I should imagine so. They've interviewed everyone here too. It was particularly stressful for Cara's secretary, of course. She's away on compassionate leave at the moment."

"Why? Were they close?"

Regan shot me a puzzled look and then shook her head. "Sorry. I presumed you knew. It was Vanessa who found Cara."

I offered my sympathies and explained that I didn't yet know the details, but was hoping to see a copy of the crime report. "Did Cara often work from home?" I asked.

"No, but there were times she preferred to work alone without the usual interruptions. We had arranged to meet in the office early that morning to prepare for an important presentation later that day. But Cara called me first thing to say she would work from home and be in the office in plenty of time for the meeting."

"What time was she found?"

"Not long after noon. When Cara hadn't arrived by then, I called her but got no reply. I sent Vanessa round to find out why."

"So she could have been killed anytime that morning?"

"Cara emailed Vanessa just after 8:30 am and asked her to email some information she needed for the meeting. So it would have been some time after that."

That would give me a timeline to work with. Now, I just needed to get my hands on the police report and check out the alibis. And I had a good idea of where I would start.

I thanked Reagan for her help and brought our meeting to a close.

Before I left, she stressed, once again, that she would be happy to help in any way she could and asked me to tell Jordan he had her full support.

I thanked her and took my leave, eager to be on my way.

Reagan's reserved responses to my enquiries about Austin Brady had piqued my interest. It was time to pay him a visit.

CHAPTER TEN

The Beefed Up gym was no more than a five-minute walk away from Springboard Creative's offices. And despite its naff name, it had a lot going for it. A bright, airy place with modern, state-of-the-art equipment. It was busy, and I had to wait in line at the reception desk. In nearby rooms, the clank and clatter of metal vied with the thump of feet on treadmills, the hiss of hydraulics, and the shouted instructions of trainers.

Once I reached the front of the queue, I asked if Austin Brady was free to speak to me on a personal matter. The limber young woman behind the desk directed me to a courtyard at the rear of the building. "He's on a break at the moment," she said. "But you'd best be quick. He has another class in five minutes."

When I caught up with Brady, he didn't seem in much of a hurry to return to his class.

He was leaning against the back wall of the building, one hand on the wall, the other on the buttocks of the shapely, black-haired woman pressed up against him. They were deep in conversation and didn't see me approach.

I could understand why Cara would fall for him. He was a hot-looking guy. One of those firm-fleshed, square-jawed types with piercing blue eyes beneath dark, heavy brows.

Under the tracksuit was a muscular, powerfully built body, and everything about the way he posed, about his confident, swaggering manner, told me he was only too well aware of his sex appeal.

But I could just as readily understand why Reagan Francis hadn't considered him relationship material. For starters, he didn't exactly fit the picture of the grieving partner. And from the way he leered and dropped his gaze to peer down the front of his companion's figure-hugging, red dress, it was a fair bet they weren't discussing work-related matters.

I interrupted them. "Austin Brady?"

As they turned to face me, Brady's leer morphed into an expression of sudden surprise and then a tight-lipped grimace. "I'm on a break here, man. You need to check in at reception."

"It's a personal matter," I said and introduced myself as Cara's ex-husband. "I dropped by to offer you my condolences on your loss."

I hoped the irony of my words wasn't lost on him.

He had the good grace to blush, and he and the woman moved apart.

She was a Latino, raven-black hair tumbling over her shoulders, smouldering good looks, and fire in her eyes.

She shot Brady a conspiratorial look and said, "I'll see you later." The look she gave me as she moved away was less friendly. Obviously, not very happy at my interrupting what appeared to be part of a familiar routine.

Brady watched her head towards the gym's rear entrance and, once the door closed behind her, he grinned and said, "It's always a good idea to stay well in with the rest of the staff. It's nothing serious."

As excuses went, it was right up there at the top of the lame list.

"Losing the person you loved must have hit you hard," I said, trying to sound sincere.

He swallowed and nodded.

"We hadn't known each other long," he said. "Just a few weeks. But we were already making plans. I was getting ready to move in with her and make it more permanent. And then this. It came out of nowhere. Bad enough it was so sudden. But murder? I still can't believe it."

"You must have been closer to her than anyone. Any idea who would want to harm her?"

His brows knitted. "They have someone up on a charge, don't they? Her son, Jordan, did it."

"My son was interviewed along with everyone else who knew Cara. But no charges have been brought against him."

He blinked. "Your son?" He sounded less sure of himself.

"I understand he had a rocky relationship with his mother," I said. "But it's only what you'd expect of a teenager. Hardly a reason for murder."

"Look, man, I'm not looking to point the finger at anyone here, but that boy of yours had a temper. That last argument he had with his mother was a real humdinger."

"You were there?"

"Sure was. But I stay clear when Jordan's around. We're not exactly buddies. But I heard them from upstairs."

"Do you know what they rowed about?"

"No. But, believe me, there were a lot of angry words on both sides. Cara was upset for a long time afterwards but she wouldn't talk about it."

"And no one else you can think of who might have wanted her out of the way?"

He shook his head. "Cara was well-liked. Everyone got on with her. I can't think of anyone who would want to kill her."

"And no changes to her routine before her death?" I asked. "Nothing out of the ordinary?"

"Nothing I haven't already told the police. We were at a party the night before, enjoying ourselves. Having a good time."

"Did you leave together?"

"No. She had some sort of meeting to prepare for the following day. She didn't want me staying over, so I took a cab home."

"So there were no problems? Everything was okay between you?"

He narrowed his eyes and there was a slight curl to his lip. "And why would you ask that?" he said.

"It's a straightforward enough question."

"I'm not so dumb I can't see where you're heading," he said. "But don't go there. Cara and I were doing just fine."

"The police must have questioned you about your relationship."

"Sure they did. And they were satisfied with my answers. And my alibi. So let's leave it to them, shall we?"

He glanced at his watch. "And now, if the cross-examination is over, I have a class to take." He gave me a curt nod and headed towards the door.

I followed behind, keeping my distance. And, once inside, made my way back to the reception.

I wasn't done yet.

First impressions of others are formed within seconds of meeting them. We may not be aware of it on a conscious level, but it happens all the same. We assess them based on their appearance, their mannerisms, their body language, and we decide, almost at once, whether we like or dislike them.

And I disliked Brady.

Intensely.

In my line of work, it's important not to let such instinctive assessments distort professional judgement. But in Brady's case, I found it hard to stay neutral.

Everything about him was at odds with the expectation of someone grieving the loss of a partner. And that made him worthy of closer scrutiny.

Once at the reception desk, I explained to the young woman on the other side of it that I was thinking of enrolling. "I'd like to join one of Austin Brady's classes if possible," I said and asked for details of times.

"I don't have any hard copy," she said, "but we have the information on our website." There was a monitor screen on the desk and she turned it around at an angle so we could both view it. "We can run through it now if you wish and book you in."

I declined. "I'll check the site later when I have more time and get back to you."

Having Brady's schedule would help me assess his movements and whereabouts over the past few days, a step on the way to determining where he was on the day of Cara's murder.

The police may have been happy with his alibi. But I wasn't.

CHAPTER ELEVEN

"Did you need to go see him?" Nathan asked.

"I wanted to offer my condolences."

"And, of course, you didn't interrogate him while you were there?"

I was back home following my visit to the gym. Nathan had just returned from shopping for groceries and household supplies. We were in the kitchen putting them away while I brought him up to date on what I'd learned from and about Austin Brady.

"He wasn't very talkative," I said. "But it's as well I went to see him. Something's not quite right there."

"How so?" He handed me a bag of cleaning products.

I crouched by the sink and found places for the various aerosols and plastic bottles in the cupboard beneath. "He was round the back of the gym coming on to one of his co-workers," I said. "The woman he's supposed to be in a close relationship with is murdered, and he's already making out with someone else. Not what you'd expect from the grieving partner, is it?"

"Perhaps not. But don't go jumping to conclusions."

"It's hard not to."

"The guy sounds like a jerk. But that doesn't make him a killer."

"Nor does it make him a blameless innocent." I pushed myself to my feet, reached for the kettle, filled it at the tap, and plugged it in. "I got the impression Cara's business partner didn't much like him either."

Nathan handed me a jar of coffee and said, "How did that go?"

I told him of my conversation with Reagan Francis while I spooned coffee into a couple of mugs. "She was worried about Jordan, but I assured her we were looking after him." I finished making the coffee and handed him one of the mugs. "Did you know he had a live-in girlfriend?"

"Yes, Sophie. Nice girl."

"You've met her?"

"Yes. You'll meet her later. She's bringing her stuff over."

"Bringing her stuff over?"

"Yes, she's moving in."

"Moving in?"

Nathan raised his head and looked around the room. "Is there an echo in here?"

I huffed. "When did all this happen?"

"Jordan came back not long after you left and we had a chat. He had a lot to get off his chest.

"Okay, so let's hear it."

"You said it yourself. The poor guy's life is a mess right now. He's been accused of murder and stuck in an unfamiliar setting with people he doesn't know. And, on top of that, he's parted from the person he's closest to and the one who's best placed to bring some normality to his life. You said we needed to support him. What better way than letting him have his girlfriend with him?"

"Okay, but should we let her move in?"

"They're a couple. They're living together. Of course, we should let her move in." He sipped his coffee.

"They're just kids. I'm not sure we should let them shack up together."

"They're not kids. They're teenagers. Just what were you doing at their age?"

I leaned against the sink, put down my mug, folded my arms, and glared at him. "I was waiting for you to make a move."

"Well, you sure made up for lost time when I did. So stop talking nonsense."

I grunted and pulled a face.

"You've left it a bit late to start playing the heavy-handed father," he said. "Not a good idea, given the current state of your relationship. Just let it be."

I picked up my mug again. "Being a father is a lot more complicated than I thought it would be."

"I'm sure you'll get the hang of it, eventually." He drained his mug and handed it to me. "Which reminds me. I called in at the station on my way back. The report's not to hand yet. But I had a chat with one of the investigating team. They're no further on than they were."

"Did you find out what they learned from Brady?"

"Sorry to disappoint you, but it seems he's in the clear. He has a verifiable alibi. He was at the gym all that day. His boss confirmed it."

Before I could reply, we were interrupted by the sound of the front door opening, and a female voice called out, "It's only me."

A moment later, we were joined in the kitchen by a young woman, introduced to me by Nathan as Sophie Barber.

She wasn't at all what I'd imagined. She and Jordan couldn't be more different. In my mind, I'd conjured up a picture of an arty type; all bright colours, zany dress style, and extravagant gestures. What I got was a sombre young woman with straight, dark-brown, shoulder-length hair, no makeup, and dressed casually in jeans and a grey sweatshirt.

"I'm a fan," she said. "I've read some of your books on psychological profiling. Fascinating. It was strange finding out you were Jordan's dad."

"Strange times all round," I said. "Let's just hope we can get this mess sorted out."

Nathan butted in. "Jordan didn't come back with you?"

"He's at his workshop. The guy he shares with wanted to know what was happening. I said I'd pick him up later."

"You work with Jordan?" I asked.

She laughed. "I leave the creative stuff to those with a talent for it."

We chatted for a while and I learned she worked as a paralegal for a large law firm in Cheltenham. She and Jordan had known each other since they were children at school and, despite having very different lifestyles, had always been close. They had finally got together as a couple and had recently moved into a shared rental.

I liked her. She was pleasant, outgoing, and easy to talk to.

Nathan said, "You'll have to forgive Mikey. He has a habit of interrogating people he's just met. Goes with the job."

She laughed again and said she was happy to chat.

I wished my son could be as happy to talk with me.

Nathan said, "Well, let's get you settled in before he gives you the third degree. I'll show you to your room." He led her through to the hall where she had dropped her cases.

I rinsed our mugs under the tap, left them on the drainer, and caught up with them as Nathan was picking up the cases.

"I'll take these up," he said and headed up the stairs.

Sophie called after him. "I'll unpack later. I'd best go pick Jordan up first. Once he and Danny get together, they start on the beers and lose all track of time."

"Tell you what," I said. "Why don't I go pick him up? It'll give me chance to spend some time with him. And he can show me around his workshop."

Sophie agreed readily enough. "I'm sure you still have a lot to talk about." Something about the way she said it told me my relationship with Jordan was an ongoing subject of discussion between them. Maybe he was finally ready for a grown-up talk. I hoped so.

She gave me directions to the workshop and followed Nathan upstairs as I headed for the door.

Jordan's workshop was in the old part of town, just over ten minutes' drive away. It turned out to be a converted double garage at the end of a row of such structures in a disused car park that now served as a workspace for various small industrial units.

I parked the Elan at the back of the long, low structure and made my way around to the front.

As I was turning down the side of the building, the sound of raised voices from inside brought me to a sudden halt. The voices were clearly audible through the ventilation grille. One I recognised as Jordan's. The other, presumably, belonged to his work buddy. They were in the middle of an argument.

Jordan's voice was loud and his tone querulous. "We're supposed to be friends," he said.

"Forget it. Not going to happen."

"I'm asking you to back me up, is all."

"Dropping me in it, more like."

Jordan was pleading now. "It's not that much to ask, is it?"

"Lying to the police? Not much to ask? You tried that already, remember? See where it got you."

"It wouldn't be lying. You just need to play dumb is all. If they come round asking questions, act as if you don't know anything."

"The only one being dumb around here is you. I said no, and I meant no."

"Well thanks and fuck you." Jordan was shouting now.

The sound of receding footsteps was followed by the rattle of the metal shutter at the front of the workshop, and then Jordan delivered a parting shot. "Nice to know who my friends are," he called out.

I ducked behind a group of canisters pushed up against the side of the building, hoping to avoid being spotted. Fortunately, Jordan stormed off in the other direction.

After a moment or so, I crept to the end of the wall and peered around the edge to make sure the coast was clear. Jordan was nowhere in sight.

Straightening up, I turned the corner to the front of the unit and stepped into the workshop.

The smell of wet clay assailed my nostrils. The young man inside was seated on a stool, elbows on the bench before him, head in his hands, several cutting tools scattered around him. Behind him, an electric kiln stood against a breeze block wall beneath a ventilation grille.

He looked up as I entered.

"It's Danny, isn't it?"

"Yes."

"I'm Jordan's father," I said. "We need to talk."

CHAPTER TWELVE

I'd spoken more sharply than intended and put the young man on the defensive. He squinted up at me, pale-faced and with a glint of alarm in his eyes.

When he spoke, his voice was strained. "What do you want?"

I crossed towards the bench, pulled back a stool from the other side of it, and seated myself opposite him. I leaned forward, stared him full in the face and said, "You can start by explaining the conversation I just overheard."

He pressed a hand against the bench and pushed himself away from it. "I don't know what you mean."

"You accused Jordan of being dumb. I hope you're not dumb too."

"Jordan's done nothing wrong."

"Lying to the police? I think they might disagree."

"I got nothing to say." He stared down at the bench, avoiding my gaze.

"You have a choice. You speak to me, or you speak to the police. Either way, you're going to explain that conversation. And believe me, speaking to me will be a whole lot easier on you."

He swallowed hard, picked up a clay-covered paddle from in front of him, and turned it over and over in his hand. "Look, Jordan can be a bit of an idiot at times, but he's no killer."

"That doesn't answer my question."

"I promised him I'd say nothing. If I go back on my word now, I'd be letting him down."

"Okay," I said and rose from my stool. "The police it is then."

"Wait." He dropped the paddle, jumped to his feet and rounded the bench. He hesitated, as if coming to a decision, and said, "There's something I want to show you."

He crossed over to a filing cabinet on the other side of the workshop, pulled some papers from the top drawer, took them back to where he'd been sitting, and spread them out before him.

"I don't want him thinking I betrayed his trust," he said, "so let's suppose that when you came in, I was sitting here going through these invoices, and you just happened to catch sight of this one." He pushed a printed sheet towards me across the bench.

I picked it up. It was an invoice from a local garage for fitting new brake pads. I was puzzled. "What's this got to do with anything?"

"We hold all our personal invoices here, as well as the ones for workshop supplies. It makes it easier to keep an eye on our individual spending."

"I don't understand."

"Just read it."

It was made out to Sophie Barber and was dated… I froze. "It's dated the day of the murder," I said.

"Now work it out."

"Sophie works in Cheltenham, so she'd need a car to get there. If her car is off the road, the most obvious solution would be to borrow Jordan's."

"You got it."

"It wasn't Jordan who visited his mother that day, was it? It was Sophie." I handed the invoice back to Danny. "So, what's the story here?"

He took the invoice from me and put it back on the bench. "I've done my bit," he said. "Now you'll need to speak to them."

"It would help if I knew what I'd be facing."

"There's nothing more I can tell you. I have no idea what happened that day. Only that Jordan wasn't there."

"I guess I'd best go find out then," I said, and turned to leave.

Danny said, "You will keep me out of it, won't you?"

I turned to face him again. Deep lines creased his forehead.

"Don't worry," I said. "You're in the clear." I thanked him for his help, said my goodbyes, and reassured him, once more, that I wouldn't say a word about our conversation.

On the drive home, I mused over what I'd just learned. First off, it took Jordan out of the frame as a suspect. Or, at least, it made it less likely. But now, Sophie was going to be under the spotlight.

And, if Jordan was covering for her, did that mean she was implicated in Cara's death? I hoped not. On first meeting, she had struck me as a mature, decent, straightforward type. So why lie? I guess both she and Jordan had some explaining to do.

Back at the house, the sounds of laughter and animated chatter drew me through to the living room where I found the three of them chilling out, Jordan and Sophie sprawled out on one of the couches, Nathan laid back in an armchair with his leg over the arm, all three of them holding glasses. They were enjoying a pleasant, relaxed chat over a shared bottle of wine.

And I was about to spoil it.

"Sorry I missed you," Jordan said. "I got a taxi back."

"I've already told him off for not waiting," said Sophie with a smile.

"No worries." I dropped into the other armchair. "Danny was busy sorting out some invoices, so I didn't stay too long."

Trying to sound casual, I said, "Is your car running okay now, Sophie?"

"My car?" She straightened herself up in her seat and frowned. "What about it?"

"I happened to spot an invoice on the desk at Jordan's workshop while I was chatting to Danny," I said. "I see your car was in for repairs recently."

When she spoke again, she sounded unsure, her voice strained. "It was nothing serious. Just some minor repairs."

"It's a long journey to Cheltenham," I said. "And there are no direct trains. I presume you would need to borrow Jordan's car to get to work that day."

Jordan interrupted. "The garage arranged a hire car."

"Really?" I said. "So if I check with them, they'll be able to confirm that, will they?"

Jordan and Sophie exchanged glances, and Jordan squirmed and pulled himself upright.

"Why would you need to hire a car," I said, "when your partner has one readily available?"

The silence in the room was deafening.

Nathan broke it. "What's going on here?"

"What's Danny been saying?" said Jordan.

"He didn't need to say anything," I said. "I can work things out for myself."

Nathan tried again. "Is someone going to tell me what's happening?"

"Sophie's car was in the garage for repairs the day Jordan's car was spotted at his mother's place, the day they found her," I said. "Now we just need to know who was driving it."

Sophie butted in. "I said this would happen." She blurted it out, her voice on the edge of hysteria. "I said it was a stupid idea."

Jordan countered. "I was only thinking of you."

Sophie turned to face me and Nathan, her gaze darting back and forth from one to the other of us, a pleading look in her eyes. "I tried to persuade Jordan to tell the truth," she said. "I knew it was wrong, but he can be so stubborn." She was shaking, and the blood had drained from her face.

Jordan said nothing. He bit his lip and looked down at the floor.

"So you've been lying to us?" Nathan sounded like he'd already decided the answer to that and wasn't too happy about it.

Chill time was over.

Nathan was back on duty.

"Start talking," he said. "And this time we'll have the truth."

Jordan and Sophie sat bolt upright, side by side, their faces showing signs of strain. It was like watching a couple of naughty schoolchildren facing the headmaster's wrath.

Sophie shot Jordan a glance and squeezed his thigh before turning her attention back to Nathan. "Jordan didn't lie to the police. He didn't know I'd been to see his mother. It was only later, when he learned his car had been seen, he realised what had happened."

"So why not just come clean about it?" Nathan asked.

Jordan took over. "After the hassle I had with the police, I didn't want Sophie to go through that, too. So I changed my mind and told them I'd visited my mother that day."

"What were you thinking?" Nathan said. "You realise you've made it a whole lot worse?"

"It didn't seem that big a deal at the time," said Jordan.

"Well it sure as hell is now," said Nathan. "Your lie made you the focus of the investigation."

Jordan chewed on his lip and dropped his gaze to the floor once more.

Nathan's tone was less harsh when he spoke again. "I'm sure you did it for the best of reasons, but we need to make this right."

I said, "And it's put Sophie in a worse position."

"I don't see why," said Jordan.

"Because you're both caught up in the same lie," said Nathan. "And now the investigating team are going to think maybe Sophie has something to hide."

"They'll want to know why you were there," I said.

"So why were you?" Nathan asked.

Sophie exchanged another look with Jordan and said, "Jordan and I have known each other all our lives. We knew we were right for each other. And once we'd moved in together, Jordan wanted us to get married. I'm eighteen, so I'm free to make my own choices, but Jordan needed his mother's permission."

"Which is why I drove over to see her a few days ago," said Jordan. "Big mistake. I've never seen her so angry. She called me an idiot and said I was throwing my life away. That I was too young. Like I didn't understand what I was getting into. We ended up shouting at each other, and I stormed off."

I sighed inwardly. The folly of youth. We're so certain of everything at that age, so impatient to get on with our lives on our own terms, so eager to ignore the advice of those who have our interests at heart. But then I'd made enough stupid decisions of my own at their age, so I recognised how easy it was to dismiss the voices of reason. And I could understand why Cara would have been so against an early marriage for her son. She would not have wanted him to make the same mistake we had.

Sophie took over again. "I needed to make the peace. There was always some friction between me and Cara. She was very protective of Jordan, and I'm sure she felt I was taking him away from her. But I needed to put things right between us. Which is why I went round to see her that day."

"And how did it go?" I asked.

Sophie said, "She didn't answer the door. I could tell she was home because her car was parked out front. And I caught a quick glimpse of her in the upper window where her office is. But when I looked up, she stepped away. She obviously didn't want to see me, so I left."

"And if you'd told this to the police in the first place," said Nathan, "Jordan wouldn't now be on bail while the police try to build a case against him."

"You need to make a new statement," I said to Jordan.

"You both do," said Nathan and sprang to his feet. "And I suggest you have a good hard think about what you're going to say on the way to the station. You have a lot of explaining to do."

"You want us to go now?" said Jordan.

"Too right I do. Get moving."

No one was in the mood to argue.

CHAPTER THIRTEEN

At the station, I let Nathan do the talking. He was better acquainted with police procedures and would be able to smooth the way for our two wayward charges.

I'd managed to contact Jordan's solicitor on the drive over and had arranged to meet him here. Now it was just a matter of waiting it out.

I left the three of them at the desk and seated myself in the empty waiting area on one of the standard-issue, metal-framed chairs. I'd always harboured a suspicion they were meant to make users as uncomfortable as possible.

Nathan joined me a few minutes later. He dropped into place at my side and said, "They've been taken to separate interview rooms. Not sure how long it will take - they have to wait until Jordan's solicitor gets here - but, in the meantime, I've asked to speak to the officer leading the investigation, Inspector Gibson. I still haven't had that report, and it might help if we knew the current state of play."

"Inspector Gibson?" I groaned. "Not the ginger guy who'd look more at home in a circus ring? That's all we need."

Nathan glared at me, a steely glint in his eyes. "Okay, what did you do this time?"

I avoided his gaze. "I didn't do anything."

"Mikey?" He was growling.

"He was the one who started it."

"I'll ask you again. What did you do?"

I bit my lip before answering. "We had a few words, is all." I told him about my earlier encounter with Gibson. "He'd already decided

Jordan was a murderer. You can hardly blame me for being annoyed."

"Perhaps. But getting on his wrong side isn't going to help, is it? When we see him, you need to apologise."

I sat bolt upright and turned to face him. "Apologise? Me? What do I need to apologise for?"

"Which is more important, Mikey, protecting your ego or getting the police onside?"

I exhaled heavily. "It's going to cost you a steak dinner at the most expensive restaurant I can find."

"It'll cost a hell of a lot more if you don't apologise."

I gave in and agreed, reluctantly, to say sorry. And when Gibson finally deigned to appear, I greeted him with a welcoming smile and tried to make it seem genuine.

In return, we got a blank stare and a curt nod.

He led us away down a cheerless, white-walled corridor to an office at the far end. Once inside, we were offered seats on the other side of his desk, and he sat facing us, his expression still the same unwelcoming stare.

"How can I help you, gentlemen?" he said. His tone of voice suggested help was the last thing on offer.

I drew in a slow breath and said, "Before we go any further, I owe you an apology."

He arched his eyebrows but said nothing.

"I was disrespectful and discourteous when we first met. I want to apologise for my behaviour."

Gibson's hard expression lightened and when he spoke, his tone was less tense. "You were upset. It was understandable."

"All the same, it shouldn't have happened. I've worked with the police many times in the past and I know from experience how difficult your work can be. It doesn't help having someone like me making it even more difficult. I should have known better."

For a non-actor, it was a good performance. I almost believed it myself.

Only when I'd finished speaking did I realise I'd been digging my fingernails into the palms of my hands. I forced myself to relax and sat back in my chair.

"Let's just forget about it, shall we?" he said. "In the end, we all want the same thing."

I wasn't so sure about that, but I agreed anyway.

"These past few days, I've learned something of your work in assisting with criminal investigations," he said. "I hear you came up trumps on that series of murders in Wood Green a few years ago. You have an excellent reputation. I'm impressed."

"I do what I can."

"Maybe we could use some of that expertise in this case," he said, and added hastily, "Of course, I appreciate that your personal connection precludes any direct involvement, but I can't see any harm in your looking over our case files."

"I'd be happy to help," I said. Perhaps it was best not to tell him I had every intention of involving myself anyway.

"Are you okay with that?" he said to Nathan.

Nathan held up his hands in a gesture of dismissal and said, "You're quite capable of handling this case without any interference from me. I'm just here as an interested observer." Ever the diplomat.

Gibson nodded, seemingly satisfied.

I said, "What's the current situation with the investigation?"

"We now have the autopsy report," said Gibson. He reached across his desk, pulled a manilla file towards him, opened it, and referred to it as he spoke. "The report confirms the findings of the preliminary examination. Ms Welles' body was found lying on the floor in her upstairs office. Blood traces suggest she hit her head on the corner of the desk during a fall."

"Would that have been enough to kill her?" Nathan asked.

"That was the initial assumption," said Gibson. "Which is why Ms Welles' death was originally thought to be an unfortunate accident. But a closer examination of the body revealed the presence of fibres on the victim's face. That alone was enough to arouse suspicions. We now know those fibres came from a cushion found on the nearby couch." He tapped the file. "A more detailed examination of the body shows the presence of microhemorrhages in the lung tissue, a clear sign of asphyxia. Ms Welles was smothered."

"Wouldn't there be signs of a struggle?" said Nathan. "Bruising of some kind?"

"Often, that would be so," said Gibson. "But, in this case, it seems the victim was knocked unconscious by the fall, and the killer took advantage of that."

I said, "Which suggests the killer acted on impulse. It's possible the encounter started as a physical altercation that got out of hand."

Gibson agreed. "That was also the conclusion our forensics team came to."

"Anything else?" asked Nathan. "Fingerprints?"

"We've matched what we found against all those who had sanctioned access to Ms Welles' office," said Gibson. "That included her son, Jordan Welles."

There was something about the way he emphasised that last remark, as if his focus was still on Jordan.

I wasn't going to let it pass without comment. "So there's nothing to suggest Jordan was involved in his mother's death, is there? Is he off the hook now?"

"Once he's made his statement, we'll need to check it out," said Gibson. "But, for the moment, I'm going to leave the bail conditions in place."

I was about to object when Nathan pressed a hand to my thigh as a warning to keep quiet.

I said nothing. My turn to be diplomatic.

Gibson said, "The young man needs to know that lying to the police has consequences."

"We'll make damn sure he won't forget," said Nathan.

"What about Cara's partner?" I asked. "Anything there?"

"Those closest to the victim are always going to be of particular interest, as I'm sure you will appreciate," said Gibson. "But Brady has a cast-iron alibi. His boss at the gym confirmed he was working during the period the murder took place. There's no question of his being our killer."

I made a mental note to check that out.

Gibson's desk 'phone rang. He answered the call, grunted a couple of times, and hung up. "Jordan's legal representative is here."

We finished our meeting and Nathan and I headed to the reception.

On the way, I said to Nathan, "I get the impression Gibson's still looking at Jordan for his mother's murder."

"I picked up on that too," said Nathan. "He seems determined to stick to his original presumption no matter what."

"Just as well we're on the case then," I said. "Not that we have anything to go on yet."

Back in reception, we met up with John Grayson. I'd already brought him up to speed by phone, explaining Jordan and Sophie's recent admission. He ran through it with me again to make sure he was fully briefed before deciding to get Jordan's interview over with first before seeing Sophie. "Jordan's interview will simply be a retraction of his earlier statement," he explained, "and I'll advise him to say no more than that. Sophie's interview may take longer."

I accepted his decision and, whilst he was arranging for access to Jordan, Nathan returned to the waiting area. A minute or so later, Grayson and I were being shown into the interview room where Jordan was waiting for us, looking suitably chastened. Grayson prompted him on how to respond to questioning and to follow his lead and we were then joined by the interviewing officer.

It proceeded much as Grayson had planned. He kept control of the interview, making sure focus was on Jordan's retraction only, and thwarting any attempt by the interviewer to change course and implicate Jordan in his mother's murder. With the interview over, Jordan went to the washroom, Grayson returned to the desk to make arrangements to see Sophie, and I rejoined Nathan in the waiting area.

As I seated myself, I explained how the interview had gone and told Nathan we may have a longer wait before Sophie's interview was over.

Nathan said, "I'm happy to stay if you want to come back later. I can call you when we're ready."

"No problem," I said and reached into my messenger bag. "I came prepared." I took out my iPad, logged in to the browser and pulled up details for the Beefed Up gym. "I asked about Brody's schedule this morning at the gym. I want to check if it coincides with his alibi."

"You seem to have your sights set on him."

"There's something about him that doesn't add up." I found details of classes, scrolled down the page, and found what I was looking for. My heart sank. "He was scheduled for classes all that morning," I said.

"It was a long shot, anyway."

"I still don't trust the guy. I have an instinct for these things."

"His boss confirmed his alibi."

I returned to the site's home page and checked the staff details. And my heart rose again.

"Look." I showed Nathan the screen. "This is a pic of Brady's boss,

Leila Rivera."

"What of it?"

"She's not only Brady's boss. She's the owner's fiancée. She's also the woman I caught Brady coming on to at the back of the gym. Seems they were both playing away from home."

"They must like playing with fire."

"An alibi from his boss is one thing," I said. "An alibi from someone he's having a fling with on the side is another thing entirely."

"It's certainly worth taking a closer look," said Nathan. "But let's not jump to any conclusions just yet."

Nathan was ever the cautious one, always needing proof positive before moving forward. But sometimes we need to rely on our instincts. And mine were telling me Brady was implicated in Cara's murder.

And I had no intention of letting it drop.

CHAPTER FOURTEEN

"You didn't need to come," I said. "I could have driven myself over."

Nathan snorted. "Like that was going to happen. I agreed to your making some enquiries. I didn't say I was going to let you loose on your own."

It was the morning of the following day, and we were in Nathan's car in the Beefed Up gym's car park at the front of the building.

The previous day had been emotionally draining for all of us. And once Jordan and Sophie had finished their interviews, we had driven back home and tried to put the day behind us and relax. Tried, but failed. To say the atmosphere was strained would be an understatement. Jordan and Sophie were still feeling stressed out following their interviews and were not very communicative, and Nathan was annoyed at having been lied to. I was still niggling over my doubts about Brady's alibi and putting Nathan in even more of a strop.

Which is why we were here.

I wasn't happy with Gibson's ready acceptance of Leila Rivera's confirmation of Brady's alibi. To take it at face value without digging deeper seemed sloppy. No doubt, because he was still focusing his attention on Jordan.

To put my mind at rest, Nathan had suggested, reluctantly, I check Brady's alibi for myself and question the staff.

"I don't know why you can't interview them in your official capacity," I said. "It would be so much easier."

"You're acting as a private citizen," he said. "So if you tread on any toes, the most you'll get is a slap on the wrist. If I step out of line, it would be a serious breach of protocol."

"I guess I'll have to do my best then."

"How will you handle it?" he asked.

"I'll do what I always do and tell a pack of lies."

He groaned and said, "Be careful."

"I'm always careful," I said and reached for the door.

He muttered something under his breath, but I was halfway out of the car and didn't catch it.

The place was busy. The early morning diehards were already lifting weights and the clash of metal from surrounding workout rooms reverberated around the building.

A different receptionist, a young man, was on duty, which would make my task easier. I followed the same tack as before and pretended to enquire about classes.

"A friend of mine recommended one of the trainers," I said, "but I don't recall the name. Would you be able to find out if I tell you when my friend had his class?"

The young man confirmed that they kept records of training sessions, reached under the counter, and produced a ledger. I gave him the date of Brady's alibi, and he flipped through the book and checked the sessions for that day. He gave me some names, none of which was Brady's.

"I think the name was something like 'Brody' or 'Brady', I said.

"That would be Austin Brady," he said. "But it can't have been him. He had some classes booked that morning, but he cancelled them. His first class that day was in the afternoon."

My heart leapt. Eureka. My instincts had been right.

"So, was he not at work that morning?" I asked.

"No. I was on duty that day and we had complaints from customers who had booked early sessions. Not sure why they were cancelled, but it seemed very last minute."

"And you're sure it was that particular day?"

He jabbed the ledger with a finger. "It's right here," he said. "All our sessions are recorded. Are you sure it wasn't one of the afternoon sessions?" As an afterthought, he added, "Austin has some classes this morning. He should be here in a few minutes if you want to wait and ask him."

That was the last thing I wanted. I told him not to worry. "I'll check with my friend and get back to you later," I said.

Given what I had just learned, together with my earlier observations of the less-than-formal relationship between Brady and Leila Rivera, I should be able to press Gibson into looking more closely at Brady's alibi.

I thanked the young man, told him I would come back later, and headed for the exit, feeling pleased with myself. Before I was halfway there, a door next to the main entrance opened and Leila Rivera stepped out.

She caught sight of me and stopped, her mouth half-open. She started towards me and, as she approached, her face hardened and she regarded me through narrowed eyes. "Is there something I can help you with?" she said, sounding anything but helpful.

I reminded her who I was, not that she needed any prompting.

"I know who you are," she said. "More to the point, why are you here?"

Her tone was abrasive. Guilty conscience maybe?

"I'm sure you'll appreciate I'm interested in learning as much as I can about my ex-wife's background and relationships," I said. "It might help throw some light on the circumstances leading to her death."

"My relationship with Ms Welles was strictly professional. We were clients of her company."

"That's not the relationship I'm interested in. She was in a personal relationship with one of your trainers."

"The police have already interviewed Austin Brady. This is a matter for them, not you."

"I'm sure the police would be grateful for any information that helps their case. Especially when I tell them what I've just learned."

She paled and opened her mouth as if to speak but closed it again, saying nothing, her lips pressed together in a tight, thin line.

"You told the police Austin Brady was here the day Cara was murdered. And yet all his classes were cancelled that morning."

She crossed her arms and thrust her chin forward. "There must be some mistake."

"Your own records confirm it."

"The police were satisfied with my statement. I see no point going over it with you."

"As you wish. I'm happy to let the police deal with it. And when they learn you're having an affair with Brady, I'm sure they won't be quite so keen to accept your support for his alibi."

She gasped and paled and raised a hand to her throat.

Her reaction confirmed what I'd already deduced.

"You should be grateful it was me who caught you out and not your fiancé," I said.

Before she could respond, I brushed past her and headed for the door.

She called after me. "You dare spread any stories about me and I'll make you pay for it. Don't come nosing around here again."

I ignored her, went out into the car park, and made my way to where Nathan was leaning against the side of the car, talking on his mobile. I waited impatiently, eager to tell him what I had learned.

He finished his call and said, "That was Karen. She was calling to catch up. I told her we were at a dead end at the moment."

"Don't be so sure about that." I told him what I had just learned. "We should be able to persuade Gibson to take a closer look at Brady's movements that day."

At that moment, we were interrupted by the squeal of tyres from a dark-blue VW Golf racing into the car park and screeching to a halt on the far side.

A scowling, red-faced Brady emerged from the car, slammed the door, and marched towards us.

"Uh oh." I mentally prepared myself for battle. "I'm guessing boyo just got a call from his not-so-bosslike boss."

I walked towards him, meeting him halfway.

He braced himself, legs apart, and poked me in the chest. "You have some explaining to do, fellah."

"Poke me again," I said, "and the only thing you'll be getting is a broken finger."

He thrust forward his chin, his lip curled. "I don't appreciate having someone sticking their nose into my business."

"I prefer to call it exposing the truth."

By now, Nathan was by my side. "You need to calm down," he said to Brady.

Brady looked him up and down, still sneering. "And who the fuck are you?"

Nathan produced an ID card from his inside jacket pocket and held it up to Brady. "DCI Quarryman," he said. "And I'm telling you again to calm down."

That threw Brady off balance. He drew in a sharp breath and backed off. "What is this?" He switched his gaze to me and then back to Nathan. "If this is about Cara's murder, I've already given a statement down at the station."

"I'm not involved in the investigation," said Nathan. "That's a matter for the local force."

"If you're not involved, why is this guy asking questions?" He nodded in my direction.

"Mr MacGregor is a private citizen and is at liberty to ask whatever questions he chooses."

"But I don't have to answer them."

"No, but that doesn't give you the right to be physically aggressive."

"Then I think we're done here," said Brady.

"For now," I said. "But I think the police may want to see you again when they learn your alibi doesn't stand up."

"My alibi is solid," he said.

"You didn't take any of your classes that morning."

"That's because I suffered a muscle strain and thought it best to cancel them," he said. "I spent the morning out of sight in the office, helping Leila with some admin work."

The smug, self-satisfied smirk told me all I needed to know about how true that was. Brady was lying and seemed not to give a damn that I knew it. He sneered, turned away, and headed towards the gym.

Such overweening arrogance riled me and I was more determined than ever to call him out.

If he thought this was over, he was sadly mistaken.

CHAPTER FIFTEEN

Nathan was still giving me grief about my confrontation with Brady on the drive home. And back at the house, he didn't let up.

As he followed me through the hall, he said, "I want you to be careful. That could have turned ugly."

"I'm no weakling. It's not like I can't handle myself in a fight." I made my way into the living room and slumped down onto the couch. "Besides, he's not likely to start something in a public car park next to his place of work."

Nathan came in and seated himself beside me. "That's not the point." He wasn't going to let it drop. "Brady could be lying for any number of reasons. But if your suspicions are correct, and he's our killer, he's a dangerous man."

"Okay, I get it. I'll be careful."

We were still arguing when Sophie appeared in the living room doorway.

We fell silent.

"Okay if I join you?" she said. She sounded unsure, as if we might turn her away.

"Of course you can." I waved her towards one of the armchairs.

"We thought you were at work," said Nathan.

"I was," she said, "but after yesterday's drama, I wasn't up to being around other people, so I brought some work home." She came into the room, seated herself, and clasped her hands in her lap. "I wanted to say how sorry I was about lying to you. It's been on my mind all day. I know you're doing all you can to help, and we should have been honest with you. I really am very sorry."

"Best to put it behind us and move on," said Nathan. "We all screw up at times. Let's just agree to be upfront with each other in future."

She nodded and looked relieved. "Jordan means well," she said. "But he's stubborn, and he doesn't always think before he acts. Once he makes his mind up about something, there's no changing it."

Nathan grunted. "It must be in the genes," he said and glanced in my direction.

"What's that supposed to mean?" I said.

"We both know the answer to that," he said.

I let it go. It wasn't the first time he'd mistaken my tenaciousness for stubbornness. An old argument we were never going to settle.

I turned to Sophie and said, "Nathan's trying to stop me getting too involved in the investigation."

"Only because I want you to be safe," he said.

Sophie smiled. "Yes, I just caught the end of your... er... discussion. I'm not sure what you think Brady has to do with it, though."

"He was close to Cara," said Nathan. "So he's bound to be a person of interest."

"He was close to a lot of people," she said. There was a trace of sarcasm in her voice. She frowned and stared at us in silence for a moment. And then, "It's not something I like to talk about with Jordan. Austin was his mother's partner, after all. But he has a bad reputation."

Nathan said, "A bit of a ladies' man?"

"Why am I not surprised?" I muttered.

"I'd seen him around before he met Cara," she said. "Down at the gym. He had a high opinion of himself and came on to several of his customers."

"And not only his customers," I said.

"He even tried it on with me once while we were over at Cara's place," she said. "It really freaked me out. But I never told anyone. I should have told Cara but wasn't sure how she'd take it. We never really got on and she might have thought I was out to cause trouble between them. But after that I kept out of his way. The guy was a total creep and I detested him."

"Join the club," I said.

"I don't want to speak ill of Jordan's mum, but when it came to choosing her men, she didn't do herself any favours."

I could vouch for that. Sophie might not have had me in mind when she made the comment, but I was definitely on that particular list.

She continued. "Austin was a scrounger." She tugged at a lock of hair and twisted it around her finger as she spoke. "Cara was always buying him presents and paying for nights out. And they ate at the most expensive places. Nothing but the best for Austin."

"So he would have had no reason to kill her," said Nathan. "Far from it. He would have lost out."

"Kill her?" Sophie sounded startled. "Is that what you're thinking?"

"He's the most likely suspect," I said. "Those closest to the victim are always top of the list. Maybe she found out he was cheating on her and they got into a fight."

Nathan said, "I don't like him any more than you do, Mikey, but you're not going to make a case against him based on mere conjecture. The police need hard evidence."

Sophie said, "It couldn't have been him, anyway."

"What makes you so sure?" I asked.

"Because I know where he was all that morning. He was on the other side of town."

For the next few moments, the only sound was the pounding in my ears as Nathan and I stared at Sophie.

Nathan was the first to speak. "So let's hear it," he said.

"It was after I visited Cara," she said and went on to explain how she had intended to travel straight to work from Cara's place but had changed her mind and returned home to finish some paperwork first. Just before noon, she had driven to work on her usual route and passed Brady's car on the way.

"I often pick up my friend Ali on the way to work and we sometimes see Austin's car parked outside the same house on London Road. Ali knows the people who live there. The Kellers. Barry and Holly. They both travel a lot for work. And it's become a standing joke between us that Austin must be staying over when the husband is out of town."

"You're sure about this?" Nathan asked.

Sophie flushed and tugged at her hair again. "Not really. But what else could it be?"

"You're aware Brady gave the police an alibi?" I said. "He told them he was at the gym that morning."

"I didn't know that," she said. "But I could have told them he wasn't there."

Nathan said, "Just because you saw him at noon, it doesn't necessarily follow he was there all morning. He could have gone round there later."

"We saw him there first thing in the morning so often, I presumed he must have stayed over," said Sophie. "It seemed the most obvious reason for being there. And everyone around here knows what Austin is like."

"Not everyone," said Nathan. "Clearly Cara didn't or she would surely never have taken up with him in the first place."

"I think people were too embarrassed to tell her," said Sophie. "Not that she would have believed them, anyway. In her eyes, he could do no wrong."

I pushed myself up from the couch and crossed over to the window. Outside, an autumn sun hung low on the horizon, casting its fiery glow across the garden.

Had I got it wrong? Had I been so determined to prove Jordan innocent, I had sought to lay blame where it couldn't be justified? I hoped not.

We needed to think this through.

I turned back to face the others. "Even if Brady wasn't on the other side of town all morning, he still lied. He claimed he was at the gym all day. And he would only have lied if he had something to hide."

"That doesn't mean it had anything to do with Cara's murder," said Nathan. "If Sophie's right, and Brady was playing away, he'd want to keep it under wraps. Especially if he's having a relationship with a married woman."

"The only way we're going to know for sure," I said, "is to check it out for ourselves."

"We can hardly go over there and ask her," said Nathan. "We'd be stirring up a whole heap of trouble. And if her husband is there, she's not likely to admit to an extramarital affair, is she?"

"If we want to know the truth," I said. "I don't see we have much choice. And it's not like we have to give anything away. I'm sure we can find some pretext to question her. And for all we know, Brady could have had a legitimate reason for being there anyway."

Nathan sighed. "I'm not going to talk you out of this, am I?"

"No."

He knew when he was beaten. "I can see you're determined," he said. "So if we're going to do this, we might as well do it as soon as possible." He glanced at his watch. "It's early yet. We're more likely to catch them in this evening, so let's leave it till then. Okay?"

I agreed.

And maybe, in the end, it would lead nowhere. But at least it was a step in the right direction.

CHAPTER SIXTEEN

"That one there," I said and pointed across the road. "The one with the blue door."

The Keller's house was part of a bay-windowed terrace, fronted by small gardens, and one of several such terraces on the main road out of town. Nathan pulled over and parked outside. He had insisted on waiting until well into the evening before driving over to London Road and, now we were finally here, I was eager to get on with it. I unclipped my seatbelt and reached for the door handle.

"Not so fast." Nathan put a restraining hand on my arm. "We need to work out a strategy. How are we going to approach this?"

"Just leave it to me," I said. "I'll think of something."

He grunted. "I'm sure you will. Your ability to come up with a convincing lie on the spur of the moment is beginning to worry me. But this time, you can leave the talking to me."

"Aren't you worried about interfering with the local investigation?"

"It's a risk we'll have to take," he said. "And if it helps disprove Brady's alibi, I'm not sure I give a damn if it's seen as interference."

We climbed out of the car, and I followed Nathan over the road and up the garden path to the front door.

The woman who answered the door was as Sophie had described her; late-thirties, carefully made up, tall and slender, with reddish-brown hair cut in a bob style, and distinctive blue eyes. I could understand why Brady might be attracted to her; she oozed poise and glamour. Sophie had also warned us that Holly Keller was known for her overbearing attitude and wasn't very friendly.

Nathan produced his warrant card and showed it to her. "We're following up on a recent local incident and making house-to-house enquiries," he said.

She looked him up and down, lips pursed, and said, "It's a little late in the day to disturb people, isn't it?"

"It's the best time to find people at home," Nathan countered. "I'm sure you wouldn't want the police to waste their time at the taxpayers' expense."

She sniffed and wrinkled her nose, but said nothing.

Nathan gave her the date we were enquiring about and said, "We need to know if you saw anything unusual that day, any strangers in the vicinity, any suspicious behaviour. It would have been early that morning."

She pressed a hand to her throat. "Is this something we need to be concerned about?"

"Not at all," Nathan said. "You don't need to worry."

What happened?" she said.

Nathan hesitated, as if unsure what to say. I butted in and said, "Someone had their dog stolen. It was right outside your house."

Nathan glared at me.

"That's unfortunate," she said. "But I can't help you. If I'd seen anything out of the ordinary, I'm sure I would have remembered."

"A dark-blue VW Golf was parked outside your house at about that time," said Nathan. "Do you know who it belongs to? Did you have any visitors that day?"

"I have no idea who might own it," she said. "It's not one of the neighbours. And I'm sure..." She stopped in mid-flow and a slight gasp escaped her lips. "I've just had a thought," she said. "Wait here a moment."

She left us at the door and disappeared into a room at the back of the hall. A moment later, she was back carrying a mobile phone. She tapped at the screen a few times and looked up at us, an expression of triumph on her face. "Thought as much," she said. "I wasn't here that morning. I met with clients in London the day before and stayed over. I didn't get back home until late that evening."

My heart sank. Yet another dead end.

"My husband was here though," she said. "He may have seen something." She turned and shouted across the hall. "Barry, do you have a moment?"

A door to the left of the hall opened, and the husband appeared; a dark-haired man sporting a stubble beard which, like his hair, was sprinkled with grey. He didn't look too happy at being interrupted. He said, "I was watching the match." As if in acknowledgement, the sounds of a roaring crowd blared out through the open door from the TV beyond. He half-turned at the sound, screwed up his face, and turned back to glare at his wife. "And I just missed a goal."

"Never mind that," she snapped. "This is more important than a silly football game."

Clearly not a fan.

Nathan, once more, ran through the reason for our visit and asked if he'd seen anything. "It would have been early that day," he said.

Barry was adamant that he had seen nothing. "That's the day Holly was due back from London. I had a lie in that morning, so I wouldn't have been up in time to see anything."

"And you wouldn't have seen a dark-blue VW Golf outside?" Nathan asked.

Again, he answered in the negative. "And I'm sure none of the neighbours has a Golf," he said.

"Sorry we can't help," his wife said. "Have you checked with the neighbours?"

"Not yet," Nathan said. "It happened outside your house, so we started here."

"Can I go watch my game now?" Barry said, glared at his wife once more, and made his way back to his TV.

Nathan apologised for the interruption, wrapped up the conversation, and we took our leave.

On the way back to the car, he said, "They seem genuine enough."

"I guess." I'd been so sure we were onto something here and felt deflated.

"And what was all that nonsense about a dog?" he said. "I was trying to be as vague as possible without telling any lies."

"Vague doesn't work," I said. "Leave the lying to me in future. I'm better at it."

He grunted.

I said, "It occurs to me that if Brady is having a clandestine relationship with someone in this neighbourhood, he may leave his car outside the Keller's house so as not to draw attention to his actual whereabouts. Neighbours gossip, after all. And he wouldn't want anything to get back."

As we reached the Astra, Nathan opened the doors with his fob. "We can't go knocking on every door in the neighbourhood on the off chance of finding the right one."

We got in the car and, as I fastened my seatbelt, I said, "If Brady is a regular visitor here, it might be worth keeping tabs on him and see if we can catch him in the act."

Nathan switched on the engine. "You're determined to follow through on this, aren't you?"

As we drove away, I said, "I just want to be sure about Brady's alibi. If he's in the clear, then so be it. But I need to be certain."

Truth be told, I still had Brady in my sights and, despite all the evidence to the contrary, I was still hoping to find a way to connect him to Cara's murder.

And if there was a way to make that connection, I was determined to find it.

CHAPTER SEVENTEEN

Most nights, I sleep soundly enough. Even Nathan's snoring doesn't keep me awake, despite sounding like a cross between a foghorn and a Boeing 737 during takeoff. But that night, I was restless, and sleep didn't come easy.

Patience wasn't one of my virtues and, after failing to either confirm or refute Brady's alibi, I had no idea what to do next. The only option was to keep tabs on Brady and hope we could catch him out during one of his visits to London Road. But that meant waiting, and I didn't like to wait; I wanted to keep things moving and didn't know how.

I had finally convinced myself there was nothing to do but wait, settled down to sleep, one arm wrapped around Nathan's sleeping form, and was dropping off when something brought me back to wakefulness. A noise from downstairs. The outer door? The bedside clock told me it was 2:00 a.m. Was someone moving around down there? I strained to hear, but all was now quiet.

Careful not to wake Nathan, I eased myself out of bed and crossed over to the window. Moonlight bathed the garden in a sheen of silver, highlighting the bushes and flowers. Over to the right, a huddled figure was seated on a wooden bench by the side fence. It was Jordan. He sat with his arms folded, leaning forward, staring down at the ground. He looked so alone, so mournful, and my heart went out to him.

Maybe it was time for that heart-to-heart chat.

Trying to build a rapport with Jordan over these past few days had been a continuing struggle, and I hadn't made much headway so far.

But I needed to make more of an effort. Focusing solely on the investigation wasn't enough. I needed to find a way to help with emotional support too, to make sure he understood he could turn to us and let us help him in any way we could. I needed to put this right. The timing could have been better, but I guess I had to take my chances when I could.

Keeping as quiet as possible, I pulled on a pair of joggers, a sweatshirt, and some slippers, crept downstairs, and made my way out into the garden. Jordan caught sight of me as I crossed towards him.

I stopped in front of him. "Can't sleep?"

He shook his head.

"You've been through a lot these last few days," I said. "And it's easy to get overwhelmed with so much going on. No time to take it all in. And when you finally do, it hits hard."

He bit his lip and looked down again.

I slipped into place beside him. "We'll get through this," I said. "Together. I promise. We're here for you. I hope you know that."

He looked up at me, eyes full of tears, and said, "I told her I hated her." He blurted out the words. "The last thing I ever said. I hated her."

My heart skipped a beat. Is this why he had been so distant these last few days? Weighed down by shame and guilt? Such a heavy burden to bear alone.

I took hold of his arm and squeezed it. "We all say things we regret," I said. "But your mother raised you and cared for you these past seventeen years and she knew who you were. She loved you. And she wouldn't have judged you for one foolish outburst."

"We did nothing but argue those last few weeks."

"That's how I know she loved you."

He shifted his position, turning toward me, his face screwed in a frown. "I don't understand."

"She wanted what was best for you," I said. "To guide you at a time when you were finding your way in the world. Why would she do that if she didn't care? I'm not saying she was right. But she did it for the best of reasons. Because she loved you."

"I was such a jerk."

"I'm beginning to understand why your mother appointed me as your trustee."

"Yes?"

"Something Nathan said the other day. About how alike we were. Stubborn, argumentative, impulsive. Ring any bells?" I finished with a smile.

He chortled and returned the smile.

I said, "Your mother and I weren't much older than you when we married. I'm guessing she didn't want you making the same mistakes we did. And she would have known I was best placed to do that. We both learned the hard way the consequences of making the wrong decisions."

"What really happened between you?"

The autumn air was beginning to cool, and I shivered. "It's starting to get cold," I said. "Let's go get ourselves a warm drink, and I'll tell you all about it."

I stood up and led the way back into the house and through to the kitchen. Jordan seated himself at the table while I busied myself filling the kettle. As I switched it on, I shot him a glance.

"I don't want you thinking I regret my time with your mum. She meant a lot to me."

"So why did you split up?" he asked.

While I considered my response, I grabbed two mugs from the cupboard, dropped a spoon of coffee into each of them, and turned to face him while I waited for the kettle to boil. I leaned back against the counter.

"Back then," I said, "I was running away from a dysfunctional family situation and in denial about my sexuality. And your mum was having her own problems. She was rebelling against the controlling grip of an overprotective father. As Nathan was keen to point out to me, it wasn't the best of reasons for a healthy marriage."

"You really didn't know about me?" he asked.

"I really didn't," I said. "If I had known, I may well have stayed and tried to make it work. Your mother would have known how pointless that would be. Which is why she kept me in the dark."

Jordan nodded. "I used to listen to your show on the radio. It's kinda weird to think all that time I was listening to my father. Bit of a shock."

"It was a shock for me too. And it saddened me. I feel like I've been missing out all these years. I wish I'd known about you."

"Me too."

The kettle finished boiling, and we both lapsed into silence while I turned away and made our coffees. I turned back, mugs in hand, and offered him one. "For what it's worth," I said, "I think your mum was wrong about Sophie. I think she's good for you."

Jordan took the mug and thanked me. "Me and Sophie have known each other all our lives. We've always got on."

"She reminds me of Nathan," I said and took a sip of my coffee. "They have the same characteristics; sensible, down-to-earth, cautious. They're the kind of people idiots like us need to help keep us grounded. We'd get ourselves into trouble without them."

He laughed and said, "I like Nathan. He's a good guy."

"One of the best."

"You met him through work?"

"No, we were friends long before then. We were at school together."

"You knew him before you met my mother?" He looked confused.

I nodded and went on to tell him something about my childhood. About how my early friendship with Nathan had grown into something more. How my homophobic father, the local priest, had disowned me and driven me away from everything I held dear, including the man I loved.

"I was in a bad place before I met your mother," I said. "I tried to leave my past behind and start a new life in London. Your mother and I met at college and hit it off straight away. She was my saviour. She helped me through a difficult time. But we should never have married. We both knew it was a mistake."

He nodded but still looked uncertain.

"It took me a while to get my life back on track," I continued. "After your mother and I parted, I went through another marriage and very public divorce before I learned to accept who and what I was and found my way back to Nathan. It was where I had always belonged. I should never have left him."

"And you work together now?"

While we drank our coffees, I explained the sort of work I did in support of police services, including witness and suspect interview analyses, and crime scene investigation. "Once the police have finished with your mother's place, I have every intention of checking it out for myself. You could come with me if you like. See how it's done."

"I'd love that." He bubbled with enthusiasm.

It seemed I was finally making headway; all that resentment was melting away and the defensive barrier was crumbling. Maybe we could make something of our relationship after all.

I said, "We need to talk about finances sometime, too. I understand your mother gave you an allowance."

He squirmed and looked uncomfortable. "I wasn't sure if I should say anything," he said. "I'm running a bit low on funds and didn't know what to do about it. Sophie's been making sure we got by."

"Of course you should have said something. We'll talk some more tomorrow and get something set up with the bank."

He nodded his approval.

"And how about your rental property?" I asked. "Now that Sophie is staying with you at the house, is your landlord okay with you leaving it empty?"

"It's not empty," he said. "We share the place with Danny and his boyfriend."

"Your fellow artist is gay?"

Jordan squirmed in his seat. He must have picked up on the surprise in my voice.

"I know I must have come across as anti-gay when we first met," he said, "but I'm not. I was just angry. I didn't understand."

"It's okay. I get it," I said. "It must have been very confusing. But we're all good now?"

"Sure we are." He sounded relieved to have put that particular issue to rest. "Danny thought it was kinda cool me having a gay dad." He shot me a sideways glance. "And he told me about your conversation. About the car."

I studied his face for a moment, trying to gauge his feelings. "And how did you respond?" I asked. "Is everything okay between you?"

"I was being an idiot, and he was just looking out for me. We patched it up, and it's all good now."

"Glad to hear it," I said. "You need your friends around you at a time like this."

I took his empty mug from him and dumped them both in the sink. "And, in the meantime, we need to get some sleep. We're going to need our wits about us for a while."

He agreed.

We made our way back to our respective rooms and parted with a whispered goodnight.

We may not yet be making any progress with the investigation, but I was, at least, making some progress with my son.

CHAPTER EIGHTEEN

It was four days before we had a possible breakthrough. Not that those days weren't well spent. I used the time to get to know my son, to catch up on all the years I'd missed, and to find out more about his present circumstances, his work, his relationship with Sophie. He was just as keen to learn more about my life and work, though I concentrated on the more positive parts.

But I was getting restless. Eager for some progress on the investigation.

And today was the day.

Sophie called a little before 7:30 am. She was on her way to work via London Road and had spotted Brady's car in its usual parking space outside the Keller's house.

I finished the call and charged into the kitchen to confront Nathan. "We have to go," I said. "Brady's on the loose." I gabbled out the details of my conversation with Sophie as I raced into the hall to grab my jacket from the coat rack. "The sooner we get over there, the more likely we are to catch him."

Nathan was in the act of filling a bowl with cornflakes and grumbled about being rushed away before breakfast. But he knew better than to argue. He followed me outside, struggling into his jacket, and said, "We'll take my car. We don't want Brady spotting us, and a bright red Elan is a bit of a giveaway."

As I climbed into the passenger seat beside him, he said, "I hope this is going to be worth it."

"Don't worry," I said. "You can have breakfast later."

"That's not what I meant," he said. "I know you, and if this is another wild goose chase, it'll put you in one of your moods."

"I don't get moods."

He snorted and shook his head.

Fortunately, Nathan had nothing to worry about. By the time we reached London Road, Brady's VW was still there.

Nathan parked up on the other side of the road.

"We have a clear view of the whole road from here," I said. "We shouldn't have a problem seeing which house he comes out of."

"Just keep your eyes skinned," said Nathan. "And be prepared for a long wait."

In the event, we didn't have to wait more than fifteen minutes. What we did get, though, was a shock. The sight of Brady emerging from the Keller house with Barry Keller right behind him.

I gasped. "What the hell."

"That guy has some explaining to do," said Nathan.

We leaned back in our seats to minimise the chances of Brady seeing us. But he was too wrapped up in his conversation with Keller to notice. After chatting for a few moments, Brady gave Keller a quick hug, raised a hand in farewell, made his way to his car, and drove away. Keller went back inside.

"Seems we were looking in the wrong direction," said Nathan. "It's not the wife Brady's interested in."

"Jeez, that man sure does like to put it about," I said.

A moment later, we were at Keller's door and Nathan rang the bell.

Keller looked surprised to see us.

"You remember us?" said Nathan.

"Sure. Something about a missing dog."

Nathan shot me a dark look. To Keller, he said, "Among other things. You may also remember we asked about a dark-blue VW parked outside your house. One you denied any knowledge of. The one just driven away by Austin Brady."

The blood drained from Keller's face. He took a step back and stared at us wide-eyed, his mouth half open. His hands trembled. "What's this about?" he said.

"That's what you need to tell us," said Nathan.

I said, "It might be best if you invited us in. I'm sure you wouldn't want to give the neighbours something to gossip about."

He leaned forward, looked both ways down the road to make sure no one was around, and then stood back and let us in before showing us into the living room at the back of the house.

Nathan said, "For starters, you should know there was no stolen dog." He shot me another look. "The dog story was a cover to save you and your wife any possible embarrassment."

"We're presuming your wife is away again," I said.

This time, Keller blushed.

"Let's get straight to the point," said Nathan. "Are you having a relationship with Brady?"

Keller swallowed hard and sank onto the couch behind him. He was shaking. "If this gets out," he said, "it would destroy me."

"As long as you're straight with us," I said, "there's no reason why we can't keep this under wraps."

Nathan said, "I presume you know that Brady is involved in a murder investigation?"

Keller nodded.

"Then you may also be aware he gave the local police a false alibi," said Nathan. "He was here, wasn't he?"

With each question, Keller crumpled even more, slumping down on the couch. "He did it for me. If the truth got out, he knew how bad it would be. He raised his head and stared up at Nathan, a pleading look on his face. "No one needs to know, do they?"

"If Brady is in the clear," said Nathan, "you have nothing to worry about. As long as his alibi stands up."

"He stayed overnight the day before his partner's murder and we overslept," Keller said. "He couldn't say where he really was without giving the game away, so he persuaded his boss to cover for him. She knows about us."

Nathan questioned him some more but, finally satisfied, nodded an understanding acceptance. "Okay, we'll leave it there," he said, and added with more emphasis, "for the moment." Keller tried to interrupt him, and Nathan held up a restraining hand. "We'll be as discreet as possible, but we will need to verify your story."

A heaviness settled inside me. It was beginning to look as though I had been wrong all along. If Keller's story stood, Brady couldn't be our man. We were back at square one with nothing to show for it.

"And it won't go any further?" Keller pleaded.

That was the third time of asking. Keller seemed desperate for reassurance. "We'll make you a deal," I said. "You don't tell Brady we were checking up on him, we'll end this here."

Keller looked relieved. "Deal," he said.

Afterwards, on the way back to the car, Nathan said, "He'll probably tell Brady, anyway."

"Of course he will," I said. "But Brady won't be able to challenge us about it without putting our agreement with Keller at risk."

He grunted. "Clever move."

Right then, I couldn't have given a damn either way. I was pissed at having wasted all this time following a false trail.

Back in the car, we sat for a while and ran over our conversation with Keller. "Nathan said, "On the face of it, his story seems to hold up."

"On the face of it?"

"I'm just thinking through some possibilities. Including Brady and Keller being in this together and covering for each other. But it doesn't seem likely."

"Agreed. Keller seemed genuinely terrified. He's hardly likely to spin us that story if it's not true. Especially given the serious harm it could do him if it got out."

"To be honest, I couldn't give a damn if it did. Men who cheat on their partners like that deserve all they get."

I stiffened.

Nathan growled. "Mikey, I'm sorry. I didn't mean-"

I cut him off. "It's okay. As it happens, I agree with you. But it's a lesson I had to learn the hard way."

In response, he squeezed my thigh.

It was my serial cheating that had led to my second divorce. Not something I was proud of. And I was still finding it hard to forgive myself for being the kind of person I was back then.

We sat in silence for a minute or two before Nathan switched on the ignition. "Seems we need to look elsewhere for our murderer," he said. "Brady was a dead end, after all."

"So it would seem. I'm so bloody angry at the way the local force has handled the investigation so far. If they'd been more thorough, they would have known about Keller and saved us all the hassle of chasing a false lead."

As he pulled away from the kerb, Nathan said, "All the more reason for us to pursue our own enquiries."

"No argument from me there," I said. "It's time to get serious."

CHAPTER NINETEEN

The following weekend, we were blessed with warmer weather. Jordan, Sophie and I were sitting in the garden, making the most of it, when Nathan brought us the news.

"I just called the station for an update," he said. "No progress so far, but they've released part of the crime scene. The house is still off-limits, but the grounds are open again."

"That's something at least," I said. "Jordan and I can go do that crime scene analysis I promised him. We can go over there now if you like."

"Oh, cool." Jordan hadn't lost any of his enthusiasm.

Nathan looked less eager.

I gave him the old what's-the-problem screwface look, but he didn't respond.

Jordan headed through to the living room with Nathan and me in tow. Once inside, I said to Jordan, "Why don't you go wait in the car? I need a quick word with Nathan." I threw him the keys to the Elan.

He caught them and left by the front door. Once he was out of the way, I said, "What?" Straight to the point.

The French doors leading to the garden were open and Nathan lowered his voice so Sophie wouldn't hear us. "You think it's a good idea taking Jordan with you? He is still officially a suspect, after all. Is it right to involve him in the investigation?"

"Sure it is. The crime scene is a done deal as far as the police are concerned. It's not like Jordan's presence is going to make any difference."

He grunted.

"Besides, it gives me a chance to spend time with him. And that's much more important."

I got a begrudging acceptance in response.

"Why don't you come with us?" I said.

"It's probably best if I take a back seat as much as possible."

I nodded, told him we'd see him later, and went to join Jordan.

On the way over to Medway House, I told Jordan what I would look for; points of entry and exit to the crime scene, ease of access, lines of sight and how exposed to view someone would be.

As we approached, I said, "See how cut off from view the grounds are? They're surrounded by high hedges. And look..." I nodded towards the turnoff to the entrance. "Those bushes and trees in front of the turnoff hide the gates from the road."

"So, what does that tell you?"

"It tells me there are a limited number of ways someone could know your car was at your mum's. If they followed behind the car and saw it turn in. If they overlooked the grounds. Or if they were already inside the grounds or house."

"Why would it matter?"

"Because the same limitations apply to any other car that entered the grounds. Including - if they came by car - that of the murderer."

I drove up to the gates via the turn-in and stopped to allow Jordan to open them with his remote. As I pulled through and followed the curve of the drive to the front of the house, I said, "And that's another limitation. Remote access."

"Not many people had remotes. Mum, of course. And me. I kept mine in the car so Sophie could use it, too. And I think Austin had one. Mum kept one at work as well, in case anyone from the office needed to come over."

"And anyone else would have to be allowed access from the house. Which means those gaining entry through the gates would likely have a genuine reason to be here. Unless there are other points of access?"

"There are a couple, yes."

"Then we'll check those out, too."

I parked up in front of the house and, as we climbed out of the Elan, I scanned our surroundings and checked lines of sight to the gates and the rest of the grounds. This spot was not visible from the road, nor was it overlooked from outside.

Blue barrier tape was stretched across the house door, a clear warning the police hadn't yet finished their forensic examination. Though there was no sign of police activity.

"Pity we can't get into the house yet," I said.

"Now we're here, I'm not sure I'd want to go in the house anyway," said Jordan. "At least, not where it actually happened."

"I can understand that," I said. "So let's just concentrate on the surroundings. We still have plenty to work with."

Jordan said, "Someone could have got in here." He led me over to a gate at the left side of the house.

The wall here, as elsewhere, was lined along the top with anti-climb spikes and the gate itself, a solid metal construction with keypad access, seemed secure enough. I tried to rattle it, but it held firm.

"Where does this lead?" I asked.

"There's a footpath on the other side," said Jordan. "I'll show you." He tapped in the access code and opened the gate. "It's not used much. Visitors always come in by the front gates."

We stepped out onto a narrow pedestrian walkway. It was bounded on one side by the house wall and on the other by a tall conifer hedge. Traffic sounds from beyond the hedge betrayed the presence of a busy road on the other side of it.

I checked the view in both directions.

"If you go left," said Jordan, "it leads back to the road running past the gates. The other way leads to an alley between a row of shops at the top and then up to the main road."

"So Springboard Creative's offices are within walking distance from here?" I said.

"Sure. But if you're driving, it's quicker to go round to the front gates."

"This path was never used?"

"Vanessa sometimes came this way if the weather was good and she fancied a stroll."

"Your mum's secretary?"

"Mum worked from home now and again. Vanessa would bring round any files she needed."

Satisfied I'd seen enough, I stepped back through the gate and said,

"Let's check out the rest of the grounds."

Jordan followed me back in, locked the gate behind us, and followed me past the house and into the centre of the grounds.

There was nothing here to impede the view in all directions. An extensive lawn, bounded on all sides by the same high walls, surrounded a large central bed of low-level flowering plants in the centre of which stood a solar-powered, barrel-and-pump water feature. Over by the far wall, dilapidated outbuildings clustered around another gate. Four tall elms stood in a group over in the far left corner.

I shielded my eyes from the glare of a low autumn sun and, turning full circle, followed the lines of sight over the top of the walls. Only one other property overlooked our position, a more modern construct than Medway Hall. Its upper storey and rear-facing windows were clearly visible, and from the middle window, a face stared out at us.

I turned away, tipped my head in the direction of the window and said, "You know the guy up there?"

Jordan took a sideways glance in the same direction. "Not really," he said. "Mum knew him. At least she knew about him. He's some sort of writer and he's housebound. Probably why he sits in that window all day."

"Does he know what car you drive?"

"I guess. Why?"

"From where he's sitting, he wouldn't be able to see your parking spot in front of the house. So if he was the one who reported seeing your car here, he wouldn't know for sure who was driving."

"Gotcha. Which is why the police presumed it was me."

"All these details matter when you read a crime scene. You never know how important they might be." I set off, walking towards the outbuildings. "Now let's go check the other gate."

Jordan followed me over to the wall at the other side of the property.

The gate itself, also of solid metal construction, stood between two brick buildings built into the wall, a small one to the left and a much larger one to the right. The smaller one was in poor condition, with crumbling brickwork, rotting door frames, and minus a roof with the wooden rafters exposed.

The larger building was a little more robust. It still had its shingle roof but was still badly in need of renovation.

"What are these buildings?" I asked.

"The larger one was a gatehouse back in the day when the landed gentry lived here. The smaller one was some sort of store."

"Are these the buildings you intend turning into a workshop?" I asked. "'Cos if they are, good luck with it."

"I'm quite handy with a trowel," said Jordan. "And Danny said he'd give me a hand."

I obviously didn't look convinced.

"This one isn't too bad." He slapped a hand against the wall of the larger building. "And look here…" He led me to the end of the building, to where a rusty metal grille had been built into the end wall. He put a hand against its surface and rattled it. "See, it's solid enough and gives the kind of ventilation I need for my work."

"Fair enough," I said. "But for the moment, the outside gate is of more interest."

We walked back to the other end of the building and I took hold of the gate handle and tried to shake it. Like the other gate, it held firm. "I doubt anyone is likely to get through here without being given access."

I checked the line of sight to the neighbouring house, but the view from here was obscured by the trees.

"I think I've seen all I need here," I said. "But it might be worth checking in with your neighbour. I'd like to know what he saw that day."

"You can get to his place through this gate," said Jordan, and opened it. "His entrance is on this road."

"Probably best if you stay here," I said. "If he's the one who reported seeing you to the police, it might make him feel uncomfortable."

"No problem. I'll wait here. But give me a shout when you come back. This gate is self-locking, and it only opens from this side.

We parted company and Jordan closed the gate behind me. A moment later, I was heading up the path of the neighbouring property.

I was more buoyed up than I had been in days. It felt good to be doing what I did best, unlocking the secrets of a crime scene. Later, back home, I would go over what I had learned so far and try to make sense of it. But I hadn't finished yet.

Hopefully, the man up there in the window could help me unlock more secrets.

CHAPTER TWENTY

The doorbell chime was answered by the sharp metallic sound of a lock disengaging and a disembodied voice from a door intercom inviting me to enter.

I let myself into a small wood-lined hall on the other side of which a flight of stairs led to an upper landing. The reason for the less-than-usual method of answering the door was now clear. The man I'd seen at the window, and who was now seated at the top of the stairs, was in a wheelchair.

"Please come up and join me in my office, Mr MacGregor," he said.

So he knew who I was. I could only hope the more wholesome aspects of my reputation had preceded me.

I made my way up to him, skirting around a raised wheelchair lift at one side of the stairs. As I reached him, he turned his wheelchair around and led me into an office overlooking the front of the house.

A large wooden desk faced the window and, from here, there was an almost uninterrupted view of Cara's garden.

"Have we met before?" I asked.

"Let's just say we're fellow travellers on a mutual quest to bring enlightenment to the masses."

He smiled up at me, no doubt enjoying my look of consternation, and held out a hand. "George Osborne. Fellow writer."

Smiling, I took the hand and shook it.

George Osborne was a rotund, middle-aged man with thinning grey hair, a florid complexion, and a face etched by lines that told of a full and active life.

"I hadn't realised I was on such an important quest," I said.

He said, "Well, your tomes on the less savoury characteristics of our more notorious serial killers certainly enlightened me." He waved a hand towards a nearby straight-backed wooden chair. "Please take a seat."

I turned the chair to face him and seated myself. "And what's your subject?" I said. "Something a little more savoury, I hope."

"History," he said. "More particularly, the history of the great and good of these sceptred isles of ours."

"Then I'm sure you've come across plenty of villains of your own," I said.

"Indeed, I have. But I suspect you're here to discuss a more recent case of villainy." The warm tone of voice faded to something more serious. "I was deeply sorry to hear of Ms Welles's demise. She was a lovely lady."

"Did you know her well?"

"Not very well, no. She led such a busy, active life. But she found the time to visit and keep me company on occasion. She knew I was on my own."

I nodded. It was just like her to find time for others when they needed it. She always was a very generous woman. "And you have an excellent view over her grounds," I said.

"Which is why I have my office on this floor," he said. "All the benefits of a beautiful garden without the need to contribute to its upkeep."

"And you must see everyone who comes and goes."

"And that's why you're here, of course. To find out what I saw." He smiled and said, "I saw you in the grounds with Ms Welles' son. I presume you're assisting the police with your expert advice? Though I'm sure you'll appreciate they've already interviewed me."

"I am helping them to some extent, yes," I said. "But I take a different approach. Reading crime scenes is one of the ways I'm able to help."

"Yes, I've heard some of your radio broadcasts on the subject. Fascinating stuff."

"I also have a personal involvement," I said. "Jordan is my son, too."

Osborne's face fell and he winced. "I'm so sorry to hear that. I had thought your interest was purely neutral."

"Cara and I had been separated for some time. But news of her death was still a shock."

"I'm sure it was. And I'm happy to do whatever I can to help with your enquiries."

"It would help if you could tell me what you saw that day."

He spun his wheelchair to face the window as if the sight of the garden would help his recollection. "I'm a creature of habit," he said. "I'm at my desk at the same time every day. Just before eight. So that's the earliest I would have seen anything of note."

"Before the day itself," I said, "the day of the murder, is there anyone who visited regularly, anyone who would be familiar with the layout of the house and grounds?"

He sat in contemplation for a few moments with wrinkled brow. "There were several regular visitors but you must understand, I didn't know who many of them were. Usually, I would see only their cars.

"Which ones did you recognise?"

He thought this over for a moment longer and said, "There were the commercial vehicles, of course. I recognised those from the signage on the sides. A local firm supplied gardeners on a regular basis, and there was a domestic cleaning contractor. Apart from those, the only ones I knew for sure were her secretary's white Honda Civic and your son's Ford Focus. I knew about the secretary because her car arrived one day when Cara was over here visiting and she had to leave in a hurry. Your son I would see in the garden with his mother." As an afterthought, he added, "There was someone else. I think she'd found herself a suitor. Just recently. I would see them together in the garden too."

"Yes, I know about him. What about the day itself, the day Cara was killed?"

"I can vouch for only two people being here that day. Her secretary and your son. And the police, of course. They were swarming all over the place not long after the secretary arrived."

"You're right about that," I said. "It was Vanessa who found Cara. But you're wrong about my son. He wasn't here that day."

Osborne looked puzzled.

"You saw his car," I said. "But it was being driven by his girlfriend that day."

"That's strange." He looked perplexed. "Then I have to assume two of us got it wrong."

"I'm not sure I understand."

"I didn't see your son's car arrive. I saw it leave later, after I was seated at my desk. But someone else did see it arrive. I am reliably informed by the policeman who interviewed me that someone saw your son's car entering the gates to Ms Welles's house that morning. And the witness identified your son as the driver."

CHAPTER TWENTY-ONE

Afterwards, on the drive home, I talked Jordan through my conversation with Osborne. Most of it. But not the reference to Jordan being identified as the driver of his car on that fateful morning.

It's not that I doubted Jordan's account. I'd been in this game long enough to know when someone was lying to me. And Jordan wasn't. Of that, I was certain. But I was loath to raise it as an issue until I had checked it out with the local police force. And, of course, Osborne could have got it wrong. Instead, I stuck to details of the crime scene itself.

I said, "I'd like to look inside the house. But it will have to wait until the police release the scene. For the moment, we'll have to work with what we've got."

"Did you learn anything?" Jordan asked.

"Enough to work out a possible timeline and make some informed assumptions," I said. "When we get home, we'll call a family conference and talk it through."

Back at the house, we found Nathan and Sophie sitting out in the garden enjoying the brief warm spell and chatting over a jug of lemonade.

We went to join them.

"You're home early, Sophie," I said.

She sighed and said, "I took the day off and came home. My mind's not on work right now. Not with all that's going on. So I thought it for the best."

"It's as well you're here. It'll save me having to go through it all again."

Jordan dropped into place on the bench at Sophie's side and I took the other garden chair next to Nathan. Once we'd settled, I briefed them on what I'd learned.

I said, "We know Osborne was at his desk just before eight and Cara contacted her office at about half-past. So the murderer can't have arrived by car or they would have entered and left under the watchful eye of Osborne."

"They could have arrived before Osborne sat at his desk," said Sophie.

"But he would still have seen them leave," I said.

Sophie interrupted again. "So the only visitors they would know about for sure are me and Cara's secretary, Vanessa."

I acknowledged this and said, "It means our killer must have entered by the side gate. And that raises some interesting possibilities."

This time, Jordan interjected. "It would have to be someone who knew mum. Someone who knew the entry code."

I said, "And someone who knew the layout of the grounds well enough to know they were more likely to be spotted if they used the front gates."

Nathan took up the thread, following my train of thought. "Which means they came with prior intent."

"Exactly," I said. "Otherwise, there would be no point in trying to avoid being seen."

"Most of mum's visitors knew they could be seen from the neighbour's house," said Jordan. "Vanessa used to say she felt as if she was under constant surveillance whenever she and mum were out in the grounds. Osborne was always at that window."

Sophie said, "Wouldn't Vanessa be a suspect? She was the one who found Cara, after all."

"Anyone who had means, motive or opportunity is going to be under investigation," said Nathan. "Even if only to rule them out. Vanessa is an obvious candidate."

"Not likely though," said Jordan. "Mum and Vanessa were good friends."

"Which would make her a useful source of information," I said. "It would be a good idea to talk with her at some point."

"At least we know Austin isn't a suspect," said Sophie. "Though I'm not sure Holly Keller would be too keen on confirming his alibi to the police."

Nathan and I exchanged glances. We had already told Jordan and Sophie we were satisfied with Brady's alibi, that he had been at the house on London Road. What we hadn't told them was Barry Keller, and not his wife was Brady's alibi.

Nathan cleared his throat and said, "There's something you need to know." He told them of our second visit to London Road, of our conversation with Barry Keller, and what we had learned about his relationship with Brady.

Somewhere in the distance, the low hum of an aeroplane broke the following silence.

Sophie was the first to speak. "I'm stunned," she said. "I'd always known Brady was playing the field. But I hadn't realised just how large a field it was."

Jordan's response had a bitter edge to it. "My mum sure did know how to pick them." He drew in a sharp breath, coloured up, and turned to me. "I'm sorry. I didn't mean-"

I cut him off. "Nothing to be sorry for," I said. "We all make dumb decisions at times." A change of direction was called for. I said to Sophie, "Osborne told us the police had another witness who saw Jordan's car that morning. Do you remember seeing anyone else around? Were you followed?" For the moment, I thought it best not to mention the witness having identified Jordan as the driver.

Sophie shook her head. "Not that I recall. That stretch of road isn't very busy at that time of day, so I'm sure I would have noticed."

"Only one way to find out for sure," said Nathan. "I'll call the station and ask. I can tell them your thoughts on the crime scene, too. And I'll chase them up on the file they were supposed to be letting us have." He dug into his pocket for his phone but came up empty. "My mobile's inside," he said and rose to his feet. "Back in a minute."

As he left us, I called after him, "While you're at it, see if they checked CCTV in the area. There might be something on the main road near the side passage to the house."

He called back to say he would and disappeared into the house.

Sophie said, "If someone had come from that direction, they could have parked on the main road and walked the rest of the way to the side gate."

"It's a long walk down the side passage," I said. "It would be quicker to drive around to the front of the house and use the gates. So if someone had come from that direction, it means they would have wanted to avoid being seen entering by the main gates."

Sophie said, "I hate to think someone came to the house intending to kill Cara. An argument that went too far, maybe. I could understand that. But not..." She cut herself short and shuddered. "It gives me the creeps."

"Everyone liked mum," said Jordan. "I can't believe anyone would have wanted her dead."

We all lapsed into silence.

Nathan returned a few minutes later. He was frowning. Not a good sign.

"What's wrong?" I said.

"Something's not right," he said. "It just doesn't add up. According to the crime report, the witness who saw Jordan's car that morning was Brady."

CHAPTER TWENTY-TWO

"Much as I try, I can't make sense of it," I said. "Brady has a lot of explaining to do."

"This time we have enough on him to force his hand," said Nathan.

It was early the following day, and Nathan was driving us over to the gym. We were determined to confront Brady and pressure him into cooperating. It was either that or have his relationship with Keller exposed. His choice.

In response to Nathan's call to the station, I'd already told him what I'd learned from Cara's neighbour about Jordan being identified as the driver that morning. We'd talked it over and decided not to question Jordan about the claim until we'd challenged Brady about it. Jordan was feeling enough of a strain without upsetting him any further unless it became absolutely necessary.

I said, "You don't suppose Keller was selling us a crock? Giving Brady a false alibi?"

"I'm sure his relationship with Brady is genuine," said Nathan. "He's not likely to invent something that has the potential to destroy his marriage if it became public knowledge."

"Sure," I said. "But he could be lying about Brady being there all morning. Perhaps Brady was blackmailing him into covering for him."

"There wouldn't be any point. Leila Rivera had already given Brady an alibi that satisfied the local police. Why go to the trouble of inventing another one? No, I'm sure Brady's only concern was to cover up his relationship with Keller."

"Which means he couldn't possibly have seen Jordan's car that morning."

"But someone must have. Otherwise, how would Brady have known? He's still mixed up in this somehow."

"Hopefully, we're about to find out."

"And you do realise Gibson's been holding out on us?" I said. "Brady's journey to work would normally take him past Cara's place, so if Gibson was prepared to accept Brady's false alibi, he probably also accepted Brady's claim he'd seen Jordan at the house."

"I get that," said Nathan. "It explains why Gibson was reluctant to drop Jordan's bail conditions. He was keeping his options open."

We reached the gym and Nathan pulled into the car park. A moment later, we were making our way to the front of the building.

The weather had taken a turn for the worse. The day was dull and dark, and a chill wind blowing in from the north brought with it the threat of winter. We hurried towards the main entrance, eager to get out of the cold.

As we stepped into the lobby, I said, "I don't think we're very popular here."

Nathan responded with a grunt.

The receptionist was the young woman I'd met on my first visit. But today, she was decidedly less cheerful. She seemed flustered.

I asked to see Brady, but learned he hadn't turned in that morning. It seems our visit had been in vain.

"I'm not sure what's going on at the moment," the young woman said. "There's been some sudden changes this morning."

"Problems?" I asked.

"Our manager didn't turn in this morning either," she said. "And then the boss turned up and told us she was being replaced."

"Elliot Garcia was here?" Nathan asked.

She nodded. "He wasn't in the best of moods, either. None of us knows what's going on."

Nathan and I exchanged glances. The same thoughts must have been going through his mind.

Had the truth come out? Had Garcia learned his fiancée was cheating on him with Brady? It would certainly explain the sudden absence of the cheating duo and Garcia's foul temper.

"We're going to need Austin Brady's address," said Nathan.

The young woman was reluctant to give out any personal data until Nathan took out his ID card and flashed it in front of her. "It's a police matter," he said.

A few moments later, we were hurrying back to the car with the information we had asked for.

As we strapped ourselves in, I said, "Looks like Brady's transgressions have finally caught up with him. It can't be a coincidence that both he and Leila are not at work."

"Can't say I feel sorry for either of them," said Nathan.

We set off and, by the time we reached our destination, a light rain was falling.

Brady's home was a brick-built bungalow, one of three sited at the end of a leafy cul-de-sac on the edge of town and backing onto open countryside. Lights were on in the windows of the two bungalows on either side of his, but Brady's place was in darkness.

His VW was out front.

"Doesn't look as though he's up and about yet," I said.

We drew in behind the VW and parked up. I was first out of the car and headed for the door with Nathan close behind. The two windows, one on either side of the door, had their blinds drawn.

"He's probably keeping his head down at the moment," I said and rang the bell.

No reply.

I tried again.

Still no response.

"Looks like he's out," I said.

We waited a few moments longer, but there were no signs of activity from inside.

I nodded towards a path trodden into the grassy ground at the side of the bungalow. "There's a trail over there leading to the open land at the back of the building. Maybe he's gone for a run."

"More likely, he's keeping out of sight and wants us to think he's out," said Nathan. "He probably doesn't want to see anyone right now."

"Tough. He's picked the wrong time to play hide and seek." I tried the door handle but to no avail; it was locked.

Nathan cupped his eyes and peered through a gap between the inner edge of the window and the side of the blind. "Can't see a thing in there," he said. "Not enough light."

I crouched and looked through the letterbox, but no luck there either. I could just about make out the shadowy outlines of three doorways leading off the hall. But nothing more.

"Let's try round the other side," said Nathan.

I followed him through a gate at the side of the bungalow to a small paved yard at the back. Here too, windows on either side of a central door had their blinds drawn.

But the door itself was ajar.

"That's odd," said Nathan.

"I don't like the look of this," I said, keeping my voice low.

Nathan took hold of the handle, eased the door open, and peered into the gloomy interior. He nodded to me and I followed him in, edging my way through to a small kitchen.

We stood in silence for a few moments, and I strained to hear any sounds of movement from the rooms beyond.

Nothing.

Nathan called out, "Police. If anyone's here, show yourself."

The only answer was the ticking of the wall clock and the hum of a nearby refrigerator.

"Something's not right here," said Nathan. He crept over to the open door leading into the hall, turned to face me, and raised a hand, warning me to stay back. "Stay here while I check out the place."

As he disappeared into the hall, I made my way over to the window and raised the blind, letting in what little light there was from outside. A clean cereal bowl sat on the side unit by the sink, a box of shredded wheat, and a spoon next to it. It seemed Brady had missed breakfast that morning.

I crossed over to the hall as Nathan was stepping out of the room to the left. "His bed's empty," he said.

He moved soundlessly over to the door on the other side of the hall, slowly turned the handle, and went inside.

The clatter of a blind being drawn a moment later was followed by a sharp command. "Mikey."

I hurried towards the sound of Nathan's voice.

He was standing by the window, silhouetted in the half-light, and staring down at a blood-splattered floor.

A dark brown leather couch stood against the adjacent wall, an overturned chair to one side of it. And in the centre of the room, face down in a pool of blood, lay Brady's lifeless body.

Nearby was a bloodied knife.

CHAPTER TWENTY-THREE

Inspector Gibson stared down at the body, his expression set firm. "Forensics are on their way," he said, "but, in the meantime, it might help if I knew why you were here in the first place." He sounded aggrieved, as if we were intruding and had no right to be here.

He had arrived within ten minutes of Nathan's call, bringing a uniformed constable with him, and was trying to make sense of the situation.

Nathan came straight to the point. "Brady lied. We came here to find out why. And, as you can see, we were overtaken by events."

Gibson drew himself up to his full height and said, "With respect, DCI Quarryman, this is a local matter and if you had new information concerning the investigation, would it not have been more appropriate to bring it to me?"

"You'd already ruled Brady out as a suspect," said Nathan. "Something you were adamant about. I thought your conclusion was premature. In the circumstances, it seemed reasonable to make my own enquiries. It now appears that decision was justified."

The two of them were locking horns, ready for battle. I had no doubt which of them would win.

"There was no reason to suspect Brady," said Gibson. "His version of events appeared to hold up."

"You were wrong," said Nathan, blunt as ever. He went on to explain the sequence of events leading to our discovery of Brady's whereabouts.

"That still doesn't make him a suspect," said Gibson. "It seems evident to me he lied to cover his indiscretions."

"You're missing the point," said Nathan. "Brady claimed to have seen Jordan's car at the crime scene. He can't have seen it. He wasn't there. So how did he know the car was there? And why did he lie?"

Gibson swallowed hard, but said nothing. He knew he was losing ground.

Nathan continued, "Does it not occur to you he was covering for someone? That he was clearly involved in some way?"

By the end of this exchange, Gibson was scowling. He was not happy at being criticised for his handling of the case and his resentment showed. So much for keeping the police onside. It was time to placate him.

"To be fair, Inspector Gibson, we did have a couple of lucky breaks," I said. "I caught Brady and his boss in a compromising situation at the back of the gym. I guess I was just in the right place at the right time."

"They were having an affair?" said Gibson.

"Whatever else it was," I said, "you can be sure it wasn't a business meeting."

Nathan said, "And that would raise concerns about the veracity of Leila Rivera's support for Brady's alibi."

I said, "And we had Sophie's sighting of Brady's car. Another lucky break."

With his mouth set firm, Gibson nodded, a reluctant acknowledgement that maybe he'd got it wrong after all. "Sometimes, all our hard work and expertise counts for nothing. It just comes down to luck."

Struggling to keep a straight face, I shot Nathan a warning glance, signalling him to keep quiet. We both knew but for his sloppy approach, Gibson could easily have discovered this new information for himself. But now wasn't the time to tell him that.

"I'll need to interview this Keller guy to confirm his claim," said Gibson. "And Ms Rivera has some explaining to do, too."

"I hope you'll go easy on Keller," I said. "If it gets out Brady was bedding him too, it would cause serious problems in his marriage."

"I'll do what I can," said Gibson, "but I'm not making any promises. He'll have to take his chances."

"It's not looking good for Leila Rivera either," I said. I explained what we had learned during our visit to the gym that morning. "It's a fair bet her relationship with Brady has been exposed."

"This guy seems to have been trouble wherever he went," said Gibson.

"I presume you'll be treating his death as a separate investigation for the moment," said Nathan. "It's probably too much of a coincidence to think his death is not part of the current enquiry, but it's best not to jump to conclusions."

"Too early to tell one way or the other," said Gibson. "We need to keep an open mind."

Pity he hadn't thought of that earlier. It might have saved Jordan the unwarranted distress.

Gibson turned his attention to the constable waiting patiently by the door. "You can start securing the scene while we wait for the rest of the team."

As the constable left the room, Gibson turned his attention back to the body. "Any ideas about how this went down?" he asked.

I crouched as near as I could to the body without disturbing the pool of blood in which it lay and pointed to two bloody patches, one at the front and one at the back of the head. "It looks as though Brady was initially hit on the head with a blunt object."

"Not stabbed?" said Gibson.

I pushed myself to my feet. "There are three knife wounds to the neck. If Brady had been stabbed while still standing, we would expect to see a wider dispersal of blood spatter from droplets thrown from the slashing motion of the knife and from the wounds themselves. But look around." I swept a hand around the room. "The walls and furniture are clear. The blood spatter is confined to a relatively small area of the floor."

Gibson followed the motion of my hand and nodded. "So he was felled by blows to the head?" he said. "And then stabbed where he lay?"

"It would appear so," I said, "but your forensics team should be able to give you a more detailed analysis. And something else." I crouched again. "There's blood spatter on or very near to the upper body, as you'd expect. But look down here." I pointed to some staining on Brady's trousers. "These drops of blood are circular, which shows they fell straight down under the force of gravity rather than from some other force."

Gibson leaned over the body to take a closer look. "They could have fallen from the knife as the assailant stood over the body," he said.

"That's one possibility," I said and stood up again. "But if Brady managed to fight back before he was downed, his assailant may have been injured too and left traces of his own blood."

Before Gibson could respond, we were interrupted by the return of the constable. "I've just been approached by one of the neighbours, sir," he said, addressing Gibson. "He reported some sort of disturbance here last night. He's waiting outside if you need to speak with him."

"Too right I need to speak to him," said Gibson and followed the constable out to the front of the bungalow, with Nathan and me following on behind.

The neighbour was a stout bespectacled man with thinning grey hair. The constable introduced him as Trevor Noakes.

"Is everything all right in there?" said Noakes, straining to peer past us into the gloom of the open doorway.

Gibson ignored the question. "Tell me about this disturbance," he said.

"It was last night, quite early," said Noakes. "Mr Brady often has visitors in the evening, but this one was shouting and hammering on the door, causing a right commotion. I came out to see what was going on just as Brady answered the door and let him in."

"Could you hear what was going on inside?" asked Gibson.

"Just more shouting." said Noakes. "But he didn't stay long. He went storming off after a few minutes."

"And did you get a good look at him?" asked Gibson. "Would you be able to describe him?"

"I can do better than that," said Noakes. "I often see him around. He owns that gym off the High Street."

"Elliot Garcia?"

"Yes, that's him."

Gibson turned towards us, chin thrust forward and a gleam in his eyes. "I don't think we're going to have any problems with this one," he said. "Looks like we have our man."

My heart sank. So much for keeping an open mind. Given the circumstances, it couldn't be denied Garcia was the most likely suspect for Brady's murder, but it wouldn't be the first time Gibson had jumped to the obvious conclusion and got it wrong. Would this man never learn?

CHAPTER TWENTY-FOUR

Nathan wasn't in the best of moods. Not that I could blame him. He'd been on edge since our confrontation with Gibson at the scene of Brady's murder the previous day. "The man's an incompetent fool," he said. "He takes too much for granted without investigating it thoroughly enough."

We were on our way to the local station in Nathan's car. No longer confident of Gibson's ability to handle either murder case effectively, Nathan had asked to be kept appraised of any progress. In response, Gibson had invited us to a debriefing.

"To be fair, speculating about suspects is all part of the process," I said. "It's something to work with. After all, I had Brady in my sights for Cara's murder."

"Sure, but you didn't leave it there," he said. "You followed up with more enquiries. And if Gibson had been doing his job properly, he wouldn't need us to do the work for him."

"In any other circumstances," I said, "I'd be inclined to focus on Garcia as the prime suspect for Brady's murder, but it's too much of a coincidence to think the two murders aren't somehow connected."

"Exactly," said Nathan. "The problem with Gibson and those like him is he'll take it no further. You saw how he reacted yesterday. He thinks it's a done deal."

"Just as well we got involved then," I said.

Once at the station, we were shown into Gibson's office. He was buoyant, full of cheer, and wearing a self-satisfied grin.

"Looks as if I was right about the Brady killing," he said, waving us to a couple of chairs in front of his desk and seating himself behind it.

Nathan and I exchanged glances. Nothing needed to be said.

Gibson continued, "Garcia has already been interviewed under caution. He's now on bail pending the forensics examination, but I don't doubt we'll find what we need to charge him."

"So, what's the story here?" Nathan asked.

Gibson leaned forward, hands clasped on the desk before him. "As you suspected, Garcia learned about his fiancée's affair with Brady. To be more precise, she owned up to it."

"She must have known it was going to come out anyway," I said. "Best to get in there first and try to minimise the fallout."

"Not that it did her much good," said Nathan.

"She confessed to Garcia that evening," said Gibson, "and Garcia went straight round to Brady's to have it out with him. He told us as much."

"But he didn't confess to the murder?" Nathan asked.

"He says he warned Brady to stay away, and he was terminating his employment with immediate effect," said Gibson. "But he claims that's all it was. Just words. Nothing physical."

"Is he likely to be the murderer, though?" I said. "If that had been his intent, he wouldn't be doing himself any favours attracting attention from the neighbours."

"Unless it was on the spur of the moment," said Gibson. "He was fired up after all."

"Fair point," I said, "but it does suggest he didn't go there intending to kill Brady."

Gibson beamed at each of us. "Even so, I don't think we're going to have any problems with this one, gentlemen."

"Whether or not Garcia's the perp," said Nathan, "Brady's death leaves us out in the cold regarding Cara's murder. We have no idea who he might have been covering for."

"Have you interviewed any of Brady's contacts?" I asked.

Gibson lost some of his verve. "There's not been much point until now," he said. "But, of course, we'll get on to it straight away."

"How about the forensics examination at Medway Hall?" I said. "Anything there?"

"Sorry, we've drawn a blank there," said Gibson. "I'm asking my team to stand down and I'll be releasing the crime scene today."

That was something, at least. I'd been eager to get in there and go through Cara's records. There was always a chance something had been overlooked.

"We also took charge of Ms Welles' mobile," said Gibson. "I'll make sure it's returned to you before you leave. And I'll let you have a copy of the forensics report."

"We need to check out Brady's contacts as soon as possible," said Nathan. "Anyone who had a connection to Cara Welles."

Before Gibson could respond, we were interrupted by a knock at the door and a uniformed constable entered the room. He apologised for the interruption. "A moment of your time, sir," he said, addressing Gibson. "Something you need to know about."

Gibson excused himself and followed the constable out into the corridor, closing the door behind him.

Nathan let out a long, slow sigh of exasperation. "If that guy had been in my squad," he said, "I'd have booted him by now. If he'd played this properly in the first place, we might have made some progress. We may even have been able to interrogate Brady before his unfortunate demise."

"No argument from me," I said. "I told you right at the beginning of this, the man was a jerk."

He grunted.

"And this is the guy you made me apologise to," I said. "Which reminds me, you still owe me a steak dinner. And I'm adding a bottle of champagne, too."

Another grunt.

A minute or two later, Gibson returned and dropped into his chair. This time, he was more sombre.

"There have been some developments," he said. "Ms Welles' business partner, Reagan Francis, has just been attacked outside her home."

CHAPTER TWENTY-FIVE

During the drive home, the wind dropped and the sun finally broke through the dark blanket of cloud that had hovered over the town all morning, bringing a welcome change of weather and brightening the day.

Unfortunately, Nathan's mood hadn't brightened any. He was still complaining about what he referred to as Gibson's inept and potentially harmful approach to investigative policing. "How many more people have to get hurt before that idiot gets his act together?"

Gibson had filled us in on what he knew of the attack on Reagan Francis. Details were sketchy, but we learned that she had avoided serious injury.

"It doesn't sound as if she was badly hurt," I said. "More shaken than anything."

"Only because she managed to get away from her attacker before he caused any significant damage. If Gibson had been on top of this, he could have prevented anyone else from getting hurt." Nathan was still fuming. "Gibson reminds me of one of those bumbling idiots you get in cheap murder mystery paperbacks. I never thought I'd see one in real life."

"I know Garcia is the obvious suspect," I said, "but I'm not buying it. We're all missing something here."

"The only thing Gibson's missing is an adequate level of intelligence. But maybe now he'll rethink his approach instead of jumping to conclusions."

Nathan's temper still hadn't improved any by the time we reached home, so I left him to stew in the living room and went to seek out Jordan, taking his mother's mobile with me.

I found him in the garden.

In compliance with his bail conditions, he'd made his weekly visit to the police station earlier that morning and then given the workshop a skip, preferring instead to return home and work on ideas for a new metal sculpture.

He looked up, pen in hand, as I crossed over to where he'd parked himself at the wooden bench beneath the shady beech tree at the side of the garden. As I approached, he folded his drawing pad and said, "How did you get on?"

He'd been eager to hear of any progress, including possible release from his bail conditions. I suspected that's why he'd chosen to return home.

I was about to disappoint him.

He listened intently as I went over our conversation with Gibson, the light in his eyes slowly fading as I continued.

Once I'd finished, he said, "If the locals think Austin's death is a separate matter, we're no further on than we were before."

"I don't think it is a separate matter. And don't forget the assault on Reagan. I'm sure they're all connected." I seated myself, facing him from the bench on the other side of the table. "We're not going to sit on this," I said. "You can be sure of that. I'm going to keep on poking my nose in where it's not wanted until we've cleared your name and caught our villain."

From somewhere nearby, a blackbird sang its joyous song.

Jordan bowed his head, staring down at his fists clenched on the bench top. "I wouldn't be surprised if they pulled me in for the attack on Reagan," he said. "I'm sure that Inspector still thinks I killed mum, so they may as well add assault to the list too." He sounded so mournful.

"None of this is easy," I said, "but it won't be forever. And once it's over, you'll get your life back on track. And then maybe we can spend more time getting to know each other."

He raised his head and looked me full in the face. His eyes were moist. "You don't mind being my dad, then?"

That came from nowhere and my hand tightened around the mobile, reminding me I was still holding it.

I gave him a reassuring smile. "I'm slowly getting used to the idea of being a dad. And if I'm going to be one, I'm sure I couldn't do much better for a son." He still seemed so unsure of himself. "Is it something you'd like to talk about?"

"We didn't get off to the best of starts," he said. "I don't want it to spoil things between us."

"It's already forgotten," I said. "Let's just move on from there."

He nodded, seemingly reassured.

"And in the meantime," I said, "we need to work on sorting out this mess." I handed him his mother's mobile. "We got this back from the police this morning. I'd like you to look through the contacts and tell me what you know about them."

"You think one of them..." The words dried in his mouth.

"It's fairly certain your mother's death was no random act," I said. "Which means everyone she knew or had contact with is a suspect."

Jordan nodded, switched on the mobile, and scrolled through the list. After a few moments, he said, "The only personal ones I know about, apart from me and Austin, are people at the office; Reagan, Vanessa, and Ian."

"Ian?"

"Ian Parks. He works in sales. I only know him 'cos he came by the house sometimes. There are some other names here, but I don't know who they are."

He handed the 'phone back to me, and I turned it off and slipped it into my pocket. "I'll get in touch with Reagan when she's feeling better and see if she can help me out. It'll give me a chance to ask her about the assault, too."

There was another pressing matter I needed to discuss with him. Why would Austin Brady lie to implicate Jordan in his mother's murder? But this was a tricky one. And I wasn't sure how to approach it.

"How well did you get on with Austin?" I asked.

He furrowed his brow and regarded me through narrowed eyes. "Why do you ask?" he said.

"Just wondered. I don't know how much you had to do with him."

"Not a lot." He hesitated and then said, "To be honest, I tried to stay out of his way. I didn't rate him much, but he made mum happy, so I said nothing."

He must have realised I was curious for a reason. He said, "What's this about?"

The last thing I wanted was to add to his trauma, but the truth was bound to come out eventually and so, on reflection, it seemed best if he heard it from me rather than the local police. But there was no easy way to tell him.

I drew in a breath and said, "He told the police he'd seen you driving to your mother's house that morning."

"But he can't have."

"I know."

He mulled this over for a few moments while the implication of what I'd told him sank in. Finally, he said, "Austin tried to blame me for killing my mother?" It was more a statement than a question.

I nodded.

Jordan paled.

I added hastily, "I don't think it was anything personal."

"What else could it be?"

"I suspect he was covering for someone. Someone who saw your car there that day. They wanted to shift the blame, and you were an easy target."

Jordan fell silent as he considered this. In a neighbouring garden, the sound of a barking dog brought a sharp rebuke from its owner, interrupting the background hum of traffic from the road on the other side of the hedge.

"You okay?" I asked.

He nodded and murmured, "It just seems to get worse and worse."

I leaned across and squeezed his arm. "Try not to let it upset you. Wherever this goes, you have me and Nathan with you all the way."

He smiled weakly but didn't seem much happier.

"It might help if you can think of anyone Austin was close to," I said. "And when Sophie gets home, ask her to have a good think about who may have seen her on the road that day. Someone must have."

He agreed.

A moment later, we were joined by a smiling Nathan. His bad temper seemed to have subsided. "You two are looking serious," he said.

We didn't respond.

He dropped into place at Jordan's side. "What are you working on?"

he said, nodding down at the drawing pad.

Jordan flipped through the pad, opened it at his most recent design, and all too soon the weight of his present cares seem to gradually fall away and he was lost in his art, eagerly explaining the concept of his latest project to an equally interested Nathan.

Watching them like this helped ease my own troubled concerns for Jordan's mental well-being. So much to cope with in such a brief space of time. Just how much could one person bear?

Now I was even more determined to sort out this mess.

And no time like the present.

I rose from my seat. "I'll leave you two to chat," I said. "I have a call to make."

I fished in my pocket and pulled out my mobile as I made my way back to the house. Once inside, I tapped in Reagan Francis's office number, got through to her secretary and asked for an appointment. Perhaps once Reagan had recovered from her ordeal and was feeling up to it, she would be happy to talk with me again.

All other lines of enquiry had run into dead ends. I could only hope Cara's business partner could give me some more leads.

CHAPTER TWENTY-SIX

Reagan Francis was made of stronger stuff than I had imagined. Despite her ordeal, she hadn't allowed it to interrupt her work schedule and agreed to see me the following morning at Springboard Creative's offices.

A young man in a rumpled sweatshirt and faded jeans met me at reception and escorted me to a basement area where, he informed me, Reagan Francis was overseeing a photoshoot.

The basement was overly warm, and I was greeted by the whirr of fans and a breeze playing across my face.

Against a white backdrop attached to one wall, a half-naked man of sculpted build stood on a circular plinth flexing his muscles as a lighting crew set up a rig around him. He winked at me as I passed by. Obviously, his gaydar was in full working order.

I crossed the concrete floor, stepping over several cables, to where Francis Reagan was waiting to welcome me. The dark glasses she wore did little to hide the bruising down the side of her face.

My escort excused himself and Reagan led me over to a lounge area on the far side of the studio, where we seated ourselves away from the working crew.

"Sorry about the unusual meeting place," she said. "Cara would normally take care of a shoot like this. But we're on a deadline, so I had to step into her shoes and move things on."

I sympathised, saying I realised what pressure she must be under, and then offered my condolences for her recent attack. She took off the glasses to show me her injuries. There was extensive heavy bruising around her right eye and on the cheekbone.

I responded with a sharp intake of breath. "That must have been quite a blow," I said. "I hope it's not as painful as it looks."

She put her glasses back on and said, "At first, it was the shock as much as anything. The attack came out of nowhere. It was only later once the adrenalin wore off, I realised how much damage he'd done and that's when the pain set in. It doesn't hurt as much now but it's not something I'm going to get over in a hurry."

"The police were sketchy on the details," I said. "What happened?"

She sighed and fell back in her chair. "I'm trying not to think about it too much," she said. "But then there's not much to think about. It happened so quickly."

She paused for a moment or two and stared into the distance as she gathered her thoughts. On the other side of the studio, cameras were clicking and someone was shouting out directions to the model.

Reagan turned back to me, her face showing signs of strain, and told me how she had returned home from the local store to find her assailant hanging about outside her house.

"I came around from the back of the house on foot and was at the door before he spotted me," she said. "The next thing I knew, he was hitting me and punched me in the face, but I managed to push him off and get inside. I slammed the door on him and locked it and called the police straight away."

"Seems you had a lucky escape," I said. "I presume you heard about the attack on Brady? He wasn't so lucky."

"That was yet another shock," she said. "First Cara and then Austin. And the police tell me they're looking at Elliot Garcia for Austin's murder. Which is even more of a shock. Some sort of love triangle. Not that I believe it for a moment. Elliot has never been anything but a perfect gentleman. He's just not capable of such a thing."

He certainly didn't fit my interpretation of a perfect gentleman. Far from it. But I had no doubt he was capable of turning on the charm when it suited him. And strong-minded and independent woman though she was, I could imagine Reagan being seduced by his manipulative ways.

She continued, "This photoshoot is for a poster campaign for Elliot's gym. I hope it won't turn out to be a waste of time. He's not going to be too concerned about promoting his business if he's having to contend with accusations from the police."

"I'm sure you're on safe ground," I said. "I'm not buying the police's version, either. I think there's a connection between Brady's and Cara's deaths."

She agreed. "I think you're right. And, after what happened to me, I'm even more certain. I don't think my attack was an isolated incident."

"What makes you so certain?"

"Something he said as he hit me. He said 'You're next bitch'." She shuddered and wrapped her arms around herself. "He was waiting for me. It was no random attack."

"Does Brady have a connection to your business?" I asked.

"Other than as the employee of a client and Cara's partner, no. Why do you ask?"

"It occurred to me your business could be a target. A disgruntled client or an employee with an axe to grind."

"The same thought occurred to me," she said. "But I can't imagine anyone being that disgruntled. I'm sure we're a target, but I have no idea why."

"It has to be someone who knew all three of you," I said. "Or at least the relationships between you." I dug into my jeans pocket. "Which brings me to the point of my visit." I pulled out Cara's mobile and pulled up the contacts page. "The police returned Cara's phone and I've been checking through her contacts. Jordan helped identify some of them, but I need your help with her business associates."

I handed the mobile to Reagan. She took it from me and scrolled through the list. "Cara wasn't very good at keeping her contacts up to date," she said. "Some of these are no longer with us."

I said, "I'm particularly interested in those who had access to Medway Hall. I know that included Vanessa and Ian Parks."

"Ian is our salesman, but he's on extended leave at the moment," she said. "He's a single father and one of his children is ill. We had to take on a replacement to cover for him, but he had no cause to visit Cara in the short time he's been in the role."

"And no one else?"

"There are one or two other employees but no one who would have access to Cara's place. We're a small, friendly team, though, so she may have entertained some of them socially from time to time. I'd be happy to make some enquiries."

"That would help," I said and pocketed the mobile.

"Let's hope we get some answers soon," she said.

"We'll have to carry on digging till we find some."

"Even though the police are keeping an eye on my place, and I'm being extra vigilant to make sure I stay safe, I won't feel totally secure until this is over."

I offered my sympathies and we brought our meeting to a close after she had confirmed she would make her own enquiries and get in touch if she learned anything useful.

As she walked me over to the door, she said, "How is Jordan taking it? He sounded despondent when I spoke with him."

I paused, my hand on the door handle. "He's much as you'd expect, but we're taking good care of him," I said. "I didn't know you'd been in touch with him. He never said."

"I called to ask him if he needed any financial support while probate's being sorted out. I know Cara used to give him an allowance."

"That's kind of you," I said. "But there was no need. We have it covered."

"I'm sure you do. I just wanted him to know I'm happy to give him whatever support he needs."

"I'm sure he appreciates your concern," I said.

"He tells me his mother had already gifted him several thousand pounds in Premium Bonds for his last birthday. So he should be fairly secure for a while."

My hand tightened on the door handle. Jordan had already made it clear his financial situation was dire. And here I was learning he had sizeable assets at his disposal.

Why would he lie to me? Something didn't add up.

CHAPTER TWENTY-SEVEN

My meeting with Reagan Francis wasn't the only reason for my visit to Almchester town centre. As I was in the neighbourhood anyway, it seemed as good a time as any to check out the area for myself.

From my parking spot on the High Street, I walked the short distance to the nearest turnoff and down past a short row of shops to where the narrow walkway between a coffee bar and a hardware store led to Medway Hall's side gate.

Anyone leaving Medway Hall from here would have to take this route back to the High Street.

Nathan had asked the local station for details of any CCTV surveillance in the area, but they hadn't yet got back to him. So I'd decided to check for myself.

The usual assortment of shops and businesses typically found in an urban shopping centre were all around me, but, unfortunately, there was a dearth of CCTV cameras.

The first I spotted was above the branch of Barclays Bank on the other side of Springboard Creative's offices, but nothing on this side until I reached the coffee bar at the end of the turnoff. Loud red signage above the plate-glass window proclaimed this to be Ollie's Place.

Fingers crossed, I headed towards it. This would be my one chance of gaining any useful video footage from the day of Cara's murder.

It was early afternoon, towards the end of the lunch break, and I was greeted by the murmur of voices, the clatter of dishes and mugs, and the aroma of freshly brewed coffee from behind a long counter holding chrome expresso and frothing machines.

On the other side of the counter, a dark-haired man of about my age whistled a happy tune as he wiped the coffee machine's warming plates with a damp cloth.

I pulled a business card from my inside jacket pocket as I made my way towards him. I offered him the card and said, "I'm guessing you're Ollie and this is your Place."

He took the card from me and grinned. "Your powers of observation are right on track." He looked down at the card and let out a short, sharp whistle. "And you're the famous Michael MacGregor." He looked up at me wide-eyed. "A pleasure to meet you. I'm a fan."

"Only mildly famous." I thanked him and, lowering my voice, said, "If you have the time, perhaps you could help with an investigation I'm involved in."

"Sure." He glanced over to the tables where a smattering of customers sat, most of them chatting over coffee and a couple working with laptops. "We're just winding down after the lunchtime rush, so I'm not too busy right now." He leaned towards me, arms on the counter. "What can I do for you?"

"I'd be interested in viewing your CCTV footage from about two to three weeks ago."

He groaned, pulled a face, and pushed himself back up from the counter. "Sorry, man. The camera's a fake. Cheaper to run than the real thing and not as much hassle. It's there as a deterrent."

My heart sank. "Not to worry," I said. "It was a long shot, anyway."

"Is this about Cara Welles' murder?"

"You've heard about it?"

"I knew her. She was one of my regulars. She came in most days for take-away. It was a real blow, what happened to her. She was one of the sweetest people."

"Was she here that day?"

Ollie shook his head and said, "A lot of Cara's people come here for lunch, but she wasn't here that day." He nodded towards a table at the far side of the room where a young woman in a grey business suit and with tied-back blonde hair sat staring down at a coffee cup. "That's Cara's secretary. She's one of my regulars. This whole thing has hit her hard."

"I've been meaning to get in touch with her," I said. "She may be a useful source of information. Do you mind if I go have a chat with her?"

"Be my guest," he said.

I thanked Ollie for his time and threaded my way through the tables to where Vanessa sat in the corner. She didn't see me approach, still staring into her empty coffee cup.

I stood over her and said, "Vanessa?"

She started as if shaken out of a reverie and stared up at me blank-eyed, a puzzled look on her face.

"Michael MacGregor," I said. "I was hoping to have a chat if you're up to it."

The blank stare faded as the light of recognition dawned in her eyes and she straightened up. "Of course. You came to our offices a few days ago."

"I've just come from there." I flipped a hand towards the empty chair facing her. "May I join you?"

She signalled her consent, and I took a seat.

"I heard you were making enquiries into Cara's death," she said. "I'm happy to help." Her eyes moistened as she spoke.

"I'm told you were close."

"She was more than my boss. She was a friend."

"You must have known her better than most," I said. "So perhaps you could tell me about her recent movements. I've been trying to find out if she was having problems with anyone or if there were any changes to her usual routine. I've drawn a blank so far."

She paused for a moment before answering. "I can't be certain, but..." She hesitated and raised a hand to her throat as if unsure of herself. "There was something, but I'm not sure how relevant it is. I told the police about it, but they didn't seem to think it was important."

Why was I not surprised? There was far too much the local force didn't seem to find important. At least, not until it was too late.

"If it gave you cause for concern," I said, "then it's important. Anything out of the ordinary, no matter how small."

"Something happened the day before," she said. "That evening. We'd just landed a big account with a local businessman. Elliot Garcia."

"That's a name that keeps cropping up," I said.

She nodded. "He has a lot of influence in the business community. Getting his account was a game-changer. So Cara and Reagan laid on a party for us at the office. A celebration. We held it in the basement. It was much roomier down there. And everything was going well. Everyone enjoying themselves."

She paused again and stared across the room, a distant look in her eyes, as she recalled the event. "About halfway through the evening, I went upstairs. I just needed to get away for a few minutes. All that pounding music. And that's when I saw them. Cara and Austin. They were in the middle of a blazing row. She was screaming abuse at him."

"Did they often row?"

"Never. I've not seen her so happy since they got together. That's why I was so shocked."

"Any idea what it was about?"

She shook her head. "They saw me and I asked if everything was okay. Austin told me to mind my own business and stormed off."

Vanessa fell silent, stared down at her empty cup, and grasped it between her hands.

The sound of laughter from a nearby table contrasted sharply with the pain in Vanessa's eyes when she looked up again.

"I'm sorry to put you through this," I said.

She nodded without speaking, her mouth set in a hard line, and when she finally spoke again, her voice trembled. "I helped her into one of the side offices," she said, "and tried to calm her down and find out what the problem was. But she was upset and sobbing and just wanted to go home. She'd been drinking heavily too - something else that was out of character - and she was in no fit state to drive. I took her car keys and sent her home in a cab." She drew in a deep breath. "It was the last time I saw her alive."

"And you were the one who found her the following day?"

"I knew she would be working from home that morning. She emailed me not long after I got into the office asking for some info she needed to work out a budget for the project she was working on. So I guessed she was okay. Reagan was in charge of finance, so I got the figures from her and passed them on to Cara. It was only later when she didn't turn up for the meeting, we knew something was wrong. We couldn't reach her on the 'phone so Reagan asked me to go over there. I found her lying on the floor in her office, unconscious, her laptop open on the desk. So I supposed she'd been taken ill whilst she was working. I called for an ambulance, but I knew it was too late."

"You didn't call the police?"

"I didn't think to. I guess the emergency service must have called them. Only later, when I learned she'd been murdered, I thought…" She blushed and looked down before continuing. "I thought maybe it had something to do with Austin. Something to do with their argument. Then when I heard what happened to him…" She shook her head. "None of it makes sense." She stared hard into my eyes, as if seeking answers.

I tried to reassure her everything was being done to catch Cara's killer. Not that I was so sure of that myself, but I thought it best to allay her concerns as much as possible.

"I'm surprised you're back at work so soon," I said. "You should be taking it easy for a while."

"I'd rather keep busy," she said. "It keeps my mind off it. which reminds me…" She looked down at her watch. "I should get back to the office."

Thanking her for her time, I gave her my business card, and told her to get in touch if she needed someone to talk to. I took her number, promised to get in touch if I learned anything new, and watched after her as she made it through the door, a sad broken figure.

Times like this, I hated my work.

The place was empty now except for one diehard throwback to the last century who rocked his head back and forth in tune to some annoyingly tinny music emanating from a pair of oversized earphones. Ollie came over to the seating area, dishcloth in hand, to clear and clean the tables.

As I rose to leave, waving farewell to Ollie, a sudden thought struck me, and I turned back to speak with him.

"It occurs to me," I said, "you'd know some of Cara Welles' colleagues by sight. Right?"

He paused and nodded. "Sure. Not all by name, though."

I nodded towards the other side of the bar, signalling my desire to move away from throwback man, as much to escape his taste in music as to move out of earshot.

Once at the counter, I said, "So if any of them were around these parts on the day she was killed, you may have seen them."

"I guess. Not sure how that helps, though."

"You know she lived not far from here?"

He said he did.

I explained that anyone visiting her on foot from the office would have to pass his coffee bar. "So, if she had any visitors that day who haven't been accounted for, they most likely would have passed this way."

He dropped the dishcloth on the table he'd been wiping down and straightened up, a look of consternation on his face. "You're not suggesting...? No way. One of my customers?"

"I'm not suggesting anything. Just trying to get a broad picture of who was where that day and when."

"Jeez, man, that's grim. One of my customers a killer."

"I'm not saying that."

He knitted his eyebrows as he ran his mind back over the past few days. "None of them was in that day, anyway. Which was unusual. I found out later they'd had a big meeting at work."

"Yes, a marketing presentation. So you saw no one?"

He opened his mouth to speak, but stopped himself. A pause, and then, "Well, maybe. Sort of." He seemed unsure.

"What's that supposed to mean?"

"Their salesman, Ian Parks. His car was down the road. But he didn't come in. I wondered about that 'cos he's a regular and he was always up for a chat." He shrugged. "Not that I expected him to be around these parts, anyway."

"Why not?"

"I heard he was on furlough at the moment. And he's not from around here. He lives on the other side of town." Ollie became suddenly animated. "But listen. I hope you're not suggesting he had anything to do with this. No way. He's the nicest of guys. Wouldn't harm a fly."

"I'm not saying..." I stopped myself short. Ollie had obviously got it into his head I was trying to pin a murder on one of his customers. "Let's just leave it at that."

Before I left, I said, "Have the police been around the area asking questions?"

"Not that I know of. No one has spoken to me."

I fought back the temptation to let out an expletive.
Seems like Nathan and I were doing their job for them yet again.

CHAPTER TWENTY-EIGHT

I arrived home from my foray on the High Street to find Nathan and the Ginger Clown seated in the living room.

I interrupted their conversation. "Pleasure to see you, Inspector Gibson," I said and held out a hand. I tried to sound like I meant it.

He raised himself from the armchair, shook my hand, and sat down again. "I was bringing the Chief here up to date on the investigation," he said.

"I hope I've not missed much," I said and dropped onto the couch at Nathan's side.

"I thought you'd be back by now," said Nathan.

"Stopped off for a coffee on the way," I said. I had no intention of discussing details of my visit to Ollie's Place in front of Gibson. That was for later.

Nathan was holding a manilla file which he offered to me. "Inspector Gibson was kind enough to let us have a copy of the crime file."

I took it from him and said, "This should make interesting reading." More likely for what it revealed about the shortcomings of the case than anything else.

I put it on the couch beside me and turned my attention to Gibson. "Any progress we should know about?"

"We're doing everything we can, but..." He trailed off and shrugged. "We've come to a dead-end on the investigation into your ex-wife's murder, unfortunately. We're presuming the attack on Reagan Francis is connected, but that's going nowhere either." He leaned forward and brightened up. "We have tracked down Elliot Garcia, though."

"Tracked him down?" Nathan said.

"He left town before we had chance to re-interview him. A business trip, apparently. But he's back now." He turned to face me. "Which brings me to the other reason for my visit. We're bringing him in for another interview this evening. I hoped we might take advantage of your expertise."

"You want me to sit in on it?"

"If you're okay with that. To be honest, I suspect it will be a done deal. But there's no harm in having another opinion."

"You have something new to go on?" I asked.

"Not yet. We're still waiting for the forensics report. But I want to keep the pressure on. Now he's had chance to reflect on his situation, he may realise it's in his best interests to cooperate and cut a deal."

My heart sank. Here we go again. Guilt was already a foregone conclusion.

"In that case," I said, "I'd be happy to help. Just say when and where." Anything to stop Gibson making a mess of it.

He gave me details of time and place and, before taking his leave, said, "Let me know if you think of anything once you've read the report," he said.

Nathan saw him out of the door while I ran through the file. He returned to the living room and said, "So, how did your meeting go? Anything useful?"

I went over my conversation with Reagan Francis, including the details of her attack. "I'm sure it's connected to Cara's murder. Just not sure how or why." I held up the report. "And there's nothing in here to suggest the ginger clown is treating Cara's murder as anything other than an isolated event."

"Don't let him hear you call him that." He dropped into place at my side.

I grunted and then told him of my visit to Ollie's Place and my chats with Vanessa and Ollie Jay. "I probably learned more in my brief talk than Gin... than Gibson did during the whole of an interview session. Which reminds me..." I opened the report and flipped through its pages. "... I need to know if they interviewed Ian Parks."

"Here," said Nathan, and took the file from me. "There's a list of interviewees at the front. You just skipped it." He found the relevant page and grunted. "No mention of Parks."

I groaned. "Why am I not surprised?"

"I'm starting to think we're better off doing our own interviews," said Nathan. "We need to find out where he lives and pay him a visit."

"I can help with that." I pushed myself up from the couch, went into the hall to where I'd left my messenger bag on the coat rack, retrieved Cara's mobile, and scrolled through her contacts as I made my way back to the living room. "Here it is," I said. "He's in the Parkside district. It's on the other side of town, but it shouldn't take too long."

"You're going to be tied up with the Garcia interview this afternoon, so let's contact Parks later and see if we can't get over there tomorrow."

I agreed. "At least I should be able to make my own decisions about the veracity of Garcia's interview," I said. "Do you want to come with me?"

"I'll hang on here," he said. "Jordan will be back soon, and he wanted to show me some more of his sketches."

My heart skipped a beat. "You and Jordan seem to get on well."

"He's a good kid."

"He's still not being completely upfront with us," I told Nathan what I'd learned from Reagan about Cara's birthday gift. "Jordan told me he was getting short of funds. Why would he tell me that when he has a large nest egg to fall back on?"

"Given all that's happened, he must still feel insecure. And suddenly finding himself financially dependent on you isn't going to help any. Having that sort of money would help him feel less dependent. A secret reserve to fall back on."

"I guess so. But I'm not sure what to do about it. If I confront him and turn it into an issue, it could stall what little progress I've made with him."

Nathan slow-punched my arm. "Tell you what, why don't you leave it to me? I can sound him out about it while you're over at the station."

With a sense of relief, I agreed. "Your relationship with him is sound," I said. "Better than mine. You both seem so comfortable in each other's company."

"Things are getting better between you, aren't they?"

"We talk, yes. And we're making progress. He's much friendlier. But there's still this distance between us. It's like he's still sounding me out, trying to decide if I'm worth having a relationship with."

"Isn't that inevitable? He still has a lot to process. And he's always asking about you. About your past. About our lives together."

"Really?"

"Really. He's working through his feelings and trying to adjust to a relationship he never knew he had. But he'll get there in the end. You need to be patient."

Something melted inside me. "You would make such a good father," I said.

"And so will you. Just hang on in there."

He pressed a hand to my thigh and squeezed it. "And you know I'm always here for you."

I responded with a smile. "I know that."

The last few days had been a nightmare, and it wasn't over yet, but right now, nothing mattered more than knowing I always had my man's support, and no matter what lay ahead, I would never have to face it alone.

CHAPTER TWENTY-NINE

It was later that afternoon, time for Garcia's interview, and Gibson was leading me down that same featureless corridor to the recording room at the rear of the station.

He stopped at a door halfway along and opened it. "This is it," he said and stepped aside to let me through.

Opposite the door, labelled monitoring stations sat along a metal desktop running the length of the wall. Only the centre one, labelled 'Interview Room 2', was turned on.

He followed me in, directed me to the one metal chair in front of the central workstation and pulled a second one over from the station to his right.

The monitor screen displayed a view of the interview room with a table at its centre and a chair on either side of it.

Gibson seated himself at my side. "Our background check on Garcia threw up some interesting details," he said. "He's not quite the bona fide businessman he pretends to be."

"Bit shady, eh?"

"The Met has had him under surveillance for some time. He's been expanding his empire recently, moving into legit businesses. But it may well be that empire is founded on dirty money. He's suspected of laundering drug money for one of the big cartels in London. They haven't been able to pin anything on him yet, but it looks as though the good times are soon coming to an end."

There was a hint of glee in Gibson's tone, and I could almost see the cogs turning in his brain as he imparted this information. Garcia was a bad man. Bad men kill people. So Garcia must have killed Brady. It was the sort of sloppy thinking that seemed to guide Gibson's investigative methods, and it was just one more indication he'd already decided on Garcia's guilt.

"Is the autopsy report on Brady available yet?" I asked.

"Just the preliminary findings. Your original assessment appears to be correct. Brady was felled by a blow or blows to the head and then stabbed to death where he lay."

As we were speaking, the image on the monitor screen changed. The door to the interview room opened and Garcia entered, followed by two uniformed officers.

Garcia walked with a swagger. He was tall, of swarthy complexion, and the expensive-looking grey wool suit did nothing to hide the powerful physique.

One of the uniforms stationed himself by the door and the other seated himself and waved Garcia to the chair on the other side of the desk.

Garcia sat where he was directed and ran both hands down the fabric of his trousers, smoothing the creases, as he made himself comfortable. A supercilious smile played across his lips.

I got the impression this wasn't the first time Garcia had faced questioning in a police interview room.

The interviewing officer signalled to Gibson that he was ready to begin recording, introduced himself as Sgt Vincent Tyler, read Garcia his rights, and reminded him he was entitled to a solicitor.

Garcia responded with a curl of the lip, and said, "No need. I don't bother my solicitor with this nonsense."

"Nonsense?" Tyler fixed Garcia with a hard stare. "We're talking murder here. A man lost his life."

"To me, this is not a concern." Garcia glanced down at his watch. "Can we do this, please? I have already told you all I know and there is places I have to be."

"You may want to take this a little more seriously, Mr Garcia," said Tyler. "You were the last to see the victim alive."

"Not so." Garcia smiled and revealed the glint of a gold tooth. "Last to see him alive was killer."

"You were seen leaving the victim's property following what was reported to have been a violent argument. This was the evening before his body was discovered."

"Argument, yes. Nothing more."

"What did you argue about?"

"He screwed my woman. This is something to argue about, is not so?"

"Sounds like a motive for murder to me."

"Brady did me favour."

"A favour?"

"Showed me she is cheating bitch. Now bitch is history. Not worth killing for." Garcia leaned forward, arms on the desk, fingers spread. "Listen to me. This was about him and me. Not her. He was supposed to be friend. This is not what friends do."

"He broke the rules?"

Garcia nodded. "Brady want to screw around? Fine. But not this. There is code of conduct among men of honour. And this is not how men of honour prove themselves. Brady crossed a line. But I did not kill him. He needed to know we were done."

"So, how did you leave it?"

"He was finished. No job. No friend."

Garcia showed no sign of unease or discomfort. He was supremely confident and at ease. And as Tyler continued to push him, challenging his version of events, Garcia remained calm, focused, and steadfast.

Long before the interview was over, I knew this was not our man.

Gibson didn't share my opinion. "We'll break him eventually," he said.

"I wouldn't take any bets on that," I said.

"You're not suggesting we have the wrong man?"

"On the face of it, he's a dead cert. He had motive and opportunity. And he was in the right place. But he shows none of the overt signs of guilt I would expect to see."

"But even so-."

I interrupted him. "You've heard the phrase 'honour among thieves'?"

"Yes, but I'm not sure how that applies."

"It suggests even those of questionable morals like Garcia live by an ethical code, one that determines how they act and relate to others. He said himself that there are standards by which honourable men live.

And I have no doubt that the standards he expects others to live by guide his own behaviour."

Gibson said, "I'm not sure where you're going with this."

I continued, "Everything I've seen so far suggests to me that Garcia is a confident, forceful man, someone capable of standing his ground in the face of opposition, the kind of man who faces conflict head-on."

"I'd go along with that."

"And, clearly, he's Brady's physical equal. You can see that for yourself. Which suggests he would be capable of handling himself well in a physical altercation."

"Agreed."

"And yet one of the blows that felled Brady was to the back of the head and he was then stabbed where he lay, probably unconscious."

I paused to allow Gibson to take this in.

"Now do you see where I'm going with this?" I asked. "If Garcia had wanted to kill Brady, he would have stood firm and taken him head-on. Someone of Garcia's mindset would not have disposed of Brady in a way that would be perceived as cowardly. It would have been dishonourable."

To his credit, Gibson was prepared to accept my analysis, albeit begrudgingly. "I can see how you may have come to such a conclusion," he said. "But we still need to be sure. We'll need to keep him in the frame."

"Of course you will. But I suggest you look elsewhere too."

I had already made up my own mind. Garcia didn't kill Brady. I was sure that Brady's and Cara's deaths and Reagan's assault were linked. And now we had to find that link.

But we were running out of leads.

Maybe interviewing Ian Parks would put us back on track.

CHAPTER THIRTY

Soft music played in the background, and the occasional clink of cutlery interrupted the hum of conversation from surrounding tables.

We were seated at a corner table in Silvers, one of Almchester's more select restaurants, Nathan suited and booted in his best grey worsted two-piece and me - not one for formality - attired in casual grey flannels and a white Emporio Armani lounge shirt.

Whilst I'd been over at the station for Garcia's interview, Nathan had made a reservation for later that evening. It was a welcome relief from the travails of the past few days.

A dapper young waiter uncorked a bottle of Veuve Clicquot Champagne, and we sat in silence as he filled our flutes and placed the bottle on the table in a stainless steel wine cooler before retreating with a smile and a brief nod.

We raised our flutes and toasted each other with a clink of glass on glass.

"To us," said Nathan.

I returned the toast.

"I finally got my steak and champagne dinner," I said.

"We needed a break," he said. "And a chance to get some time to ourselves."

"Well, make the most of it," I said. "I can't see this train wreck of an investigation ending any time soon."

"All the more reason to enjoy it while we can."

"I'll be happier when we've got our lives back on track," I said. "We still have a wedding to plan, remember?"

Nathan said, "Have you said anything to Jordan about that?"

"Not yet. I think he has enough to grapple with at the moment." As an afterthought, I added, "You realise you'll be getting a stepson as well as a husband?"

He grinned and a warm light danced in his eyes. "If I can cope with the father, I'm sure the son will be no problem."

I laughed. "As long as you know what you're letting yourself in for."

"Which reminds me," he said, "I talked to Jordan about his finances while you were at the station. You have nothing to worry about. He wasn't holding out on you."

"So what was all that about the bonds?"

Before he could reply, our waiter returned with our starters, a shared platter of chorizo croquettes. I waited patiently as he arranged our plates and cutlery before expressing a hope we enjoy our food and retiring.

Nathan forked several croquettes onto his plate and said, "Reagan got in touch with him, suggesting she keep him in funds till probate was settled. He declined, but she was insistent. He appreciated the thought. It was kind of her. But he was embarrassed. So he spun her a tale about the bonds to put her off. It was a fiction."

I heard him out as I chewed on a croquette and then said, "She and Cara were close. I guess she feels obligated to help out."

"Maybe," he said, digging into his food, "but I can understand his reluctance to accept her offer."

"He's a good guy. I just wish Gibson would drop the bail conditions. Jordan has enough to contend with."

"Gibson's the type who doesn't like to admit he's wrong. He'll keep those conditions in place to the bitter end. Until Cara's killer is behind bars."

"Might help if we were anywhere near that," I said. "I'm still trying to make sense of what we have so far." I pushed my empty plate to one side and raised my glass. "Something happened to Cara the day before, something that had a profound effect on her. There has to be a connection."

I sipped from my glass as I ran back over my conversation with Vanessa and then, "Cara was never much of a drinker. She must have been particularly..." I trailed off mid-sentence, struck by a sudden thought. "The car."

"What?"

"Something's been niggling away at the back of my mind and it just hit me. It's the car. Vanessa told me she wouldn't let Cara drive home. She sent her off in a taxi."

"Is that important?"

"Sophie told us she knew Cara was home the following morning because her car was parked in front of the house. So how did it get there?"

Nathan frowned. "It would have to be someone from the party. And whoever that was, they would surely have seen or spoken with Cara."

"Someone who may have been the last to see Cara alive. And yet they never came forward. Doesn't that strike you as odd?"

"It needs following up," said Nathan. "That's for sure. So now we have two lines of enquiry."

"I'll call Vanessa in the morning," I said, "and find out what happened to Cara's car keys."

"And I'll contact Ian Parks," said Nathan. "I wouldn't raise your hopes, though. I'm not sure we'll get anything useful from him."

"He was parked near Cara's place on the day of her murder," I said. "That alone is cause for concern. He shouldn't have been anywhere near. And don't forget he sometimes visited Cara at Medway Hall, so presumably, he had the access codes."

Before we could continue our conversation, the waiter returned, pushing a metal trolley laden with two large platters of food and several small side dishes. The smell of freshly grilled steaks wafted over to us and my mouth watered. I hadn't realised how hungry I was.

Once the remains of the starters had been cleared away and replaced by our mains, the waiter retired, leaving us to enjoy our meal.

Nathan raised his glass. "No more shop talk for today," he said. "We have enough to keep us busy for a while. But for now, let's relax and enjoy the rest of the evening."

Once again, I clinked glasses with him. "I'm all for that." I put down the glass and took up a set of cutlery, ready to attack my steak.

The last few days, we'd both struggled to make sense of what we'd learned. The local investigation had been careless at best. But nothing we had learned since had moved us any closer to a solution, and there were still no clear patterns to guide us. We had a lot of work ahead of us and brief respites like this were a welcome relief. And so I pushed all those tangled thoughts to the back of my mind and made the most of a pleasant evening in the company of my man.

I suspected moments such as these would be few and far between over the days to come.

CHAPTER THIRTY-ONE

"Come on. Time to start the day."

Nathan's words crept into my consciousness, prompting me into wakefulness. I half-opened one bleary eye to find him sitting up in bed and leaning over me. He prodded me in the chest.

I groaned. "Why do we always have to get up at the crack of dawn?"

"It's eight o'clock."

"Exactly. The crack of dawn."

It was long after midnight when we got back home from Silvers Restaurant the night before, somewhat the worse for wear, and the last thing I needed was being booted out of bed any time before noon.

"The day's half gone," said Nathan. "Get up, you lazy sod."

I rolled over and pushed myself up into a sitting position. "Is this what married life's going to be like?"

"You'd better believe it." He was already out of bed, bounding around like a demented bear on hot coals. "Jordan and Sophie were up and out over an hour ago. You should be setting a good example."

He grabbed his bathrobe from the hook on the back of the door and headed for the bathroom.

I rolled out of bed, grabbed my own robe from where I'd dropped it on the bedroom chair, and called out after him. "All the more reason to stay in bed," I said. "Our sex life has faded into oblivion since they moved in."

I donned my robe and followed him into the bathroom.

He was in the shower soaping up and grinning. "Their bedroom is right next door," he said. "I wouldn't want them to be scared away by your carnal grunting."

"I do not grunt." I checked my reflection in the mirror above the sink, decided not to bother shaving, and reached for my toothbrush and a tube of toothpaste.

"Yes, you're right," he said. "It's more of a howl than a grunt."

"It sort of depends on the action. If I had my mouth full, I wouldn't be able to grunt or howl, would I?" I brushed my teeth and rinsed out my mouth under the tap.

He stepped out of the shower, pulled a towel from the rack, and dried himself. "Tell you what," he said. "If we're back in time, I'll give you a chance to practise your verbal repertoire."

"Back? Back from where?"

"We're going to see Ian Parks, remember? I'll call him after breakfast. See if we can't set up a meet today. We need to move this on as quickly as possible."

"Sorry, I'd forgotten. My brain's not in gear yet."

Seems my carnal needs would have to wait.

"And I'll call Vanessa," I said and stepped into the shower. "See if she knows what happened to those car keys."

Later, once breakfast was out of the way, I took over the responsibility of calling Ian Parks. "It'll be better coming from me," I said. "I can tell him I'm working as a psychological profiler for the local police. Which is almost true."

"Do you know anything about him?" Nathan asked.

"Just his name and occupation. But nothing about him as a person."

"We need to be careful how we play it. We're looking at him as a possible suspect, after all."

"We'll say we're interviewing everyone who knew Cara. He's not to know we have an ulterior motive."

Nathan grunted his agreement.

Ian Parks was surprised to receive my call but agreed to see us readily enough. He was at home and I arranged for us to go there later that morning.

Nathan drove. On the way, I called Vanessa on her mobile. She didn't pick up. I left a message on voicemail asking her to call me.

Ian Parks lived in a typical leafy Almchester suburb, row after row of bay-windowed semis standing back from tree-lined roads behind carefully trimmed privet hedges and cultivated front gardens.

Not sure what sort of reception I'd expected given the nature of our visit, but Parks was friendly enough. Affable and charming, he was a middle-aged man with thinning grey hair and a wide smile. He invited us into his home and made us feel welcome. "Terrible news about Cara," he said. "Though I'm not sure how I can help."

He showed us into a comfortable living room off the hall and, once we were seated, I explained our involvement in Cara's investigation and why we'd asked to see him.

"We're trying to account for Cara's exact movements on the days leading up to her murder," I said. "Anyone she may have spoken to or who may have visited her. Any concerns she may have discussed with them. Anyone she was having problems with."

"I don't recall having spoken to her recently. And I certainly haven't seen her in person for a while. I've been stuck at home these last few weeks."

"That's odd," said Nathan. "We were told your car was seen near Cara's place on the day of the murder."

Parks looked at each of us in turn, a puzzled look on his face. "My Car? I don't think so. I was nowhere near."

Nathan and I exchanged glances, and I said, "The proprietor of Ollie's Place recalls seeing your car outside his coffee bar that morning."

"Ahh, right." Parks' look of concern faded. "Ollie wouldn't know, but that isn't my car. It belongs to the business, and I handed the keys in when I started my leave. I'm guessing the new guy would have used it that day."

My shoulders slumped.

Seems we'd come up against another brick wall. Any hopes of Ian Parks leading us to a solution had proved futile, merely muddying the waters.

And we were fast running out of leads.

Nathan persisted. "So, when did you start your leave?"

"It was a couple of weeks ago. Though I wouldn't call it 'leave' exactly. Our computer system allows for two-way remote access, so I'm doing all my admin work from home. And the new guy is covering my outside visits until I return to the office."

"How about the office party?" asked Nathan. "You didn't go?"

"My kid's health is more important than some party."

"How is he?" I asked.

"He's good. He's recovering from an appendectomy. Bit sore. Bit sorry for himself. But he's getting there."

"Glad to hear it," I said.

"Your son's going through a bad time too," he said. "It can't be easy dealing with all the crap that's going around."

"Crap?" I said. "Not sure what you mean."

"Ah." There was something about the way Parks uttered that single word, and the accompanying frown, that told me I was missing something here.

"Is there something we need to know?" I asked.

He exhaled slowly and shook his head. "You know how it is when something like this happens. Some wild rumours are going around back at the office."

From the way he shuffled in place and avoided my eyes, it didn't take a genius to see he was deeply embarrassed.

"So, what are we up against?" Nathan said.

He stared at us both, tight-lipped, for a few moments. And then, breaking his silence, he addressed me and said, "I'm sure you realise people like you, people in the public eye, come in for some flack at times." It sounded as if he were preparing me for worse to come.

"Believe me," I said. "I've been in the firing line so often, I've become bulletproof. So what am I looking at now?"

"There's some stupid idle gossip going around the firm. People talk. Some nonsense about Jordan being his mother's killer and you interfering in the police investigation and trying to cover up for him."

My face flushed, betraying my anger. Parks raised his hands in a conciliatory gesture and said, "Hey, I'm just the messenger here. I take people as I find them. And I don't have a problem with you."

I nodded, not trusting myself to speak.

He continued. "We stand by our kids no matter what."

"If my son had killed his mother, I'd make damn sure there was no cover-up."

Nathan joined in. "You might consider telling these gossips the consequences of making slanderous accusations."

"No way am I defending them," said Parks, "but you know Cara was a popular, well-liked woman. What happened to her shook everyone to the core. She was everyone's friend and her colleagues are still in shock."

"Her son is suffering too," I said. "And the last thing he needs is having the finger pointed at him."

"Of course," said Parks. "And I sympathise. But Cara's colleagues are still trying to come to terms with what happened. And all these recent changes at work aren't helping any. They're unsettling."

"Changes? What changes?" I asked.

"You've not heard?" he said. "Reagan Francis is taking on a new partner. She's going into business with her new client, Elliot Garcia."

I gasped, unsure how else to respond. It seems it was a day for shocks and surprises.

CHAPTER THIRTY-TWO

I checked my mobile a couple of times on the journey home.

Still no reply from Vanessa.

I was starting to get edgy. Now we had lucked out on our visit to Ian Parks, Vanessa was our only hope of making progress.

Jordan's car was parked out front when we reached the house. So that was another of my anticipated needs put to boot. My sex life was more of a fantasy than a reality at the moment. Not that I was in the mood, anyway. Park's revelation about my perceived interference in the police investigation had annoyed me, and I was still fuming as we got out of the car.

"Have people nothing better to do than spread malicious gossip?" I said.

"There's always going to be speculation about an event like this," said Nathan. "Just ignore it."

"Not easy to do when you're the one being accused of unethical behaviour."

Nathan grunted in response.

I wasn't finished. "And what was all that about Reagan taking on Garcia as a partner? What the hell is she playing at?"

"Why wouldn't she? She probably just sees him as an opportunistic businessman. She's not likely to know anything of his less reputable side."

"Maybe someone needs to tell her."

"And you said yourself she's feeling a financial strain. She's probably grateful he came along at the right time."

"More like he's taking advantage of a bad situation."

Once indoors, Nathan headed to the kitchen to make coffee - probably as much to get away from my moaning - and I went to the sitting room, parked myself on the couch, and tried Vanessa's mobile again.

Still no reply.

I tried the office number instead and finally got through to one of her colleagues who told me Vanessa was in a meeting. She promised to pass on a message as soon as possible.

Seems it was a day for being thwarted in oh so many ways.

Nathan came back, mugs of coffee in hand, and gave me one before going into the hall and calling up to Jordan. "Coffee down here if you want some."

A shouted reply came back. "Be right there."

As Nathan returned to the living room and seated himself on the couch beside me, my mobile rang. It was Vanessa. At last.

She apologised for not getting back to me earlier. "It's been one of those mornings," she said.

I explained the reason for my call, asked her if she gave Cara's car keys to anyone else, and told her why it was important.

That seemed to fluster her. "I gave them to Austin," she said. "Cara drove them to the party so he would have been without transport. I understand he wasn't staying with Cara that night, but he would have needed to get home."

I said, "Austin told me he'd taken a cab home, so I'm guessing he must have passed the keys on to someone else before he left the party."

She offered to ask around the office and get back to me.

As I finished the call, Nathan said, "Anything useful?"

"Not so far." I went over my conversation with Vanessa and added, "It's bloody frustrating. So many questions only Brady knew the answers to. I was right about him. He's at the heart of this mess."

Nathan said, "I'll be glad when it's over and we can put it all behind us."

"I'm with you there," I said and pocketed my mobile. "If only to get more time to ourselves."

"And then we can think about returning home."

"And start planning our wedding," I said. "That's if Karen lets us get involved."

We were interrupted by a familiar voice. "Wedding? You're getting married?" It was Jordan. He was standing in the doorway, a puzzled look on his face.

Nathan and I rose and turned to face him.

Jordan shifted his weight from one foot to the other and a floorboard cracked beneath him, breaking the silence. He said, "I've not thought much about the future."

"It's something we'll need to think about eventually," I said.

Jordan nodded imperceptibly and lowered his gaze to the floor. "You said you were looking forward to having more time to yourselves." He made it sound like an accusation.

Nathan and I were still holding our mugs. Nathan took my still-full mug from me and said, "I'll go freshen these up and make some more coffee." He shot me a meaningful look and went to the kitchen, leaving me to face Jordan alone.

I said, "I don't want you thinking you're not included in our plans."

He looked up and stared at me as if searching for answers in my expression. "Everything's a bit weird right now. And I'm not sure where I fit in."

"You're family. We're all in this together."

"Are we?"

"Of course we are."

"It's like everything has been turned upside down and I don't know where I am anymore."

I seated myself back on the couch and patted the space beside me. "Come sit." Once he was seated beside me, I said, "I know things are tough right now. But it won't be forever."

"Once it's over, you'll have your own lives to get on with."

"Sure, we're going home. Eventually. But there's no going back to the way things were. My world's changed too. We're family now."

"Really?"

I smiled. "I'm not sure we have a choice. It is what it is. It's how we deal with it that matters."

"And how do we deal with it?"

"I don't know about you, but I suppose, like me, you're still coping with the fallout. It's still a shock. So maybe when we've both had time to come to terms with our newfound status, we can talk it through and work out the way forward."

He nodded, but still seemed unsure.

"And, in the meantime," I said, "we're in this together. As family." I emphasised that final word.

He nodded and smiled. "It's kinda weird," he said. "All these years I didn't have a father and now I'm getting two."

"That's not a problem, is it?"

"I'm okay with it. I like Nathan. And it'll be kinda cool having a Police Chief as a stepdad."

Nathan interrupted us, returning with a tray bearing mugs of coffee. "I was listening to all that." He put the tray on the side table and passed a mug to Jordan. "And it's not as if we'll be far away. Besides, we have to introduce you to our friend Karen, so you'll have to come stay, anyway. She'd never forgive us otherwise."

"Yeah, I hadn't thought of that," I said. "If we don't introduce you, she'll come over here and hunt you down."

Jordan chortled. "She sounds scary."

"Oh, believe me," I said. "You have no idea."

Nathan handed me my mug of coffee and seated himself in the facing chair. "So we're all good?"

Jordan beamed. "All good," he said, leaning back in his seat.

And whatever tension there had been between us faded away.

Another hurdle crossed.

CHAPTER THIRTY-THREE

Early the following morning, Gibson called Nathan to bring us up to speed on the various investigations, and we agreed to come straight down to the station for a briefing.

We arrived to find Gibson wasn't his usual annoyingly buoyant self. Indeed, he seemed dispirited and so I guessed not all was going well.

He showed us into his office and took up his place behind the desk as Nathan and I seated ourselves on the other side of it.

A couple of manilla files were stacked on the desk before him. He tapped the top one and said, "We have the preliminary findings from Forensics on the Brady crime scene and the final forensics report for the Cara Welles case."

He pushed the top file to one side, opened the other one in front of him, and referred to it as he briefed us.

He said, "We'll start with the Brady case. It seems you were right in your assessment, Mr MacGregor. DNA analysis of the bloodstains on the body shows not all of it was his. Unfortunately, it wasn't Garcia's either."

"So Garcia is in the clear?" Nathan asked.

"There's too much circumstantial evidence connecting Garcia to the crime," said Gibson. "Just because he wasn't in for the kill doesn't mean he's not connected somehow. For the moment, we're keeping him in our sights."

I said, "Do you have a match for the DNA?"

He didn't. "Nothing on file," he said. "And with a lack of suspects, there's little chance of obtaining DNA samples from other sources."

"Are you still treating Brady's murder as a separate case?" I asked.

Gibson nodded. "We have no clear leads on either case, so at present, there's nothing to link them."

"And what about the Welles case?" asked Nathan.

Gibson pulled the other file towards him and opened it.

"There's nothing in the report I haven't already discussed with you. It gives a more detailed analysis of the cause of death, but despite a thorough investigation, we can't tie the crime to anyone. That being so, there's little point in keeping the crime scene locked down. So, you're free to go back at any time."

My heart sank. Yet another dead end.

Even so, I was determined to check the crime scene out for myself and, once we were back at the house, I called Jordan down from his room and asked him if he wanted to go with me. "You know the place better than anyone," I said, "and it would help to have a familiar eye look over it with me."

Jordan bit his lip while he thought it over. He opened his mouth to speak and closed it again.

"I know how difficult it would be," I said, "so it's okay if you'd rather not."

He was silent for a moment longer and then said, "Can't say it's something I'd look forward to, but I think I should go if I can be of some help."

He wanted to get it over with as soon as possible and so we set off shortly before noon.

It was one of those bright but cold late autumn days and by the time we reached the house, a low weak sun had done little to dispel the chill. The interior, unheated for so many days, was cold and damp.

We climbed the stairs to Cara's office on the first floor. Unlike the other rooms, this one was small and inviting.

Pale pink walls were matched by a darker thick wool carpet. A highly polished wooden desk stood against the wall adjacent to the door and faced a well-padded multicoloured zigzag-patterned couch pushed up against the facing wall. It was a bright cheerful room, and I suspected Cara spent a lot of her time in here. The muffled tread of our feet on the soft carpeting was a welcome relief from the echoing clatter our shoes had made on the hard marble floors as we passed through the rest of the house.

A glass-fronted black flame-effect electric fire stood in the recessed hearth next to the door. I crouched down and turned it on.

On the desk was a silver-framed photograph. I picked it up for a closer look. Against the backdrop of a woodland clearing, a smiling Cara, her arm around the shoulder of her son, looked back at me. The carefree smile was one I remembered well.

"This was one of mom's favourites," said Jordan.

I offered it to him and he took it from me, ran a finger over the glass as he gazed down at the image, and put it into his jacket pocket. "I'll take it home with me," he said.

I ran a hand over the top of the desk and then crouched by its side and examined the edges and sides of the protruding desktop more closely. A dark stain marred the corner where Cara had hit her head and another small, dark patch on the floor.

I noted its position in relation to the area at the side of the desk where the body had lain.

The positioning accorded with the findings of the forensics report. Cara had either tripped or been pushed, had banged her head on the corner of the desk as she fell, and had lain incapacitated by its side.

I grasped the top of the desk, pulled myself to my feet, and said, "Who would be allowed in this room?"

"Mum spent a lot of time in here," said Jordan. "It was her favourite room, not just her office. So she would have her friends up here." He scanned the room as he spoke and when he turned back to me, he was frowning. "Did the police clean the place up once they'd finished?" he asked.

"That's not part of their remit," I said. "They would have left it as they found it."

"Strange," he murmured.

"Something wrong?"

"It doesn't look right. Mum would have papers and files scattered all over her desk. At the end of the day, she'd put them away, but not while she was working."

"She was supposed to be preparing for a presentation that morning," I said. "She even asked Vanessa for some information she needed."

"Exactly. So why is the desk clear?"

I waved a hand towards the laptop. "Couldn't she have just been working online?"

He shook his head. "That's not how she did things."

"So what does this suggest to you?" I asked.

"It suggests she wasn't working that morning."

"Then it really is strange. She was supposed to be on a deadline."

He didn't respond.

"Something for us to think about." I reached down and turned off the fire. "I think I've seen all I need to for the moment. Let's get out of here."

As we made our way downstairs, I said, "You'll need to make a decision about this place once probate is settled. Do you want to keep the house?"

"No." He was emphatic. "It's too large for one thing. And after what happened...." He trailed off.

"Understandable," I said.

"I might want to keep hold of the gatehouse, though. It would make a good studio."

"Bit run down," I said.

"Nothing that can't be fixed. And it has a decent-sized cellar. I could keep my gas cylinders down there."

I said, "I'm sure we can sort something out eventually."

"I played in the gatehouse as a kid," he said. "And whenever me and mom rowed, I'd go hide over there in the cellar. The trapdoor bolted on the inside to block access to the storeroom in the other building before its cellar door was bricked up. So I'd lock myself in and refuse to come out. Mum called it my sulking room and made some joke about me being in a dark place right then."

He laughed at the thought and then, just as suddenly, his face sagged. "I miss her so much."

"Of course you do." I didn't know what else to say.

On the way to the car, he seemed subdued, lost in his own thoughts. We didn't speak much on the drive home.

CHAPTER THIRTY-FOUR

"Anyone dare say a bad word about Jordan," I said, "and I swear to God..."

"Calm down," said Nathan. "It's not going to happen. It's his mother's funeral. You seriously think anyone would be crass enough to start throwing around accusations?"

"Not if I have anything to do with it."

It was the day of Cara's funeral, several days since our discussion with Ian Parks, and I was still fuming about the baseless allegations thrown in our direction.

Both Nathan and I were attired in dark suits - not something I was used to - and I was standing at the mirror in the hall, trying to knot my tie with shaking hands and making a poor job of it.

"Here, let me help you with that," said Nathan. He turned me around and re-knotted the tie. As he fastened it in place, he lowered his voice and said, "And keep it down. We don't want Jordan hearing anything."

I glanced up the stairs towards where Jordan and Sophie were getting ready in their room. "He'd better not hear it from anyone else either, or they'll have me to deal with."

In line with Cara's wishes, her solicitors had arranged for a cremation with a simple ceremony on-site and no advance funeral procession.

Nathan drove us over to the crematorium where the other mourners would be gathering, and none of us spoke much on the way.

It was another bright crisp autumn day. When we arrived, a small group was already standing outside the building suitably wrapped in coats and scarves, one or two of whom I recognised from my visit to Springboard's offices. I was surprised to see Elliot Garcia among them as we drove past towards the car park. He hadn't struck me as the type to show compassion to others, especially as he hadn't really known Cara. I presumed he was there to ingratiate himself with the Springboard staff now he was about to be part of their team.

Nathan parked up, and we walked over to where the others waited. I noted with dismay that the only ones who approached us and offered Jordan their condolences were Reagan, Vanessa, and Ian Parks.

The wary glances coming our way and the widening space around us were a clear sign that Jordan's unfounded reputation as a possible matricidal killer had preceded him, keeping the naysayers at bay. Fortunately, Jordan didn't appear to notice. I kept a watchful eye on those around us, ready to ward off any unwarranted attention.

Ian shook hands with Jordan and wished him well before moving away to join some of his colleagues, leaving us in the company of Reagan.

Reagan was still wearing her dark glasses, but I was glad to see the bruising on the side of her face had faded.

I asked if there was any progress in identifying her assailant, only to learn there wasn't. Being reminded of her ordeal seemed to unsettle her, so I offered my further condolences and changed the subject.

"I hear you're taking on a new partner," I said.

"News travels fast," she said. "We haven't even signed the agreement yet."

"I have to say, I was surprised," I said. "I wouldn't have thought your line of work would be of any interest to Elliot Garcia." In truth, I was more surprised that she was willing to take on a partner of Garcia's dubious character and wondered if she knew anything of his reputation. Not something I felt comfortable asking about directly.

"I'm not sure Elliott cares too much about the nature of the businesses he invests in," she said. "He's just looking for a good return on his investment."

"You're a successful business," I said. "I wouldn't have thought you needed more investment."

"You have to understand," she said, "a business like ours rests on its prestige. And that prestige relied heavily on Cara's creative input."

To Jordan, she said, "Your mum was one of the best. She was a creative genius. I'm glad to see you inherited her talent."

Jordan acknowledged her words with a smile and nodded.

She continued, "Now we're no longer able to take advantage of Cara's creative input, it may well affect the quality of our output and, consequently, our income stream. Having Elliot's financial support during what may be turbulent times ahead is a Godsend."

I understood her worries, but could have hoped she'd found a better way to secure her business. But what would I know? She'd been in business long enough to know what she was doing. And I had more immediate concerns.

I said, "Did Vanessa tell you I'd met up with her?"

"I knew you'd crossed paths somewhere," she said. "Vanessa mentioned it. A local coffee bar, wasn't it?"

I told Reagan of my more recent conversation with Vanessa and went over what I'd learned of Cara's emotional state at the firm's party, and her violent argument with Brady.

Reagan's hand went to her throat, and she gasped. "I had no idea. Vanessa said nothing about it."

I went on to tell her about the confiscation of Cara's car keys and the subsequent return of the car the following morning. "I'm sure you'll appreciate why it may be important."

"Of course." Reagan furrowed her brow. "But you are sure the car was returned that morning?"

Sophie butted in. "It was there when I called in on my way to work."

"Vanessa didn't say anything to you about it?" I asked.

Reagan shook her head. "Not a word. I knew Cara had driven Austin to the party that night and I presumed they'd driven home together afterwards. But I'd be happy to make some enquiries around the office. Someone must know what happened."

Before we could carry the conversation any further, one of the crematorium attendants called us all in to the service.

Nathan and I sat at the front, with Jordan and Sophie between us. The soft background music was interrupted only by the rustle of fabric and creaking of pews as other mourners took their seats.

Jordan had been unusually quiet the whole of the morning and clung on to Sophie's hand during the proceedings.

It was a civil ceremony, a reading by a Celebrant commemorating a happy successful life well spent, followed by the transporting of the woven wicker coffin by six dark-attired poll bearers to the plinth in front of the curtained-off cremator. We all rose as the coffin made its final journey through the curtains accompanied by Mahler's Adagietto. From somewhere behind us came the quiet sound of weeping and the occasional clearing of a throat.

Afterwards, as we stepped out into the bright autumn day, I took in several deep lungfuls of clean, cold air, grateful to be out of the claustrophobic confines of the crematorium.

We made our way to the car park, where Reagan sought us out again and invited us to a gathering at the Springboard offices. "I've laid on a small buffet for Cara's friends and colleagues," she said. "The least I could do."

I exchanged a quick glance with Jordan. A slight shake of his head told me what I needed to know. "That's kind of you," I said. "But it's been an emotionally draining day. We'll give it a miss, if you don't mind."

She accepted my explanation, saying she understood how wearing it must have been. "There is something else I need to ask," she said. "It may not be the most appropriate time to raise the matter, but Cara was working on company files at home, which included some signed customer agreements. I was hoping I could send Vanessa over to pick them up. It's not urgent, but we'll need them back, eventually."

I told her it wasn't a problem and I would call Vanessa and let her know when I was over there.

She thanked me, wished us well, and left us to carry on our way.

Before we reached the car, we were brought to a halt again. This time by Elliot Garcia.

He greeted me with a smile, but his eyes were cold. "A moment of your time, Mr MacGregor," he said.

"I'll see you over at the car," I said to Nathan.

He knitted his brow. "You sure?" He cast a dark look in Garcia's direction.

"Sure," I said.

I watched as the three of them walked away before turning my attention back to Garcia. I waited to hear what he had to say.

"They tell me you ask questions best left unasked," he said.

"They?"

"It is what I hear."

"Is it indeed? And what does it have to do with you?"

"I think it better not to get involved in matters not your concern. It would be a shame to find yourself in unnecessary trouble, Mr MacGregor." He smiled again, treating me to a glint of his gold tooth.

"Trouble?" I said. "And what kind of trouble did you have in mind?"

He pressed his lips together and narrowed his eyes.

"Are you threatening me?" I said.

"I am concerned for your welfare, Mr MacGregor. It is friendly advice."

"Well, let me give you some friendly advice of my own," I said. "I'll be making whatever enquiries I choose and I'll be keeping a close eye on anyone who tries to stop me."

He opened his mouth to speak again, but I cut him short. "I think we're done here," I said and walked away.

Garcia had just made a big mistake. He had just announced his involvement in this whole sorry saga. I wasn't yet sure how, but I had every intention of finding out.

CHAPTER THIRTY-FIVE

It was the day after the funeral, and Nathan was still worrying over my clash with Garcia. It was mid-morning. Jordan and Sophie had already left for the day and I was settling down to work on my laptop at the kitchen table when Nathan started in again.

He stood over me, arms folded. "Men like Garcia are dangerous," he said. "We're talking high-level criminal type here. Not the sort you should tangle with."

I pushed the laptop to one side. "Guys like Garcia aren't stupid either," I said. "He must know everyone's eyes are on him. He's not dumb enough to make a move that puts him at loggerheads with the police."

"Even so, it's not a good idea to make an enemy of him. Best stay out of his way."

"Not sure we can. He's mixed up in this somehow. Why else would he bother to threaten me?"

"We can still keep digging away without confronting him directly."

I held up a hand, fingers crossed, and said, "I'll be careful. I promise. And if I do want to dig any deeper, I'll run it past you first, okay?"

"Make sure you do," he said. "And in the meantime, I'll go call Gibson for an update and let you get on with some work." He dug his mobile out of his pocket and called back to me as he headed into the living room. "Not that I'm expecting anything."

I grunted and pulled my laptop towards me again. I was working on a new book series based on my radio broadcasts on the psychological aspects of crime scene analysis. As ever, I was on a deadline, and even in the midst of our current investigation, important though it was, I tried to snatch the occasional half hour or so to work on my project.

Unfortunately, it wasn't to be. This time, I was interrupted by my mobile.

It was Reagan Francis.

She sounded troubled.

"I'm sorry to bother you," she said. "But I was worried about Jordan. Is everything all right with him?"

I stiffened. "As much as it can be given the circumstances. Why do you ask?"

"I spoke with him earlier," she said. "He seemed… not sure… very down. And he said some things that bothered me."

"What sort of things?"

That morning, Jordan had been quieter than usual. But we were all subdued after the funeral and so I had tried to dismiss his sombre mood as the result of increased pressure, putting it down to the added burden of laying his mother to rest. Reagan too must have noticed he was more than usually out of sorts.

She paused for a moment. "Look, I might be overreacting," she said. "It could be nothing. I just wanted to make sure he was all right."

"Now you've taken the trouble to call, you may as well tell me what he said. Otherwise, I'm going to worry."

She sighed deeply before replying. "When I spoke with him recently, he told me he had no intention of moving back to Medway Hall, that he wanted to put it on the market as soon as possible."

"Yes, we'd already discussed that."

She continued, "I know Elliot Garcia is looking to move to the area, and I called Jordan to ask if I could show Elliot around the house."

"And he was okay with that?"

"He didn't seem to care either way. That's what worried me. He said it would soon be out of his hands, anyway. When I asked him what he meant, he told me everyone would find out soon enough. And when they did, they would regret they ever tried to help him." She hesitated. "You don't suppose…? He couldn't have…?" Another pause. "Sorry, I'm probably letting my imagination run away with me. Forget I said anything."

A tightness gripped my chest. My mind churned as the words sank in. Hardly something to be forgotten. It was obvious Jordan was in low spirits, but maybe I had underestimated how low and, more importantly, the reason for it.

"Hello? Are you still there?"

Reagan's words interrupted my thoughts and brought me back to the present. "Sorry, I was thinking over what you said." I told her of my own concerns about Jordan's current state of mind and promised to talk to him on his return home. "It sounds to me like he's feeling weighed down by all that's going on. I'm sure it's nothing more than that. He's just feeling very sorry for himself."

"I'm sure you're right," she said. "But please let me know how it goes once you've spoken to him. Or I'll worry about it."

I told her I would and added, "By the way, if Elliot Garcia is interested in buying Medway Hall, he needs to discuss it with me, not Jordan."

Garcia was the last person I wanted to do business with, and I had no intention of letting him buy Medway Hall. But he was the least of my concerns, right then. I was more concerned about Jordan's fragile emotional state.

Long after I'd finished my conversation with Reagan, I sat staring over the top of my laptop, unable to concentrate on work, still trying to make sense of Jordan's words. And I didn't like where my thoughts were taking me.

I needed to discuss this with Nathan.

As I rose from my chair, my mobile rang again. It was Cara's neighbour, Frank Osborne. I took the call as I made my way through to the living room where Nathan was seated in one of the armchairs listening to the radio.

Osborne reminded me I'd asked him to call if he had any new information and wanted to let me know he'd just seen someone crossing the grounds at Medway Hall, someone he hadn't seen there before. His description fitted Garcia.

"He didn't stay long," Osborne said. "Just crossed the grounds and left again."

I explained who he was and why he was there. "It was just a cursory look at the house and grounds but you won't be seeing him there again."

I finished the call and sank onto the couch, facing Nathan.

He picked up the remote from the arm of the chair and turned off the radio. "You look worried," he said.

"I am. I'm worried about Jordan." I went over the details of my conversation with Reagan, but kept my misgivings to myself.

He fell back into his chair with a sigh and took a moment before responding. "I'm getting a bad feeling about this," he said.

"It sounded as if he meant…" I stopped short, unable to continue.

He opened his mouth to speak, hesitated briefly, and said, "I think we both know what it means." He stared at me long and hard before continuing. "Right from the beginning of this debacle, I've tried to take an objective view. You know that. But I've had time to get to know the young man and, like you, I find it hard to believe he could have killed his mother. Even so, we have to accept we may be wrong and be prepared for the worst. He had opportunity and motive, and we've heard from several people he has a bit of a temper when roused." He held up a restraining hand as I tried to interrupt. "I'm not suggesting he's a cold-blooded killer, but it could have been an argument that went too far. I think we should-"

Before he could go any further, I cut him off. "No way," I said. "Cara's neighbour would have seen him arrive and leave if he used the front gates. Whoever did this used the side entrance to avoid being seen. That suggests intent and I refuse to believe Jordan capable of that. He loved his mother."

"Well something's not right," said Nathan, "and we have to face up to the possibility we got it wrong. When Jordan gets back this evening, we need to have a serious talk with him."

I agreed. "But we need to be careful how we approach it."

The rest of the day dragged. I tried to get down to some work, but my mind kept drifting away, going over and over all that we'd been through and trying to make sense of it.

Was I fooling myself? Had I blinded myself to the possibility Jordan had been deceiving us all along?

I was beginning to doubt my own judgement.

Given the timeframe within which Cara's murder had taken place, and given what we had learned of everyone's movements, there may well have been the opportunity for Jordan to have done the deed and avoided detection. But I would need to talk with both Jordan and Sophie to confirm their exact whereabouts at the relevant times. One of the things we could discuss that evening.

But we never got the chance.

Jordan usually arrived home around five o'clock, and Sophie an hour later. But Jordan didn't show. What we got instead was an early evening visit from Gibson and one of his constables.

Gibson was his usual officious self. "You're aware of Jordan's bail conditions," he said. "and your responsibility to make sure he complies with them?"

We assured him we did.

"I'm here to tell you he's in breach of those conditions," said Gibson. "And we're here to take him into custody."

CHAPTER THIRTY-SIX

Gibson faced us with a look of grim determination on his face and waited for a response. Nathan and I stared back at him, not sure what to say. The only sound was the churning of the dishwasher in the kitchen.

Finally, Nathan spoke. "You'd better explain," he said.

Gibson drew himself up to his full height and said, "Were you aware that Welles is in breach of his bail conditions?"

"Of course not," I said. What sort of dumb question was that?

"He failed to check in at the station today," said Gibson. "I'm sure you'll understand it's a serious matter. He needs to explain himself or face the consequences."

Nathan said, "Jordan would have no reason to break his bail conditions. If he didn't show, he must have had a very good reason."

"It was his mother's funeral yesterday," I said. "With all the pressure he's under at the moment, he must have got his dates wrong?"

"Then why don't we ask him," said Gibson. "Is he here?"

He glanced around as if expecting Jordan to suddenly materialise out of thin air.

"He's not back yet," I said. "I'll call him." I pulled my mobile from the pocket of my jeans and speed-dialled Jordan's number. It went to voice mail. I left a message. "You need to call me pronto. You missed your check-in at the police station. Get back to me as soon as you get this."

I finished the call and shoved the mobile back into my pocket.

Nathan said, "Jordan is usually at his workshop at this time of day."

"We're aware of that," said Gibson. "Which is why we called in there before coming here. He's not been near his workshop all day."

Nathan and I exchanged worried glances. This wasn't looking good.

"Sophie may know where he is," said Nathan. He glanced at his watch. "I don't want to call her while she's driving, but she should be home shortly."

"I need to get back to the station," said Gibson, "so I'll leave you to get it sorted. I'm off duty in a couple of hours. If you can get Jordan down to the station before then, I'll let it pass. Otherwise..." He left the threat hanging in the air.

"Jordan's been doing some structural repairs on the outbuildings at Medway Hall," I said. "Perhaps he went over there and lost track of time."

I was clutching at straws. If Jordan had been anywhere near Medway Hall, Reagan or Frank Osborne would surely have mentioned it. But I didn't know what else to think.

"We still have the access codes for Medway Hall," said Gibson. "I'll call in on my way back to the station. If he's there, I'll get back to you."

Once Gibson was on his way, I called Osborne. It was a long shot, but maybe he'd seen Jordan at the house and not mentioned it.

No such luck. "If he came this morning," Osborne said, "it must have been before I started work at my desk. In which case, he may be in the house, but I've not seen him in the grounds."

My next call was to Reagan. No luck there either. "He told me to make my own arrangements and give Elliot access," she said. "So we had no reason to meet. Is everything okay?"

I had no intention of letting it be known he'd disappeared. "All is well," I said. "He's not answering his phone, but he should be home soon enough, so nothing to worry about."

I finished the call before she could question me further.

In the silence that followed, Nathan and I stared at each other without speaking. Neither of us needed to say anything to know what the other was thinking.

Nathan said, "Sophie will be back soon. She may know something."

"I hope so."

Sophie was due home sometime in the next half hour. In the

meantime, I tried to keep busy, emptying the dishwasher and putting away the dishes, but glancing at my watch every few minutes, willing the time away.

I could only hope Sophie had a simple explanation for Jordan's disappearing act. But it wasn't to be. When she eventually arrived home, she burst through the door, ashen-faced and plainly distressed. "Where's Jordan?" she demanded. She was shaking and her breathing was laboured.

"What's wrong?" I asked.

She was holding her mobile and waved it at me when she replied. "I just got this strange text message from him." She looked down at the screen as she read it out. "I'm so sorry. I hope you can forgive me one day." She looked up again. "I don't understand. What does it mean?"

Nathan took her by the arm, eased her down onto the couch and seated himself beside her. "There have been some developments," he said.

I dropped into the facing armchair and sat in silence as Nathan went over what we had learned during the past few hours. "We were hoping he was with you," he said.

Sophie stared at Nathan, eyes wide, as if unable to comprehend what he was saying. She turned and faced me with the same confused expression on her face.

"I'm sorry, Sophie," I said, "but it's not looking good." I didn't know what else to say.

Her face crumpled. She was crying now, the tears streaming down her face. "I don't believe it." She covered her face with both hands and sobbed.

"We don't want to believe it either," said Nathan. "But we can't deny the implications of what we're hearing."

I leaned towards her. "This is hard, Sophie. But we need to think this through as calmly and objectively as possible. We need to think about means, motive and opportunity. It will help us determine if there is any possibility of Jordan being involved in his mother's death."

"No." She shouted the word and matched it with a rapid shake of the head. "It's not true."

I tried to calm her. "This is as much about proving his innocence as anything else. The more we know about his movements that day, the more it can help us."

She nodded and brought her breathing under control.

"Let's start with opportunity," I said. "You must know more than anyone what Jordan's movements were that morning. So let's go over the timeline, shall we?"

Sophie sniffled, wiped her eyes with the back of a hand and nodded her agreement.

"We know Cara was alive after you visited her," I said, "because you spotted her at her office window before you left."

Sophie nodded again.

"And you went straight home from there?" I asked.

"Yes, I worked from home for a while and then left for the office shortly before noon."

"And where was Jordan?"

"He was at home with me. I was going over some papers in our room, and he was..." She stalled momentarily as she cast her mind back. "As far as I can remember, he was out in the garden."

Nathan said, "Wouldn't Jordan normally go to his workshop during the day? Why would he change his routine?"

"He sometimes drove in with Danny," said Sophie. "But Danny was going over to Colton Drey later that afternoon to pick up his boyfriend, Steven - he was helping set up an exhibition over there - so Jordan wouldn't be able to get back as I had his car. He decided to take the day off and work on some drawings at home."

"Did you see anything of him that morning?" I asked.

Sophie wrinkled her brow, as if straining to remember. "I don't think so. He knows I don't like to be disturbed when I'm working, so he left me to it."

"This next step is important," said Nathan. "So you need to think hard about it." He took a breath. "At some point during the morning, would there have been an opportunity for him to have taken the car and driven over to his mother's without your knowing about it?"

Sophie cast her gaze to the floor and nodded.

When Sophie raised her head again, her eyes were full of tears. "Jordan could fly into a rage at times, and he and his mother had some major arguments those last few days, but I don't believe he would kill her. He just wouldn't."

"None of us wants to believe it," I said. "But we're having a hard time explaining Jordan's behaviour right now."

"Could he be covering for someone?" Nathan asked.

"Why would he?" said Sophie. "It doesn't make sense."

"None of this makes sense," I said. "We still don't know why Brady lied about seeing Jordan that morning. And I still think his murder was connected somehow. But we keep going round in circles."

Before we could discuss it further, my mobile rang. It was Gibson. I put the call on speaker so the others could hear it.

"Have you heard from him?" Gibson asked.

I told him we hadn't and said, "I'm presuming he wasn't at the house."

"You presume right," said Gibson.

"You checked everywhere?" I asked. "The house and the outbuildings?"

"Everywhere," said Gibson. "We drew a blank. Now we have to hope he comes to his senses and turns up soon."

I ended the call.

"So what now?" said Sophie.

"Is there anyone Jordan could have turned to for help?" said Nathan. "Any of his friends? We need to start there and contact anyone he may have reached out to."

Anything was better than sitting around and doing nothing. But I had a sinking feeling we would be wasting our time. There were too many imponderables here, too many loose ends that didn't make sense.

We were no nearer to solving this case.

And time was fast running out.

CHAPTER THIRTY-SEVEN

Gibson was being his usual obdurate self. Once he'd made up his mind, that was it. No point considering alternatives.

He sat facing Nathan and me from the other side of his desk, his posture rigid, arms folded across his chest. He was in defensive mode. "If Jordan Welles was in the clear," he said, "why is he on the run?"

"We don't know he is," I said. "He may have had an accident. Anything could have happened to him."

It was the morning after Jordan failed to check in at the station and, despite our best efforts, we'd been unable to track him down. With Sophie's help, we'd contacted not only those with whom he had current relationships but with many from his past, friends from his college days and fellow artists in the local community, anyone he could have reached out to. But we'd drawn a blank.

And now here we were, trying to buy some time before Jordan was officially declared a fugitive.

I tried again. "Surely, you can appreciate the amount of pressure Jordan is under? He's just buried his mother, the woman he's under investigation for murdering, and all while suffering restrictive bail conditions that act as a constant reminder of his presumed guilt. Any wonder he may have found it all too much. Perhaps he couldn't cope. And instead of treating him as a criminal on the run, we should think of him as someone in need of help."

My impassioned pleas fell on deaf ears. Gibson set his jaw firm and stared back at me, stony-faced, unmoved by my words.

Nathan said, "And we need to consider other aspects of the

investigation. The connection to Brady's murder, for instance. You're not suggesting Jordan had anything to do with that?"

"I'm not suggesting anything of the sort," said Gibson. "Right from the beginning of the investigation into Brady's murder, I've been of the opinion it's a separate matter."

I tried to interrupt, but he held up a restraining hand and spoke over me. "I know you think it's too much of a coincidence," he said, "but coincidences happen. I'm as convinced as ever that Garcia is responsible for Brady's murder. Everything points to it."

"What about the anomalous bloodstain on Brady's clothing?" I said. "It wasn't Garcia's blood."

"Garcia's a slippery customer," said Gibson. "He's not the sort to get his own hands dirty. We know from our enquiries with the Met in London, he has a network of underground contacts who would be only too happy to do his dirty work for him. Which is why he's managed so far to avoid having anything pinned on him."

"And are you any further on with that investigation?" Nathan asked.

Gibson shuffled uneasily in his chair. "Not yet. But I'm sure we'll get there in the end."

"There's something else to consider," I said. "What about the attack on Reagan Francis?"

Gibson's expression changed to one of gloating confidence. "In light of the current situation, I'm sure we're near to a solution in that particular matter. We've questioned Ms Francis more closely about the assault, and she's been able to give us a better description of her assailant."

"You know who it is?" I asked.

"Ms Francis didn't get a look at her assailant's face, but from what we've learned of his build and height and the way he carried himself, he seems to be a good fit for Jordan Welles."

"Bullshit." The word exploded out of me and my muscles tensed. "If it had been Jordan, Reagan Francis would have identified him. She's known him long enough to recognise his voice and body posture."

"Like you, Ms Francis is reluctant to believe Jordan capable of his mother's murder or of her assault. She refuses to accept the possibility of either. But I'm of the opinion she's allowing her relationship with him to cloud her judgement."

"Why would he even do such a thing?" asked Nathan.

"To divert attention from himself, of course," said Gibson. "By targeting his mother's business partner, he hoped to throw suspicion on someone involved in his mother's business and put himself in the clear."

"You've obviously made up your mind," said Nathan.

"I accept that it's all conjecture at the moment," said Gibson, "but my explanation brings all the various threads together into a coherent whole and gives us a reasonable and realistic account of what happened."

"A very convenient one," I said, "based on a lot of presumptions."

"I'll admit there's still work to do," said Gibson, "but I think we're on the right path."

"So what now?" said Nathan.

Gibson said, "Jordan's details will be posted on the National Police Computer where he will be listed as a person of interest. I doubt he will avoid detection for long."

"Did you put a trace on his mobile?" asked Nathan.

"Indeed we did," said Gibson. "His mobile has been turned off, but the last trace we have puts him at a location near Romford. We're working on the assumption that Jordan was making his way to London by train."

So that was it. The matter was out of our hands and the future was looking bleak for Jordan, wherever he may be.

Long after our briefing with Gibson, Nathan and I sat in the car outside the station going over what we had learned, trying to piece it all together.

"One thing's for sure," I said. "We're wasting our time with Gibson. He sees it as a done deal. Jordan is a heartless killer. End of."

"Let's face it," said Nathan, "we both came close to the same conclusion, so we can hardly blame Gibson for taking the line he does. There's no denying his interpretation of events makes sense. And it's not as if we've come up with any sound alternative."

My heart jumped and my voice went up an octave. "You're not buying it are you?"

"Calm down," he said. "It's persuasive, but no, I'm not buying it. Sure, Jordan looks right for the crime. At first sight. But once there's been time to think it through, it makes less sense. Jordan's a hothead for sure. But Gibson paints a picture of a cold and callous killer. And that's not Jordan."

I settled back down in my seat. "And all that crap about the assault on Reagan Francis. I'm not sure Jordan has the wherewithal to think up something so devious. Or harm someone for such a reason. And no way would he hurt someone he knows and gets on with so well."

"We still need to figure out how his disappearing act fits into all this," said Nathan.

I said, "I'm worried about his state of mind. I'm guessing he couldn't cope with the pressure. I hope he's not going to do anything stupid."

"For the moment, there's not a lot we can do about it. We'll have to count on the police tracking him down. At least back in custody, he'd be safe."

Nathan switched on the ignition and a moment later, we were on the main road heading back to the house.

On the way, Nathan said, "What about the Brady murder? You've already had a chance to check out Garcia. You think he could have killed Brady?"

"I've already ruled him out," I said. "Gibson knows that. Admittedly, Garcia's guilt seems obvious and reasonable at first sight. But, yet again, Gibson fails to take account of Garcia's nature. Brady's murder was an act of passion. And that's totally out of character for someone like Garcia."

"He strikes me as the cold, dispassionate type."

"Which is what he is. The exact opposite of Jordan. Garcia is a sly individual. He's clever. He thinks things through. Which is probably why, despite his dirty deals, the police have been unable to pin anything on him. And he's not going to risk falling foul of the law by killing someone in a fit of jealous rage. Not his style at all."

Nathan said, "I'd like to know how he fits into all this."

"Perhaps he doesn't."

"What about his proposed partnership with Reagan Francis?"

"I'm sure he sees Cara's death as an opportunity to take advantage of a tragedy. Another example of his heartless approach."

We reached the house, and Nathan drew up outside and turned off the engine. "I'm dreading speaking with Sophie," he said.

Following Jordan's disappearance, Sophie had taken time off work and was in the house waiting to hear details of our briefing with

Gibson. It wasn't a meeting we were looking forward to.

"There must be more we can do," I said. "We can't just sit around and hope for the best."

Nathan said, "The last time we saw Jordan, he was setting off for his workshop. So let's follow his trail. We can go over there and talk to Danny. Maybe he knows something."

"And we know Jordan spoke with Reagan Francis. We should talk to her, too."

"We may not get anywhere," said Nathan, "but it's worth a try."

"And in the meantime," I said and reached for the door handle, "let's go get this over with."

Nathan was out of the car before me. I braced myself for what was to come and followed him up the garden path.

CHAPTER THIRTY-EIGHT

It wasn't the easiest of conversations. Fearing the worst but hoping for the best, Sophie had awaited our return from the police station with what must have been a growing sense of dread. And now we had no choice but to confirm her fears.

She slumped down on one of the armchairs in the living room, feet up on the seat, arms wrapped tight around her legs, face ashen and creased with concern. Her eyes were red from crying.

We faced her from the couch and went over our exchange with Gibson and did our best to console her.

"Not for a moment do we believe Jordan capable of such an act," said Nathan. "No matter what Gibson thinks."

She seemed to be only half-listening, her mind focused elsewhere.

"I know it looks bad," I said, "but now we've had time to give it careful consideration, we're convinced it can't be Jordan."

"I'm so scared." Sophie blurted out the words and her face crumpled. "I'm frightened he'll do something stupid."

Nathan and I exchanged worried glances. We both knew what must be going through her mind, and it was difficult to know how to allay her fears right then.

"We're not giving up on him," said Nathan. "We'd already decided to follow through on his recent movements and see where it takes us." He lowered his voice, turned to me, and said, "One of us should stay here with Sophie. Why don't you head off to the workshop and see what you can find out?"

I nodded and rose to my feet. As I made towards the door, I glanced back at them. Sophie was staring out in front of her, oblivious to what was happening. Nathan crossed over to her, sat on the arm of the chair, and wrapped an arm around her shoulder.

I nodded to him again, grim-faced, and left the house.

It was still early afternoon, and the traffic wasn't too heavy at this time of day. The drive over would take about fifteen minutes and I used the time to think through Jordan's recent behaviour and try to come to terms with all that it implied. Now we'd ruled out the possibility of his involvement in his mother's murder, his actions pointed to just one thing. Which meant that Sophie's unspoken fears were justified. I tried to push the thought away, but kept coming back to it. And in the end, it had to be faced. The pressure had been too much and Jordan was contemplating suicide. I could only hope that we found him before it was too late.

I arrived at the workshop to find Danny standing out front in conversation with some guy from the bicycle shop next door.

He caught sight of me as I crossed the tarmac towards him. His expression changed to one of hopeful expectation and he stepped towards me and away from his companion.

"Any news?" he asked.

I took him by the arm, signalled to the bicycle guy to excuse us, and guided Danny to the workshop entrance. "Let's talk inside," I said.

Once inside, I said, "I take it the police filled you in on the current situation?"

He nodded. "Have they found him?"

He was clearly distressed, and I was sorry to disappoint him. "'Fraid not. I'm trying to establish what his movements might have been yesterday, where he was and where he might go. This seemed the best place to start."

Danny slumped back against the bench behind him and his shoulders dropped. "I haven't the faintest idea what the fuck's going on with him."

"Was he here yesterday?" I asked.

"I don't know. He usually gets here before me. An early starter. But not yesterday. At least, I don't think he was here."

"You're not sure?"

"The front shutter was down, but it wasn't locked. And I definitely locked it the night before. I'm always careful about such things.

Especially around here."

"So, he could have been here before you arrived?"

"I'm not sure what else to think. he's the only other one with a key, so he must have opened up. But it's not like him to leave the place unlocked, either." He shrugged. "But he's not himself right now, so I'm guessing he forgot."

"Did you tell any of this to the police?"

Danny snorted. "No chance. They were more interested in getting me to bad-mouth him. And trying to pressure me into saying he was violent. I kept shtum. They're not getting anything out of me. Jordan's a good guy. Wouldn't harm a fly."

"Where might he go from here?"

"Not a clue. This is the only place he would come to."

Seemed like there was nothing else to learn.

I made to leave and said, "There are other leads I need to follow up. If I pick up anything new, I'll let you know."

He thanked me and said he'd do the same. "Jordan has been my friend for as long as I can remember," he said. "I don't understand why he couldn't talk to me first before running away."

"Let's hope we can figure it out." I said my goodbyes, leaving him still slumped up against the bench, and made my way back to the car.

It seemed odd Jordan would make it to his workshop, open up, and then run away. What happened to upset his usual everyday routine and make him change his mind so dramatically? And why would he not at least turn to us or his friends for help? Something was wrong.

Back in the car, I called Nathan to bring him up to date. I recounted my conversation with Danny and he shared my opinion that the circumstances seemed odd.

He asked if I was on my way home, but I told him I would contact Reagan first and see if she was available for a meet-up. He agreed it was best to keep the momentum going and so I promised to contact him again later and then made the call to Reagan.

Once I'd explained the progression of events since her talk with Jordan, she agreed to meet me straight away, voicing her concern for Jordan's welfare and, less than thirty minutes later, we were face to face in her office.

She waved me over to where a couple of armchairs faced each other on the other side of the room from her desk and once we were seated, she said, "I was so sure something was wrong when I spoke to him. I wish he'd confided in me. I could have helped him."

"That's something we all wished for," I said. "But all we can do at the moment is go over what we know of his actions and conversations yesterday and hope to pick up any clues as to his whereabouts."

"I'm not sure what else I can tell you," she said.

"Tell me what time you called him," I said, "and where he might have been at that time."

"It was early," she said. "About seven. I wouldn't normally call at such an early hour, but he's usually on his way to the workshop at that time, and I wanted to catch him before he started work. I was hoping he might come over to Medway Hall and show us around. But he chose not to."

"Did he say why?"

"No, and I didn't ask. He didn't seem to care and told me to let myself in. And he sounded so despondent. Which is why I called you. I was worried. Especially after my more recent interview with the police. They seemed determined to blame him for my assault, so I presumed they were pressuring him to confess to it."

"I heard about that," I said. "What did you tell them?"

"I refused to accept it was Jordan. It's true my attacker was around the same height and build as Jordan. I couldn't deny it. But I know Jordan. And I know he would never do such a thing. And if it had been Jordan, then I would surely have recognised him."

"They've obviously decided Jordan is a murderer and are determined to prove it at any cost."

"And if anything happens to Jordan," she said, "they'll be to blame. The poor boy must be at his wit's end. I do hope you find him soon."

Given how little we had to go on, I was fast losing any hope of finding him. And as much as Reagan sympathised with Jordan's predicament, there was nothing she could tell me that would help.

I questioned her some more, but gained no useful information and eventually gave up and finished the discussion. I promised to let her know how things progressed.

Before I could leave, she asked me if I had any problems with Garcia's interest in Medway Hall. "When I told you about it," she said, "you didn't sound too keen on the idea."

"I was surprised, is all. I'd always had him down as a London type.

But I guess he could be looking for a change of scene."

Or an escape from his dubious past more like. Maybe that's why he was so keen on setting up a partnership with Reagan. Maybe he was looking for legitimate business opportunities as a way to put his past misdeeds behind him. Or maybe to cover them up.

I said, "You're aware he has a somewhat dubious history in the business world? I understand some of his more questionable dealings have drawn the attention of the police."

She flushed. "I wasn't aware of it. Not at first. But when he first approached me about setting up a partnership, he was frank about his past operations. And it's certainly true that he's cut a few corners in his time. He also made it clear the police were involved from time to time but found nothing of note. If he had been involved in any sort of criminal activity, surely they would have charged him by now?"

I couldn't tell if she was just naïve or if she wanted to think the best of Garcia and chose to push his less wholesome activities to one side. Either way, it wasn't my concern, and I let it drop and took my leave.

As before, I called Nathan once I was back in the car and told him of my talk with Reagan and that I had no idea where to go next.

"There may have been fresh developments," he said. "Gibson just called to say he needs to talk with us. He's on his way over. So you need to get back here pronto."

"What did he tell you?"

"Nothing. He said he wanted to talk in person."

"How did he sound?"

"Triumphant."

My heart sank. "That's not a good sign. But they may have got Jordan in custody. And if they have, at least he'll be safe."

"We'll find out soon enough. Just get here as soon as you can."

By the time I was back on the road, the early evening traffic had built up and my journey home took longer than expected. I reached the house to find Gibson already there, and when I joined him, Nathan and Sophie in the living room, it was obvious from the strained atmosphere and the looks on their faces that I'd walked into something bad.

"Well?" I asked. "What's happened?"

"We received a letter at the station," said Gibson. "It was from Jordan and addressed to me personally." He braced himself and drew up to his full height. "It appears to be a suicide note in which he confesses to his mother's murder."

CHAPTER THIRTY-NINE

The words were a hammer blow, a gut-wrenching jolt that slammed hard into me and left me speechless. I stared at Gibson, mouth agape, trying to absorb what I'd just heard.

I found my voice and said, "Appears to be? What's that supposed to mean? What does he say?"

Nathan held out a hand. "We need to see the letter."

Sophie broke in too, insisting on more information and now we were all talking over each other, demanding attention.

Gibson dismissed our demands with a wave of the hand. "I'm sorry I don't have the letter with me. All I will say is it's now evidence in a criminal investigation and I can't yet allow its contents to be made public."

"Made public?" Nathan spat out the words, all pretence of professional respect now gone. "We're his Goddam family. You either produce that letter or I'll file a complaint against you, and I'll make damn sure it hits you hard."

I interrupted. "I'm waiting for an answer. What did Jordan say? Did he say he intended to kill himself?"

Gibson stammered and said, "Not exactly." Nathan's outburst had stunned him and his tone had lost its condescending, officious edge.

"Then what the hell did he say?" My temper was getting the better of me.

"His state of mind was clearly implied in much of what he wrote," said Gibson. "For instance, something about a financial settlement. He had personal assets of several thousand pounds he wanted to pass on to Ms Barber here. Mostly in the form of bonds. If that's not a clear indication he was thinking of taking his own life, I don't know what is. Why else would he divest himself of any financial security he might have?"

"It doesn't make any sense," said Sophie. "He doesn't have that sort of money. I'd know about it if he did. Jordan lives off a small allowance."

"In his letter, he clearly stated his father knew about it," said Gibson.

My mind went into overdrive, pulling together threads of information and rearranging them into a coherent pattern.

"I do know about it," I said. "I also know it's a lie. And maybe that's the point."

Gibson frowned. "I don't understand."

I said, "A few days ago, he was offered some financial support by his mother's business partner following his mother's death. He didn't want to feel obligated to her, so he made up a story about having several thousand pounds worth of Premium Bonds to draw on. It was a lie. One meant to persuade her he didn't need her help."

"Then why would he refer to it in his letter?" Gibson asked.

I said. "Don't you get it? He's sending us a message. He's telling us it's all a lie, a setup."

"We need to see that letter," said Nathan. "And we need to see it now. It's beginning to sound like Jordan's in big trouble. And we need to act."

Gibson must have known he was beat. He caved. "I'll get a copy sent to my mobile," he said. He called the station and minutes later, he handed me his mobile with Jordan's handwritten letter displayed on the screen.

I showed it to Sophie and asked if it was Jordan's handwriting. It was.

Satisfied the letter itself was genuine, I ran through its contents.

"There has to be something else here," I said. "Something he's trying to tell us."

The letter started with a confession, a clear and straightforward account of how he had driven over to see his mother on the morning of her murder, how they had argued violently, how it had escalated when he knocked her to the floor and how he had then suffocated her.

I closed my eyes for a moment and drew in a deep breath. I didn't believe a word of what I'd read. But seeing it spelt out like this was an emotional jolt that left me shaken.

I opened my eyes and ran over the rest of the text. It included details of the supposed financial settlement on Sophie and finished with what, on the face of it, appeared to be a statement of remorse and regret.

But something was wrong. It didn't ring true. "Jordan didn't write this," I said. "It's not his style." One phrase, in particular, stood out. "Listen to this," I said, reading from the text. "I'm in a dark place right now and can see no way out."

"If that's not a clear indication of suicidal intent," said Gibson, "I don't know what is."

"You couldn't be more wrong," I said.

Gibson didn't look convinced.

I explained. "We all have our own recognisable speech patterns," I said. "The words we use, our dialect and idiolect, the way we use figurative language, particular phrases and idioms we regularly use. I've known Jordan long enough to recognise his pattern of speech and word usage. His language fits a particular distinctive style. It's direct, unadorned."

I tapped the screen. "He says here he's in a dark place. That's not the sort of figurative language Jordan would use. But his mother did. He told me recently how he would hide out in the cellar of the outbuilding at Medway Hall when he and his mum argued. And his mother would describe it as his dark place."

I held up the mobile and shook it. "Don't you understand? This isn't an expression of regret. He's telling us where he is. And this also tells me he's being monitored and probably being held against his will. We need to find him fast."

"You looked for him there," Nathan said to Gibson. "Did you check the cellar in the outbuilding?"

Gibson looked confused. "Cellar?" He shook his head. "We checked the outbuildings, yes. But we didn't find a cellar."

I thrust Gibson's mobile back into his hand. "We need to get over there. Now. If I'm right about this, Jordan's in danger."

CHAPTER FORTY

It was a race against time. That's the one thing I was sure of. Every second counted. But despite the added advantage of being escorted by Gibson's speeding police cruiser, lights flashing and siren wailing, the journey seemed to take forever.

Nathan and I followed in Nathan's car, Sophie sitting behind us, still in shock, still not quite believing what was happening. I glanced back at her from time to time, unsure what to say to console her, hoping against hope we would find Jordan safe and unharmed.

Nathan asked, "Who else has access to Medway Hall?"

I could tell he was thinking ahead, assessing the situation and preparing himself for what and who might be waiting for us at our destination.

I said, "Apart from the domestic help and gardening staff, it was mainly Cara's work colleagues. But one other person had access recently. Garcia."

"You think he's involved?"

"What we know for sure is he had ties to both Cara and Brady. Either as a client or employer. Plus, he was at Cara's office party the night before her murder. And he was at Medway Hall the day Jordan disappeared. There are too many connections to think he's not involved somehow."

"Seems we may have been right about that guy. We'll need to question him some more."

"Right now, I'm more concerned with finding Jordan."

I shot another glance over my shoulder at Sophie. But she wasn't listening. She had a faraway look in her eyes, as if her thoughts were elsewhere. I lowered my voice and said, "Dear God, I hope we're not too late."

Two uniformed officers were waiting in another police cruiser at the gates to the house. Gibson must have radioed for assistance on the way over. I used my fob to open the gates and Nathan followed the other two cars into the grounds, where we abandoned the cars on the drive.

I urged Sophie to wait for us in the car and Nathan and I followed the others over to the outbuildings on the far side of the grounds.

It was now early evening and daylight was fading fast. A light was on in Osborne's study next door, and I glanced up at where he sat in his usual place by the window as we hurried across the garden. He must have wondered what the sudden activity was about.

One of the uniforms was first through the entrance to the larger of the two buildings, the metal door screeching on its rusted metal hinges as he forced it open.

We all followed him through to the gloomy interior.

For several moments, we stood in silence, listening for signs of movement. We were interrupted only by the constant drip of water from above, where a gaping hole in the roof had let in the rain from a recent shower.

The building had once been a gatekeeper's residence, back in the days when the landed gentry employed servants and ground staff. It had since been converted into some sort of storage unit, but its dilapidated condition suggested it had not been used for years. And there was little sign Jordan had carried out his intention to renovate the old place. Though, to be fair, I'm sure he must have had more pressing matters on his mind.

The evening temperatures had dropped, and a cool breeze blew in from where the remnants of a window frame, held in position by crumbling brickwork, exposed the entrance hall to the elements.

In the fading light, we explored the large room, skirting around those places where rotting floorboards had given way to expose more solid oak beams beneath.

The floor was caked with grime, and dirty puddles of water had formed where the floorboards had warped into hollows.

Gibson pointed to where several muddy footprints covered the floor. "Well, obviously someone's been here recently," he said.

Three open doorways with rotting frames led into darkened rooms beyond and, acting on Gibson's instructions, we all split up and set off to explore other parts of the building.

I was checking out what appeared to be a scullery with a broken, dirty ceramic sink unit against one wall when we were summoned back to the entrance hall. "Over here," someone called out.

It was the younger of the two uniforms.

"Someone's been in here recently," he said before leading us into one of the adjoining rooms. He pointed to a chair in the centre of the floor.

"You can see where the chair has been dragged through the dirt, and if you look closely enough, you can see more footprints. And look there." He pointed down to where two short lengths of rope lay near the chair. "Looks like someone may have been tied up."

In the half-light, it was difficult to see much, but once it had been pointed out, we could just make out the signs of activity he spoke of.

"And over here..." he said and led us into another room beyond where several of Jordan's gas bottles lay heaped in the middle of the room. "These are fairly new, too."

"They're Jordan's," I said. "He told me he was storing his welding equipment here."

"No sign of a cellar, though," said Gibson. He sounded frustrated, as if this was all a waste of time. "Are we sure there is one?"

"No question," I said. "Jordan knows this place better than anyone. He told me he was going to make use of the cellar here, so there has to be one."

Nathan said, "We've searched everywhere, so the only possible place must be under the pile of gas bottles. It's the only part of the floor not exposed. So I suggest we roll up our sleeves and get them moved."

The only one who didn't "roll up his sleeves" was Gibson. Obviously, the task was beneath his pay grade. But the rest of us muscled in and set to work while Gibson looked on.

Four of the bottles were laid out side by side with another two placed on top. Nathan and I and the two uniforms heaved away the upper two bottles, moving them to the side of the wall. And once we shifted the remaining four, the trapdoor we had hoped to find was exposed to sight. It was of solid metal construction and, presumably, was fitted when the building had been converted into a storage unit.

"Looks like someone was trying to hide this trap," said Nathan.

The young constable knelt, grasped the metal ring pull, wrenched open the trap, and slammed it over onto the floor with a resounding crash that echoed through the building.

I dropped to a crouch beside him and peered down into the Stygian depths. A sickening stench of rot rose to greet me.

The stairs leading down into the cellar were broken, the remains of splintered treads sticking out of the wall to the right and hanging loose from the partially collapsed bannister to the left. I could just barely make out the remnants of the displaced steps on the concrete floor below.

I leaned forward, fell onto my knees, and called down through the trap. "Hello? Is anybody there?" I strained to hear, but the only sound that came back to me was that constant drip of water.

I pointed to the broken treads. "See the wood where it splintered. Those breaks are new. It must have happened recently."

"If there is anyone down there," said the constable, "they wouldn't have been able to get back up."

"We need a ladder," I said to the constable and then called back over my shoulder.

"I recall seeing a ladder by the building next door. We're going to need it."

"On it," said Nathan, and he and the older constable hurried away.

I fished my mobile out of my jeans pocket, turned on the flashlight and shone it into the darkness below, swinging it back and forth through the gloom. The feeble light revealed nothing within its range other than the scattered remains of the steps directly below.

Nathan and the other constable returned with the metal double-extension ladder. I helped Nathan extend it and we lowered it into place through the trap.

Gibson insisted on letting the younger constable go first, but I ignored him and took the lead.

Fetid, dank air pressed against my skin as I clambered down the ladder and I wrinkled my nose against its stench.

At the bottom, I used my mobile to light my way through the gloom.

The sound of dripping water was louder down here, and the odour of damp and mildew assailed me from all sides. The whitewashed walls were grimy and, in places, covered with mould.

I called out again, "Hello? Anyone there?"

Still no reply. I hoped I hadn't got it wrong. That Jordan wasn't somewhere else. And in danger.

In the dim light, I could just make out three doorways, one leading straight ahead and two on either side. The one to the right had been bricked up. It must have been the entrance that had once led to the other building.

The ladder creaked again behind me as someone else descended and a moment later, I was joined by the young constable. He carried a flashlight and shone it around us, bringing the room into sharp relief. He flashed his torch in the direction of the door to the left and said, "You go that way and I'll check out the other room."

The light dimmed again as he headed away, and I inched my way slowly over the slippery floor towards the left-hand doorway. From somewhere behind me, several squeaks and a rustling sound betrayed the presence of a rat. I shivered and made my way through to the smaller room beyond.

It was darker in here, and the light from my mobile did little to dispel the gloom. But as I shone it around, I caught a slight movement over by the far wall. I shone my mobile in that direction and picked up what appeared to be a heap of rags. But I was sure I had seen movement. Another rat maybe? I closed in and dropped to a crouch.

Slumped against the wall and wrapped in a tarpaulin sheet, pulled halfway up the face, lay a figure, its eyes fixed on me. It was Jordan.

He opened his mouth, struggling to speak, and managed a single word. "Dad?" It was barely audible, a mere whisper.

I dropped to his side and wrapped my arms around his shivering frame. "Everything's going to be okay," I said. "We're going to get you out of here."

I called out into the darkness. "Over here. He's over here."

The young constable's torch beam hit me in the eyes as he hurried towards us.

"We need an ambulance," I said.

"You stay with him," he said. "I'll go let the others know."

As he hurried away, Jordan tried to speak again, but I couldn't catch his words.

"It's okay," I said. "You don't need to say anything."

In response, he eased an arm from beneath the tarpaulin, slowly raised a hand to my neck and pulled me down so his mouth was close to my ear.

He said just one thing. "Thank you."

And then he closed his eyes and his body went limp.

CHAPTER FORTY-ONE

A couple of days' rest in a hospital bed and Jordan was looking a damn sight better than when I'd found him in that godforsaken hole. The dreadful pallor had gone and his eyes sparked with life again. Not that he was exactly in the best of health; dehydration and hypothermia had worked their joint evils on him. But, fortunately, we'd got him in time and he was showing signs of gradual improvement. At least physically, that is. His mental state, however, was still a cause for concern.

"I don't understand," he said. "Why can't I remember anything?" The question was directed to Jordan's physician, Dr Welby, who stood over Jordan at the foot of the bed.

We were in a side room, off the main ward, where Jordan was being kept under observation. Sophie and I had taken turns sitting by Jordan's bed over those two days but were now both here, seated on either side of the bed, and waiting for a response from the doctor.

Dr Welby looked down at Jordan, shot him a reassuring smile, and tried to alleviate his fears.

"You suffered a nasty blow to the head," he said, "and any resulting concussion from that injury can cause memory loss. But there's no permanent physical trauma, so no need to worry unduly."

"Will I get my memory back?" Jordan asked.

Dr Welby grimaced and shook his head. "We can't know that. There's always a chance, of course, but it's by no means certain. All we can do is wait and see."

Jordan sighed heavily, flopped back onto his pillow, and stared up at the ceiling.

Sophie reached out and took his hand and squeezed it, but said nothing.

"It's not something you need to worry about right now," I said. "Let's get you back into good physical shape first."

"Quite right," said Dr Welby. "You need to get plenty of rest, young man. So I'll leave you to it for now."

Welby caught my eye as he made for the door and tipped his head in the direction of the corridor, signalling a wish to speak in private.

"Back in a sec," I said and followed Welby out of the door, closing it behind me.

A uniformed police officer sat by the door on a plastic chair, looking bored. We exchanged brief nods before I followed Welby to where he had stopped further down the corridor, out of earshot of the room.

"Everything okay? I said.

"Nothing to worry about," said Welby. "I wanted to let you know we're keeping him in for a day or two more to be on the safe side. The X-rays and MRI came back normal, so what we're dealing with here is a cerebral contusion, basically a brain bruise. We've put him on steroids to lessen the effects of any potential swelling but, other than that, it just needs time."

"What are the chances of him recovering his memory?"

"No idea." The look on my face must have shown how dissatisfied I was with his answer. He went on to explain. "You'd be surprised how little is known about amnesia. Retrograde memory loss can go back mere minutes, many years, or anything in between. It's impossible to say. And if and when it does come back, it can come back slowly over time or it may return quickly."

"Is there anything we can do to help it along?" I asked.

"I wish I could say 'yes', but I can't. It can be triggered by anything, whether it be seen, heard, smelled, touched or tasted. Even a word in a conversation, or an image on TV. Anything is possible."

I accepted his words with a frown.

"I understand the young man was the victim of some sort of attack," said Welby, "so I know how important it is. The police have been putting pressure on me. But there's no magic solution. Just give him time and see what happens."

He reassured me again Jordan was well on his way to recovery and left me to go on his rounds.

I returned to Jordan's room and seated myself by the bed once more.

"What did the doc want?" Jordan asked. He was sitting up and sounded concerned.

"Nothing to worry about." I went over my discussion with Welby, assured him his tests were all clear, and said, "He's happy with your progress."

"I'd be happier if I could remember what happened."

"What's the last thing you do remember?"

He paused and screwed up his face. "I was on my way to the workshop. I remember that well enough. Next thing I know, I'm in that cellar and no idea how I got there. But there were bits in between. Sort of vague and shadowy. And other things. Strange smells."

He tried to piece together fragments of the disjointed memories hovering on the edge of his awareness, trying to make sense of them; voices, shouting, a sense of falling. His speech accelerated and his voice quavered as he spoke, signalling the stress of trying to recount his ordeal. He halted in mid-sentence and closed his eyes, his breathing laboured, his jaw clenched, the tendons standing out on his neck.

From somewhere out in the corridor, the motorised whoosh of doors opening and closing signalled the presence of a nearby lift, and a muffled voice made an announcement over the tannoy.

I leaned over and rubbed his arm. "Don't sweat it," I said. "You need to rest awhile."

"No, I need to do this."

"There'll be time later," pleaded Sophie. "When you're feeling better."

"They must have taken my mobile," he said. "I can't find it."

"Its signal was picked up from several miles distant," I said. "An obvious attempt to make it appear you'd run away."

He stiffened as if caught by a sudden thought. "My car. Where is it?"

"It's at the workshop," I said. "So you made it to work. The police are over there now, checking for witnesses."

"I always get there early before anyone's around."

"We're presuming your attacker was waiting for you," I said. "Which means he would have needed transport to get you to Medway Hall. Someone may have spotted him on the way. You should know the police have Elliott Garcia in their sights as a suspect but, so far, there's no hard evidence to tie him to your attack. We're hoping someone may have seen him or his car at or on its way from the workshop."

"Why him?"

"He was at Medway Hall the day you were attacked. Your mother's neighbour observed him in the grounds. It's possible his interest in buying the place was a ruse to get inside."

"Buying the place?" Jordan sounded surprised.

"You don't remember?"

"Remember what?"

I reminded him of Reagan's call and his agreeing to let Garcia look around the property. I had hoped my attempts to refresh his memory might help his recall, but no such luck.

"He was sighted in the grounds early that morning," I said. "So if he grabbed you at the workshop and drove over to Medway Hall, the timing would be right. Trouble is, we don't know for sure when you got there. You could have been held elsewhere for a while."

"You said Reagan was going to show him around?" he said.

"That was the idea. But he persuaded her to let him have the access code for the gates so he could check out the grounds on his own and said he'd be happy to let her show him around the house another time."

"That's weird. Why not both at the same time?"

"That's what the police thought, too. They questioned Reagan this morning, and it seems he was quite adamant about going on his own. Which gives us even more reason to suppose he's your attacker."

"If only I could remember," he said. "Then we could be certain one way or the other."

"I'm sure it will come, eventually."

"Every time I think back over the day, I get this strange sensation." He wrinkled his nose. "A smell. Sort of sweet."

"Could be chloroform. He would need to incapacitate you."

"No, it's not that. Something else." He screwed up his face. "Flowers. The scent of flowers."

"Not sure what that could have been, but at least it's a start. Maybe you'll remember more in time. And once you're up to it, the police will want to talk to you."

"It's not like I can tell them anything right now. Someone's out to get me, that's for sure, but we don't know who it is. Not for certain. It may not be Garcia."

I tried to put him at ease. "It was an attempt to frame you for your mother's murder. A failed attempt. I doubt you'll be targeted again."

He didn't seem convinced.

"You don't need to worry," I said. "We have it covered. There's a police guard on the door, and we'll make sure you're protected once you're home."

"And I'm going to take more time off work," said Sophie. "You'll be well looked after."

"Garcia's being taken in for questioning this afternoon," I said. "And if there's enough evidence to charge him, he'll be out of circulation for a while. I'm meeting Nathan over there later, so I'll let you know how it goes."

Of course, there was always the possibility the police wouldn't have enough on Garcia to charge him, and despite my reassurances, I wasn't totally convinced he was no longer a threat. Garcia was a man used to getting his own way and wouldn't take kindly towards those who thwarted him.

We needed to stay on our guard.

CHAPTER FORTY-TWO

Nathan's bad moods always followed a predictable pattern. They started with a tight-lipped, stony silence and maybe the occasional grunt in response to any attempt to engage him in conversation and ended with an outpouring of anger.

For once, fortunately, I wasn't on the receiving end.

By the time I caught up with him at the police station, he had already progressed to knuckle-cracking mode and seemed ready to explode.

He was in the otherwise empty waiting room and greeted me with a glare as I crossed towards him.

I dropped into the chair at his side. "I'm not late, am I?"

He ignored the question. "Let me ask you something," he said. "If you were conducting this interview, how would you play it?"

"I'd start by asking Garcia about his movements on the relevant day and then I'd let it drop that Jordan has been found safe and well but without telling him of Jordan's loss of memory. If he is our man, he'd be thrown off guard, think the game is up, and either try to justify his actions or confess. Voilà. Job done."

In response, Nathan grabbed a newspaper from the chair on his other side and thrust it at me.

I took it from him. It was the previous evening's Almchester Sentinel. The headline read, "Amnesia Victim's Kidnap Ordeal".

My grip tightened on the paper and I screwed my eyes shut. Once my breathing was back under control, I said, "I think that headline tells me all I need to know." I opened my eyes and tossed the newspaper onto the chair beside me. "Just as I think Gibson's level of incompetence can't get any lower.... Have you spoken to him about this yet?"

"Not yet. I just got here a few minutes ago."

Before I could respond, Gibson appeared from the other side of the reception area and made his way towards us.

I picked up the newspaper as Nathan and I rose from our chairs and held it up before him as he approached. "Have you seen this?" I didn't try to hide my annoyance.

He pulled up short in front of me, the welcoming smile dissolving.

I didn't give him chance to reply. "You realise the implication of releasing this information?"

He took a step back, disconcerted, and said, "You have to understand that once Jordan was identified as a person of interest to the police, the media were bound to take a more active interest in the case. And we were obliged to follow up on that once Jordan had been found. It was inevitable the circumstances of his rescue would become public knowledge."

"You're the one in charge of the narrative," said Nathan, "not the media. By releasing information about Jordan's amnesia, you've not only wasted an opportunity, but you've also put Jordan's safety at risk. His attacker may now see Jordan as a potential threat."

"Jordan is being well protected," said Gibson. "And I'm sure we have our man this time. Garcia won't be stupid enough to make any false moves."

"There's no guarantee Garcia is the perp," said Nathan. "And even if he is, you may not have enough on him to bring charges."

I took up the argument. "And the attacker will know Jordan could recover his memory at any time. He may be desperate enough to make a move against Jordan despite the risk of discovery."

"Garcia's waiting in the interview room," said Gibson. "Let's get his interview over with first, shall we? If all goes well, all these potential problems will go away." His tone had hardened. He must have known he'd made a bad move, but he wasn't about to admit it.

He led us through to the recording room where the middle monitor of the three was switched on and displaying the interview room. Garcia was already seated in front of the desk. He was leaning back in his chair, one leg crossed over the other, and picking at his fingernails with all the casual indifference of someone completely at ease. If Gibson thought he was going to have an easy time with Garcia, he was badly mistaken. A uniformed constable stood to attention in one corner.

Back in the recording room, Gibson drew up some chairs around the monitor and we settled into place.

We didn't have long to wait. On the screen, Garcia was joined by the officer I recognised from the earlier interview, Sgt Tyler. He nodded to the constable on guard and seated himself opposite Garcia on the other side of the desk.

Garcia greeted him with a smile and a flash of gold. "Good afternoon, Sgt Tyler. What a pleasure it is to see you again."

Tyler ignored the greeting, looked down at the desk, and opened the file before him.

He looked up at Garcia, read him his rights, and reminded him he was being interviewed under caution and was being recorded.

"I understand you don't wish to have your legal representative present," said Tyler. "Is that correct?"

"Correct."

Tyler went on to explain the interview was in connection with an incident at a time and place Garcia was thought to be present.

He began his questioning by reminding Garcia of the relevant date and location. "Were you at Medway Hall on that particular day, Mr Garcia?"

"I have many calls on my time," said Garcia. "It is difficult to remember exactly."

"You were seen in the grounds on that day by a neighbour," said Tyler.

"If you already knew that, Sergeant, why waste time asking me?" Garcia grinned. He was enjoying this encounter, treating it as a game.

Tyler ignored the question. "We have it on record you had an interest in buying the property. And yet you insisted on being admitted to the grounds on that particular day despite not having access to the house itself. That seems a little strange." He paused, waiting for a response. But none came. "Well, Mr Garcia?"

"Well what? Sergeant. You have not asked question."

There was a hard edge to Tyler's voice when he spoke again. "Why were you so insistent on looking around the grounds? And why in such a hurry?"

Garcia shrugged and pulled a face. "I am busy man, Sergeant. I like to move quickly. As for interest in grounds, if you knew property market, you would not need to ask question. It is large plot, near city centre, valuable land ripe for development. Of course I have interest."

"And you had no other reason to be there?"

"What other reason could there be?"

"Were you aware of anyone else at the property during your visit?"

"If anyone else was there," said Garcia, "I would have known." He tilted his head to one side and faced Tyler with a questioning look on his face. "This is about young man held captive in cellar, yes?" He grinned in response to Tyler's hardened expression. "I read all about it in local paper." He creased his brow in a show of concern and leaned forward with his arms on the desk. "But surely he can tell you himself what happened?"

Before Tyler could reply, Garcia sat upright, clicked his teeth together and tapped the side of his head as if struck by a sudden thought. "But of course, he can't, can he? He has - what you call it? - amnesia. That is so very unfortunate. But surely you have some idea when did this terrible thing happen, no?"

Tyler stared at Garcia, jaw clenched, before replying. "The details are unclear at present."

"So it could be any time before he was found? A matter of days?"

"One day at most."

Garcia leaned back in his chair and clasped his hands behind his head. "It is unfortunate I was not there to witness what happened to this young man," he said. "I so regret not being able to help."

By this point, I had long since lost interest in listening to Garcia's interview. He had played this game before and played it well.

"This isn't going to plan, is it?" I said.

Nathan grunted, his usual response when he wasn't in the best of moods.

Gibson squirmed in his chair and said, "It isn't over yet. Let's see where it goes."

"A blind man could see where this is going," said Nathan. "Garcia is on top of this. He knows you have nothing on him."

"And you must see it too," I said. "You're going to have to let him go."

We watched the rest of the interview, but it was clearly going nowhere. This was nothing new to Garcia. He was used to navigating his way through difficult interrogations and was clearly enjoying the verbal sparring. Tyler did his best but having nothing to work on, he had no option but to bring the interview to a close, and we knew that Garcia would soon be on his way.

Nathan and I left the station immediately afterwards, turning down an invitation to follow up with a debriefing from Gibson. Just as well, given Nathan seemed ready to explode.

We didn't talk much on the way home. It was only as we drew up outside the house, Nathan aired his concerns. "Once we have Jordan back home," he said, "we need to keep a close eye on him."

He didn't need to explain why.

Jordan was now a target.

CHAPTER FORTY-THREE

Now Jordan's ordeal had made the local and national press, it was inevitable it would attract the usual motley bunch of reporters to our doorstep. Even minor public figures like me became major persons of interest when the media had a juicy tale to tell. But their presence wasn't the real problem. The real problem was not knowing who might be hiding amongst them. Someone, somewhere, was living every day with the fear of exposure. Someone who knew Jordan could recover his memory at any time and would see him as a threat that needed to be eliminated. And that person could be hiding in plain sight among the media hacks who were trying to get close to us.

I still had Garcia at the top of my list, but he would never be dumb enough to do his own dirty work. Nor would he need to. I didn't doubt he would be well acquainted with the sort of lowlife types who would be only too happy to handle his problems for the right price.

Gibson had finally seen sense and dropped Jordan's bail conditions. But instead of returning to their apartment, Jordan and Sophie had chosen to stay on with me and Nathan. Safety in numbers, I guess. We kept Jordan indoors as much as possible and a police patrol car kept a watch on the house, but we could never be sure of being completely safe.

And so we needed to decide on a strategy to move matters along. It was Nathan who came up with the idea. "I've been thinking about what the doc told you," he said to me. "About the sort of things that could kickstart Jordan's memory. Why don't we try to help it?"

"What did you have in mind?" I asked.

It was almost a week since Jordan's release from hospital and the four of us, Nathan, Jordan, Sophie and I, were trying to make the best of our enforced seclusion and the warmer weather by chilling out in the garden as much as possible. We had finished breakfast and had taken our coffees outside and were seated around the garden table.

Jordan said, "I've been wracking my brain for days. But no luck. I keep getting this image of flowers and I don't know why. It seems important for some weird reason."

"What do you remember about being trapped in the cellar?" Nathan asked.

"A few hazy moments," said Jordan. "But nothing that makes any sense."

Nathan said, "How would you feel about going back?"

Jordan drew in a sharp breath and stared at him.

"After what happened there," Nathan said, "I can't think of a better place to help jog your memory."

"He's right, of course," I said, "but we'd understand if you don't want to." I shot Nathan a warning glance. "We don't want to put you under more pressure."

Jordan's gaze fell to the tabletop and we waited, anxiously, for a response.

Finally, he looked up and said, "It has to be worth a try. Anything is better than sitting around and doing nothing."

"Are you sure?" said Sophie. "You've been through a lot these last few days."

He pulled a face and said, "What else can I do? I can't keep looking over my shoulder, wondering if someone out there has still got it in for me." He nodded his consent. "Let's do it."

"Great," I said. "We'll do it today. Might as well get it over with as soon as possible. Which reminds me..." I reached into my jeans pocket and dug out my mobile. "I promised Reagan I'll let Vanessa know when we were over at the house so she could pick up some files." I tapped in Vanessa's office number and got through to her.

She was about to go into a meeting and wasn't able to come over to the house that afternoon, so I offered to pick up the files for her and take them round to the office. "We're in the neighbourhood," I said, "and Jordan will know where his mother kept her files, so it will be no bother."

She thanked me and said, "Reagan would like to see you, anyway. She's anxious for news about Jordan. We all are."

"I suspected as much," I said. "Tell her I'll be over later."

We drove to Medway Hall after lunch and once we'd picked up the files, I asked Jordan if he wanted to meet with Reagan. He declined. "I'll drive round to the office with you," he said. "but I'll wait in the car. You know what a fuss she makes. I can do without it right now."

I smiled. "She's worried about you. But I know what you mean. She can be a bit over the top at times."

And I was right. Once I'd handed the files over to Vanessa, I was shown up to Reagan's office, where she was waiting to greet me with a barrage of questions.

Even before we had seated ourselves, she was pressing me for information. Was Jordan fully recovered? Did he remember anything? Did the police have any leads?

I brought her up to date as best I could as I dropped into the proffered chair while she seated herself facing me. She leaned towards me, face creased with concern. "The police told me what happened," she said. "I was mortified. How could anyone be so callous? I dread to think what sort of long-term effect it might have on him. Why would anyone do such a thing?"

"Clearly, someone was trying to take the heat off themself by framing Jordan for his mother's murder. Which suggests to me whoever it is thinks the police were closing in. It seemed like a final desperate attempt."

"And does he have any idea who it was?" she asked. "Does he remember anything?"

I shook my head and pulled a face. "It's a complete blank."

"And you have no idea where Jordan was during those two days? Is there no one else he could have had contact with?"

"We know he left for his workshop as usual. That was the day you spoke with him on the phone. And that's the last anyone saw of him. In fact, his conversation with you was the last contact anyone had until we found him the evening of the following day."

"Is there any chance he'll remember, eventually?"

"We don't know. There's a possibility he may never recover his memory."

I told her of our discussion with Jordan's doctor about the ways in which external stimuli could help with recall and told her of our plan to help it along. "Jordan's not exactly looking forward to it, but he's prepared to do whatever it takes to get his memory back. We're heading on over to Medway Hall from here."

"Let's hope it bears some results," she said.

"It's all we have right now," I said. "Unless you've had any feedback on what happened to Cara's car keys?"

"Sorry to disappoint you," she said. "Vanessa asked around, but we came up blank. We have no idea who Austin Brady gave them to."

"We seem to have hit several brick walls," I said. "And the police are no further on with their investigations."

"You know they've interviewed Elliot again?" she said.

"I was there."

She stiffened and sat upright.

I explained. "Analysing witness and suspect statements is part of my skill set as a Forensic Psychologist. I've sat in on many police interviews in my time."

"Surely they don't think Elliot is involved?"

What was I supposed to say? I didn't trust the man but, so far, there was no hard evidence against him. And until there was, I had to be careful how I responded to such questions. Especially questions from someone whose very livelihood may rely on her relationship with Garcia.

I said, "Elliot was in the grounds of Medway Hall at a time when Jordan may have been imprisoned there. It was inevitable he would be questioned. But he had a verifiable and legitimate reason for being there."

The deep frown told me she was not fully convinced by my explanation. "Do you have any reason to think otherwise?" I asked.

"Not about Cara's murder or Jordan's kidnapping. Not for one moment do I believe he's involved in either incident. But I do wonder if I've been a little too hasty in bringing him into the business. You're not the only one who's expressed concerns about his business practices."

I shrugged. "I don't know what I can tell you," I said. "In the end, it has to be your decision."

She sighed. "There's so much going on at the moment, it's difficult to know what to do for the best. But we've not signed a formal business agreement yet, so maybe I should postpone any decision on the way forward for the moment. I'm sure I'll be able to think things through more clearly once the police investigation has been laid to rest."

"I'm sure you're right," I said.

"And, hopefully, if you can help Jordan regain his memory, we'll be a step nearer to that. And I know I've said it before, but please let me know if I can help Jordan in any way."

I thanked her before taking my leave, and she walked me over to the lift.

As we waited for it to arrive, she said, "Let's hope your plan works."

After stepping into the lift, I turned to face her and noted how strained she looked. It was easy to forget she too was a victim of circumstance. First through the loss of her close friend and business partner and now through the added worries of saving her business and the possible risks in taking on Garcia as a partner.

Too many of us had suffered throughout this ordeal.

CHAPTER FORTY-FOUR

The smell of mould and mildew drifting up from the open trapdoor was as strong as I remembered it, a malodorous stench that hung in the air and clung to our clothes.

Jordan peered down through the square black hole to where the ladder disappeared into the impenetrable darkness and wrinkled his nose. When he spoke, his voice quavered. "Can't say I'm looking forward to going down there."

Once I'd finished my conversation with Reagan and left her office, Jordan and I had made the short journey to Medway Hall and were now back in the squalid confines of the crumbling weather-damaged outbuilding standing on either side of the trap and peering down into its unwelcoming depths.

Although Jordan had agreed to this undertaking, it was not without some misgivings, and the last thing I wanted was to put him through another ordeal. I can't say I was taking much pleasure in it myself.

"We don't have to do this if you'd rather not," I said.

"I have to do something," he said. "Not knowing is far worse."

He stepped back from the open trap and I followed his gaze as he looked around the room, glancing from the rotting wooden beams to the dusty spiderwebs hanging in shadowy corners and against the flaking whitewashed walls, from the gas bottles now lying in haphazard disarray at the far side of the room to the rusted pipes running down one wall. He looked around studiously, as if seeing everything for the first time. Finally, he settled his gaze on the old wooden chair in the centre of the room.

"I don't think that was there before," he said. "It was in the other room."

"It seems your assailant had you tied to the chair. We found coils of rope nearby, and there were rope burns on your wrists when we found you."

"That's just great." He stared at the chair for a few moments longer and then shook his head. "I don't remember a thing."

"Let's try the cellar," I said and added hastily, "if you're sure you're ready."

"As much as I'll ever be."

I took a deep breath and said, "I'll go first."

Crouching by the trapdoor, I peered down into the gloom and steeled myself.

After what had happened down here and the image it conjured up of Jordan lying seemingly lifeless on the damp, grimy floor, I wasn't looking forward to going back down there any more than he was.

From my shoulder bag, I retrieved a torch and switched it on before grabbing the top rail of the ladder and lowering myself through the hatch. I clambered down the metal rungs to the concrete floor below, the sound of my progress breaking the ominous silence around me.

At the bottom, I held the ladder steady while Jordan made his descent.

Once we were on solid ground, I flashed the torch around to get my bearings. I needed to remind myself of the extent of our surroundings and the positions of the two doors leading into darker recesses beyond.

Down here, the smell was worse. Pungent, moist air pressed in around us, leaving its taint on our skin. Damp patches on the walls glistened in the light, and pools of water on the floor caught the beam and threw it back. I turned the torch towards the open doorway to the left. "We found you in there," I said. "That's probably the best place to start."

Jordan grunted his agreement.

I took the lead, guiding us with the torch. Making sure we avoided the larger puddles, we squelched our way across the uneven floor towards the black, gaping doorway and into the small room beyond.

Darkness closed in behind us, and shadows danced and japed against the walls as I shone the torch around. I found the spot I was searching for, aiming the torch at a muddy patch by the far wall.

"We found you over there," I said, "wrapped in a tarpaulin sheet."

"Is it still here?" he asked. "It might help stir my memory if I could see it."

"The police took it away, along with the ropes and other loose debris. They're hoping to find traces of DNA or fingerprints, but I'm not holding out much hope."

Jordan shivered. "It's freezing down here. It's a wonder I survived."

I wasn't sure if Jordan knew how close to death he had been, but I had no intention of reminding him. "You're safe enough now. That's the important thing."

He clasped a hand to the back of his neck and glanced about him. "It never used to bother me being down here," he said. "But it seems so creepy now. Like something is watching us, ready to pounce."

"Hardly surprising," I said. "After what you went through, it's bound to play on your imagination."

"I'm beginning to think losing my memory wasn't such a bad thing after all. I'm not sure I'd want to remember being trapped down here."

"So, nothing is coming back to you?"

He shrugged. "'Fraid not."

"Why don't you take a look around?" I handed him the torch. "You never know. Something might catch your attention and help you remember."

"Worth a try, I guess." He took the torch from me and, moving cautiously, traced a path around the walls, directing the beam into dark corners and across the rough, uneven floor as he moved.

The only sounds apart from the squelch of Jordan's boots were the occasional groan of the building settling and the constant drip of water.

As Jordan moved further away, the darkness pressed in around me, and I clasped my arms to my chest, guarding against the chill air. I dreaded to think how Jordan must have felt trapped for so long in this damp squalid hole. I couldn't begin to imagine how alone and afraid he must have been.

A gnawing anxiety gripped me, a sense of foreboding I couldn't place but couldn't shake off. I called out, "Everything okay?"

There was a heart-stopping silence. And then, from somewhere in the darkness, Jordan called back, "I don't think this is going to work."

A moment later, he was back by my side. He handed me the torch and said, "I remember being down here, but not recently. It was weeks ago. I'm picking up some bad vibes, like there's something at the back of my mind wanting to get out. But nothing is coming through."

"You never know," I said. "It might help your recall later. But right now, I'm all for getting out of here."

Before I could move, Jordan gasped and grabbed my arm in a tight grip. "What was that?" He sounded alarmed and his voice had risen a notch. Even in the semi-darkness, I could see how his face had paled.

I tensed. "What's what?"

"I thought I heard a noise from upstairs."

I strained to hear, but only the odd creak of a timber and the constant drip of water reached my ears.

"It's nothing," I said, but my heart was still pounding. "Just this old place creaking as the weather cools."

He slowly relaxed his hold and let go of my arm. "Sorry," he said, "I guess I'm getting jumpy."

"Hardly surprising. Let's get out of here. I think we've seen enough."

I guided us back to the trapdoor, shone the torch on the ladder, and held it as Jordan climbed up and out. Once he was out of the way, I followed him back to the upper room.

I switched off the torch and put it in my shoulder bag. "That's one place I'm happy to leave behind," I said and moved towards the outer door.

Jordan followed me. "It was worth a try," he said, "but I'm glad it's over."

But maybe it wasn't.

I stopped in my tracks, my senses on high alert. Had I heard something? That feeling of unease was back. And now it was stronger than ever. I strained to hear, certain I had caught a sound from the outer room, a shuffling, as if someone was out there waiting for us.

Jordan heard it too. He lowered his voice to a whisper and said, "I don't think we're alone."

For a moment, I stood my ground and listened. All was now silent, but I still had that sense of foreboding. I took a step forward and called out, "Who's there?"

We stood and waited for a response. At first, there was nothing. Just a pounding in my ears. And then the shuffling again followed by the sound of footsteps echoing back to us and, from the other side of the doorway, a familiar voice said, "Good afternoon, gentlemen." A shadow crossed the threshold and a grinning Garcia stepped through the door.

He was holding a gun. And it was aimed at me.

My stomach churned, and I froze.

"So sorry to interrupt your little escapade," he said, "but we have some unfinished business to deal with."

"How did you know we'd be here?"

From behind him, another voice answered. "I told him."

Garcia's companion walked into the room and moved to his side.

It was Reagan Francis.

CHAPTER FORTY-FIVE

We stood transfixed, staring at each other across the room. Garcia was still grinning, enjoying the moment. Reagan's expression was hard, her mouth set in a tight, thin line.

A scattering of dead leaves, blown in from outside, was caught by a light breeze making its way in through the open doorway. The faint rustling was the only sound that broke the silence.

Jordan took a step towards Reagan, his eyes wide and questioning, as if seeing her for the first time. "Flowers." He murmured the word, half under his breath.

She knitted her brow and stared at him through narrowed eyes, but said nothing.

"Flowers." Jordan repeated the word, louder this time, and added, "Your perfume. I remember now. I was kneeling by the chair with Garcia standing over me. And you were there, telling me what to write. And I remember your scent."

Garcia said, "You see? Didn't I tell you something like this would happen? It was only a matter of time."

I was finding it hard taking this in. "You made him write the confession?" I said. "Why?"

"Austin Brady is why," said Reagan.

"You want to explain that," I said.

"Cara was naïve. She thought he was the real deal. The man of her dreams. But she was wrong. He used her. A parasite. Used her connections and her money. And spread his sexual charms around behind her back."

"Ah, now I get it," I said. "You were one of those women within easy reach, and he spread his sexual charms your way. And I'm guessing Cara found out."

There was an increasingly bitter edge to Reagan's voice as she spoke. "She was about to end our partnership. Dissolve the business we had built up over the years for some pathetic man who didn't give a damn about her. We were riding high. The business was growing and our fortunes with it. I wasn't going to give up all that without a fight."

"Is that how it started?" I said. "A fight?"

"She was the one who started it. She lashed out at me. I pushed her away, and she fell. It could have all been so different if she'd listened to reason. But she wouldn't."

"So you finished her off."

Garcia laughed. "I tell you, Mr Macgregor, there is nothing more dangerous than a woman crossed in love. But let us not waste time going over old ground. It is history."

"And how did you get involved in all this?" I asked him. "A knight in shining armour riding to the rescue of a damsel in distress?"

He laughed again. "Let's just say I like to make the most of my opportunities. It was a fair exchange. A majority shareholding in Ms Francis's business in exchange for my silence."

He saw the questioning look in my eyes and said, "On the night Mr Brady met his untimely demise, I was lucky enough to pass Ms Francis on my way from his house. I leave it to you to figure out why she was on her way to see him."

"You killed him too?"

"He knew too much and was going to talk," she said. "I had no choice."

"And now we have yet another mess to sort out," said Garcia. He scowled. "My new partnership with Ms Francis is proving more troublesome than I anticipated. But let's not dwell on that, shall we? Now we need to figure out what to do with you two."

He was clearly running out of patience. He turned to me with a look of pity and shook his head slowly in a show of mock concern. "You really should not have interfered, Mr MacGregor."

This was not going well. But there had to be a way out. I needed to think it through and think fast. There was no point making a run for the door. I looked around the room, checking for anything that might help.

Garcia must have read my mind. "Don't waste your time, Mr MacGregor," he said. "There's no way out."

But maybe there was. Just maybe. But I had to be careful how I played this. It was going to take all my skill.

"And how do you plan to deal with us?" I said. "A convenient accident?"

As I spoke, I crossed the room in front of him, moving slowly and keeping my distance so as not to put him on guard until I was between him and the door.

He turned to keep me in his sight as I moved. "I hope you're not planning on making a run for it. That would be a mistake."

"I'm not that stupid," I said. "I wouldn't get far, would I?"

"Very wise," he said.

I stopped and turned to face him, judging our positions relative to each other and the layout of the room. I had him where I wanted him. Now I could carry out my plan. But first, I needed to assert control. Not an easy task against someone like Garcia, especially given our situation. But this is where the subconscious came into play.

I changed my stance, legs apart, hands on hips, head raised, and stared him full in the eyes. "So what now?" I stepped towards him, hand raised, as if soliciting a response.

It worked. He took a step back. Just as I'd hoped.

Within us all is a deeply ingrained survival instinct. The need for personal space. It's a need to keep others at a safe distance. And when that space is invaded, when someone gets too close for comfort, we do whatever is necessary to regain control of that space. And Garcia had reacted as I'd wanted him to.

Now I had to put the rest of my plan into action.

There is a technique used by psychotherapists to overcome resistance and gain control of the patient's subconscious mind. The Confusion Technique. By using language meant to confuse, by the use of homophones and non-sequiturs and other forms of wordplay, the subject's conscious mind is caught up in an attempt to make sense of what it is hearing, leaving the unconscious mind open to suggestion. But more than that. Confusion focuses the mind fully and to the exclusion of everything else. And that's what I needed to make use of.

I said, "Are you sure you've thought this through? The police already have you in their sights. You surely don't think you can dispose of us and get away with it, do you?"

"Your concern is touching, Mr MacGregor," he said. "But do not worry yourself. I have everything under control."

This was my chance.

"You're not thinking clearly," I said. "There's a part of you that stands apart from the part that's thinking logically. The part that wants to take part in the process is only partially involved and comes at the cost of sound judgement."

As I spoke, his face creased, confusion written large on his face, and his eyes glazed over as he tried to make sense of my words.

I continued. "You need to take apart your individual thoughts and let the logical part of you take part in the reconstruction of those parts into a logical whole."

He shook his head as if trying to clear his mind. "What the hell are you talking about?"

That was my cue. That's when I knew I had him.

"You really do need to think again," I said. I moved towards him, moving quickly, arms spread wide as if imploring.

He raised his gun and shouted out, "Move away!"

But he was the one who moved, an automatic reaction to regain control of his personal space. Momentarily confused, he took several steps back.

And it was only then, with the final step, as his foot hit dead air where solid ground should have been, he realised his mistake. His eyes widened in a fleeting show of disbelief and shock, as it must have dawned on him how he had been manipulated. I smiled at him, and his face contorted with anger.

But it was too late.

He fell back and dropped through the open trap with a howl of rage that ended abruptly as he hit the concrete floor below with a hard, bone-crunching thud.

And then just the sound of dripping water.

Reagan Francis gasped and looked around, first at the inner door and then to the one leading out to the front of the building.

"Don't embarrass yourself by trying to make a run for it," I said. "It's over."

I kept my eye on her as I reached into my pocket for my mobile and speed-dialled Nathan. "We have a situation," I said.

Before long, we were caught up in a rush of activity, of squealing tyres and sirens, of handcuffs and ambulances. And while Reagan Francis was being taken into custody and Elliot Garcia rushed to hospital with a fractured skull, Jordan and I were explaining our near-fatal encounter to Nathan and Inspector Gibson.

At one point, Gibson looked down through the trap and shook his head. "Just think," he said. "If it hadn't been for a timely accident, the outcome could have been very different."

"Yes," I said. "A timely accident."

CHAPTER FORTY-SIX

Our next encounter with Gibson was less formal and a little more relaxed. He had lost the belligerent attitude. Most likely because he now saw Jordan as a victim rather than a mindless killer.

It was the day after Reagan's arrest and we were all gathered together in our living room, Jordan and Sophie huddled together on the couch with me perched on one of the arms and Nathan and Gibson taking up the two facing armchairs.

Gibson was here to let us know what progress was being made and to learn what he could of our skirmish with Reagan Francis and Elliot Garcia at Medway Hall.

"I'll take formal statements from you later," said Gibson, "once you've had a chance to recover. But for now, if you could run over what happened."

I talked him through our face-off with Reagan Francis and Garcia and, once I'd finished, he asked Jordan if he had anything to add.

"I can't think of anything my…" He hesitated. "…that dad hasn't already told you."

That word again. It didn't yet roll easily off his tongue. But it sounded good even so.

Gibson then asked Jordan how much he remembered of his earlier abduction and captivity.

"It all came back quite suddenly," said Jordan. "The moment I saw Reagan. It was like a switch being flipped in my brain."

Gibson asked if he would talk us through it.

"Garcia was waiting for me outside the workshop," said Jordan.

"He wanted to talk about buying the house. I told him I wasn't interested and went to open up. Before I could get inside, he's grabbed me from behind and I've got a wet rag over my face. Sort of sweet and sickly."

"Sounds like he used chloroform," said Gibson.

Jordan continued. "It's kinda vague after that. I came to in the boot of Garcia's car and my hands were tied. I think he must have driven in through the main entrance and opened the gate over by the outbuildings. It could only be opened from the inside. The next thing I know, I'm being carried through the Gatehouse entrance. Reagan was already waiting for us there and followed us in. I had no idea why she was there or what was happening. I was confused."

"That would explain why Garcia was seen crossing the grounds," I said. "Those outbuildings are out of sight of the neighbour's window, so there would be no chance of being overlooked from there. Garcia wouldn't have known that, but Reagan would."

"Did Reagan Francis explain herself?" asked Gibson.

"Not at first," said Jordan. "It was Garcia. He made some crack about women crossed in love being more vicious than any man. Looks like mum found out Reagan had been screwing around with Austin and they had a massive fight at the party the night before. Garcia laughed about it. Like it was some sort of joke. Reagan tried to make out it was an accident."

"We know that's not true," said Gibson.

"She was still playing the blame game this morning," I said. "Putting it all on Cara."

"What about Reagan's phone call?" Nathan asked. "She says she called you that morning."

Jordan shook his head, his forehead creased. "It never happened. I'm sure I would have remembered."

"I did wonder about that," I said.

"Is it important?" asked Gibson.

I said, "She called us to say she'd spoken to Jordan that morning and wanted to know if he was okay. She told me he had sounded depressed, and she was concerned."

"It was obviously a ploy," said Nathan. "She wanted us to think Jordan was at the end of his tether and weighed down with remorse. It was meant to support everything that followed and convince us of

Jordan's guilt." He turned to Jordan with a rueful look. "And I'm sorry to say, it almost had us fooled."

"Until we read your letter," I said. "Clever move."

Jordan smiled. "I knew you'd understand it."

"Is that why Garcia kidnapped you?" said Gibson. "To force a confession from you?"

"That was the start of it," said Jordan. "Reagan wanted to know what would happen to me. Garcia told her not to worry, that he'd deal with me later. Doesn't take much guesswork to know what that meant."

"So he locked you in the cellar and left you to die?" said Gibson.

"That's not what happened," said Jordan. "Garcia untied me and had me kneel on the floor and use the chair as a surface to write my confession on. Reagan told me what to write and then went into the other room - I don't think she could face me - and once I'd written my piece and signed it, Garcia took it through to her so she could check it and make sure it read okay. That's when I made a break for it and locked myself in the cellar. They weren't expecting that. I could hear Garcia trying to force open the trap, but it held fast. I thought they'd have to go eventually and I would be able to get out again."

"So they made sure you couldn't," said Gibson.

"I tried to get out later when I thought the coast was clear, but I couldn't raise the trap. And while I was trying to open it, the stairs gave way, and I fell. I don't remember much after that."

I said, "That must have been when you were concussed."

"So what happens now?" I asked. "Did Reagan confess?"

"Not at first. But once we'd matched her DNA with the blood sample from the scene of Brady's murder, she wasn't left with much choice."

Nathan said, "Why did she kill him?"

"He knew she intended to visit Ms Welles that morning to return her car and try to talk her round. She later told Brady it was an accident, and he agreed to keep quiet. It was only when he learned it was murder, he refused to cover for her anymore. She went to see him to try to change his mind, but he was having none of it. So she struck him from behind with a clock she picked up from the mantlepiece as he was about to show her the door. He tried to fight back, but she got the better of him and felled him. She then stabbed him with a kitchen knife."

Nathan said, "So I'm guessing she got her injuries from him and lied about being attacked outside her house?"

"It was clever," I said. "She gave a description of her assailant that exactly matched Jordan and, at the same time, rejected any suggestion that Jordan had attacked her. Very clever."

"We had nothing to connect her to Ms Welles's murder," said Gibson. "But once she knew we had enough to charge her with Brady's murder, she came clean."

"I don't understand the timing," said Nathan. "We know Cara was still alive later that morning while Reagan was at the office. She had contacted her secretary."

"Another clever move," said Gibson. "Ms Welles's laptop had remote access to the company's computer network. All Reagan Francis had to do was access it from the office and send an email to Ms Welles's secretary asking for information that only she, Reagan Francis, could provide. That way, Ms Welles's secretary was able to confirm the time of the email and that Francis was at the office."

"So Cara was already dead when Sophie drove round that morning?" I said.

Gibson confirmed this and added, "Reagan Francis saw Sophie from Ms Welles's office window and ducked out of sight when Sophie looked up at her. It was her Sophie saw when she looked up and not Ms Welles."

"And Reagan would have left by the side gate and walked to the office," I said. "Which is why Cara's neighbour didn't see her leave."

Gibson's mobile rang before we could continue. He checked it and said, "Sorry, I'd best take this. It's the station."

The call was mostly one-sided with Gibson making the occasional grunt. Once he'd finished and pocketed his mobile, his expression was solemn. "We just heard from the hospital," he said. "Garcia didn't make it. They just turned off his life support."

"Can't say I'm sorry," said Jordan.

Much as I hated to think it, I had to agree with him.

CHAPTER FORTY-SEVEN

Those last few days following Reagan's arrest were filled with a flurry of activity; police interviews and statements, initiating the start of probate now Jordan had been vindicated, putting the house on the market.

All these things would take time, of course, but once I'd set them in motion with the help of Nathan, Jordan and Sophie, it was time for us to take a break, a time to unwind. Nathan and I were driving home that evening and this was our chance to make our peace with Jordan and Sophie and say goodbye. For now, at least.

During that final day, Nathan and I had moved out of our temporary accommodation, Jordan and Sophie had returned to their apartment, and now we were gathered at Jordan and Danny's workshop that evening, six of us, me and Nathan, Jordan and Sophie, and Danny and his boyfriend, Steven. Jordan and Danny had wanted to show us around their workspace before we left, but the occasion had turned into a farewell meal. We were tucking into numerous cartons of food from the nearby Chinese takeaway and washing it down with several cans of ale while Jordan and Danny showed off their work. Not one of the most sophisticated dinner dates I'd ever had, but one that would stay in my memory forever and one I would always recall with mixed emotions. At the back of all our minds was the tragic event that had brought us together in the first place. Cara's untimely death.

Danny was showing Nathan his kiln and some of the pottery he had made in it while Sophie, Jordan and Steven chatted over a shared bowl of noodles.

For a while, I watched them from the other side of the workbench, taking pleasure in their lively chat, before wandering out into the open courtyard. I looked up into the clear, star-filled night and sent out a silent prayer of thanks to whatever gods may be listening for granting me a life of joy and love, a life I'm not sure I had always deserved.

A moment later, Jordan was by my side. "It's weird," he said. "We've been through so much together and know hardly anything about each other."

"I wish we'd met in better circumstances," I said, "but now we have, there's time enough to get to know each other."

"I still can't believe what happened," he said. "Mum and Reagan were so close. They'd known each other forever."

"We like to think we know someone well," I said, "but I'm not sure we ever can. Reagan only showed her true colours when she had to choose between friendship and self-interest."

"I miss my mum." His shoulders slumped, and he stared down at the ground.

I turned to face him fully. "She'll always be a part of our lives. I hope you know that. I'll always be grateful to her for helping me through a difficult time in my life. And for raising a son we could both be proud of."

"I wasn't always a good son."

"And I wasn't always a good husband. But I'd like to think it was her love and support that helped me eventually find my way. And the love she gave you will help guide you too. And for that, we must honour her memory and be grateful."

He smiled and nodded his agreement.

I wrapped an arm around his shoulder and hugged him. "And we both have weddings to look forward to," I said.

"Sophie and I are going to leave it for a while," he said. "We thought it best to let things settle down a bit before making any big plans."

"Probably for the best," I said.

Before we could continue our conversation, we were interrupted by Nathan. He was accompanied by Sophie. "Sorry," he said. "It's time we were making a move."

"I guess so," I said.

Jordan and Sophie followed us over to where our cars were parked on the far side of the courtyard. Nathan and I hugged Jordan and Sophie in turn before getting into our cars. I wound down the window and signalled farewell over to Danny and Steven, who waved to us from the workshop entrance.

As I started the car, Jordan said, "See you soon, dad."

"You can bet on it, son," I replied.

This time, the words tripped easily off our tongues.

IF YOU ENJOYED THIS BOOK

I'm hard at work writing the next title in this series which continues to follow the ups and downs of Mikey and Nathan's troubled relationship. If you enjoyed this book, you may wish to add your name to my mailing list to receive notification of publication.

Please see details on my Website
GrantAtherton.co.uk

And I'd love it if you could post a review about the book on Amazon or another website. Getting reviews would give me a lot of pleasure and I look forward to reading what you think. Perhaps you could mention which parts you liked best.

I look forward to hearing from you

Grant Atherton

Printed in Great Britain
by Amazon